PRAISE FOR DARK DUDE

...ook Award
...Year finalist

"Sherman Alexie did it with ... ...er,
The Absolutely True Diary of a ... ...er
Prize–winning author Oscar Hijuelos is adding his name to the
list of literary heavyweights turning their talents to minority-
themed, young-adult fiction."   —*Los Angeles Times*

"Like Huck Finn and Holden Caulfield, Dark Dude is our streetwise
guide to the universe, the outsider with a changing view of what it
means to be inside. Oscar Hijuelos knows how to kick around the
big questions: Who are we? Who do we want to be?"   —Amy Tan,
          New York Times bestselling author of *The Joy Luck Club*

★"Frank, gritty, vibrant, and wholly absorbing."
          —*Booklist*, starred review

★"Themes are classic—alienation, the search for identity—
but his approach is pure Hijuelos: Cuban American, musical,
and very, very funny."   —*Publishers Weekly*, starred review

"In Oscar Hijuelos's *Dark Dude*, we fall in love with the engaging
Rico and his friends. We worry about them and we applaud their
small and big victories as they journey to the ends of their worlds
to find themselves."   —Esmeralda Santiago,
          author of *When I Was Puerto Rican*

"Dark Dude's journey toward self-discovery is a compelling read.
Today's teen will be thrilled to discover a voice as authentic and
accomplished as Oscar Hijuelos's."   —Ellen Hopkins,
          New York Times bestselling author of *Crank* and *Glass*

"Oscar Hijuelos, the first Hispanic writer to win the Pulitzer Prize
[for *The Mambo Kings Play Songs of Love*], offers a powerful, street-
smart, coming-of-age novel."   —*USA Today*

"Hijuelos . . . adds some much needed color and verve to teen fiction."
          —Matthew Moyer,
          Jackson Public Library, on LibraryJournal.com

DARK DUDE

DARK DUDE

OSCAR HIJUELOS

ATHENEUM BOOKS FOR YOUNG READERS
NEW YORK LONDON TORONTO SYDNEY

For Lori Carlson

ATHENEUM BOOKS FOR YOUNG READERS • An imprint of Simon & Schuster Children's Publishing Division • 1230 Avenue of the Americas, New York, New York 10020 • This book is a work of fiction. Any references to historical events, real people, or real locales are used fictitiously. Other names, characters, places, and incidents are the product of the author's imagination, and any resemblance to actual events or locales or persons, living or dead, is entirely coincidental. • Copyright © 2008 by Oscar Hijuelos • All rights reserved, including the right of reproduction in whole or in part in any form. • ATHENEUM BOOKS FOR YOUNG READERS is a registered trademark of Simon & Schuster, Inc. • For information about special discounts for bulk purchases, please contact Simon & Schuster Special Sales at 1-866-506-1949 or business@simonandschuster.com. • The Simon & Schuster Speakers Bureau can bring authors to your live event. For more information or to book an event, contact the Simon & Schuster Speakers Bureau at 1-866-248-3049 or visit our website at www.simonspeakers.com. • Also available in a hardcover edition. • Book design by Polly Kanevsky • The text of this book is set in HoeflerText. • Manufactured in the United States of America • First paperback edition September 2009 • 10 9 8 7 6 5 4 3 2 • The Library of Congress has cataloged the hardcover edition as follows: • Hijuelos, Oscar. • Dark Dude / Oscar Hijuelos.—1st ed. • p. cm. • Summary: In the 1960s, Rico Fuentes, a pale-skinned Cuban American teenager, abandons drug-infested New York City for the picket fence and apple pie world of Wisconsin, only to discover that he still feels like an outsider and that violent and judgmental people can be found even in the wholesome Midwest. • ISBN: 978-1-4169-4804-9 (hc) • [1. Self-perception—Fiction. 2. Coming of age—Fiction. 3. Cuban Americans—Fiction. 4. Wisconsin—History—20th century—Fiction.] I. Title. • PZ7.H5448Dar 2008 • [Fic]—dc22 2008000959 • ISBN: 978-1-4169-4945-9 (pbk) • ISBN: 978-1-4169-9475-6 (eBook)

acknowledgments
With many thanks to my editor Caitlyn Dlouhy,
and to Jennifer Lyons, Karen Levinson,
and John Giachetti.

DARK DUDE

Part 1 **HANGING ON THE STOOP**

DARK DUDE n. 1. What a male of light skin is derisively called by persons of color (colloquial, Harlem 1965–1970). 2. A person considered suspect because of his light complexion, especially in criminal circumstances. 3. Someone who is not considered "streetwise." 4. A white person considered not to be "hip." Cf. "Straight." "Uncool." 5. An outsider, particularly in the context of ghetto society.

—THE HYPOTHETICAL DICTIONARY OF
AMERICAN SLANG

one

WELL, EVEN IF they say life can be shitty, you really don't know the half of it until you've dug up an outhouse. This was the fourth time in twelve months that I'd gotten down into the nitty-gritty and goop of it—and I'd had enough, for crying out loud. But I was doing it for my old neighborhood bro Gilberto, not just 'cause he'd have smacked me in the head if I didn't, but as a thank-you-man for letting me stay on his farm for so long. That's right, a farm.

Anyway, let me tell you about how this New York City kid ended up around the corner from where he lived, about a thousand miles away, in Wisconsin.

First of all, you've got to be hearing music just now—not with corny-assed violins and trumpets, but maybe some cool Motown—you know, something way better than the kind of diddly country or polka music you can go nuts trying to avoid on the radios out here. Then you got to imagine *time going backwards*, and everything slipping into reverse, not to when there were dinosaurs or medieval-assed knights trying to slay dragons, but just a few years.

Now picture me on my stoop, on a hot New York City summer afternoon, with two comic books—a *Spider-Man* and a *Fantastic Four*—rolled up in my back pocket and dying to be read. While some kids are playing stickball down the street, I'm fused to the stoop 'cause I'm supposed to be going to the A&P with my Moms, but she's been taking forever to get back from wherever she's been.

I'm on my former altar boy best behavior, despite the comics I've just "borrowed" from the stationery store, and I have a pious look on my face, the one I always put on while wishing I could be doing something really devious instead, like tossing water balloons or dumping out a full garbage can at unsuspecting strangers from the rooftop, stuff I never have the nerve to do.

So I was just sitting there when my pal Gilberto Flores, all six foot two of him, came bopping up the hill from Amsterdam Avenue, wearing the biggest grin I'd ever seen in my life.

No one else looked like Gilberto. He wore a giant Afro, had a scar down the side of his face, big ears, and smiled all the time.

I was always glad to see him.

"So, Gilberto, why you looking so happy?" I asked him.

He could barely contain himself. "Rico, my man," he said, a toothpick between his lips, and stroking his goatee the way he did whenever a girl with a nice butt went walking by, "I'm rich!"

"What do you mean, 'rich'?" I asked, used to hearing all kinds of BS from him.

He strode over to me and planted one of his size-twelve feet on the highest step. "You remember that lottery ticket I bought a few weeks back at Jack's stationery?"

"Sure, I was with you," I said, nodding.

"Well," he started, bending his lanky frame closer to me. "I hit that jackpot. *And I do mean hit it!*"

"No shit?" I said, jumping up. "You mean like a million?"

"Nah, man. I didn't get all the numbers," he said,

shaking his head. "But enough of them to make me some beaucoup bucks!" And he slapped me five.

"Like how beaucoup?" I expected him to say maybe a couple of thousand.

"A lot!" he said. "Enough to get me the hell out of here!"

"Yeah? How much?" I asked again.

He looked around the street. Then he pulled a little pad out of his back pocket and wrote down a number.

"Say what?" I smacked my forehead. "Damn, Gilberto, are you being for real? Like seventy-five thousand bucks?"

"Hey, not so loud!" he said. "And keep it under your hat, all right?"

"But for real?" I could feel my face heating up.

"You best believe it," he said, his smile stretching from ear to ear. "Anyways, I got something for you, my little bro."

Reaching into another pocket, he pulled out some bills, his fist tight around them, like they were drugs, slipping them into my hand.

"That's two hundred, but don't let on that I gave this to you, all right?"

Two hundred dollars! I didn't even look at them, just stuffed those bills into my pocket.

"But why you giving me this?" I asked.

"Because you were with me when I bought the ticket! Remember how I rubbed your head? It worked, man! You brought me the luck!"

"Yeah?" I asked, feeling proud of my scalp.

"You most certainly did!" Then he grabbed me by my neck and started rubbing my head as if to relive the moment. I hated the lame-o, itchy-ball crew cut my Moms insisted I get every summer, but hey, didn't it turn out to be his lucky charm?

He spun me around a few times, then said, "Go buy your Moms a new dress, or whatever you want. Buy some of those sci-fi books you're so crazy about, all right?"

"Damn," I said. "Nobody's ever given me these kinds of bucks before." I felt like jumping up and down. "Thanks for the solid."

"Ah, it's nothing." He rapped me on my shoulder. "You're just my little bro, that's all."

Well, that was kind of true. At eighteen, and being three years older than me, Gilberto was like the big brother I never had. I mean, he was always teaching me things.

Like how to fly a kite from a tenement rooftop without tumbling off the edge.

And to tame pigeons with a broomstick and red handkerchief.

To carve toy cars from balsa wood, and to whistle really loud.

The way to sneak into the movie theater on 110th Street on Saturday afternoons.

How chicks trust guys who wear penny loafers.

And how to tell if a girl is wearing falsies. ("Their boobies get this crumply thing happening.")

Gilberto even tried to get me into ice skating once (sort of), taking me down to Wollman Rink in Central Park, where he, an ace speed skater, used to meet his fancy, East-Sidey girlfriends. No matter how many times I wiped out, he was always there to help me up, telling me, "Try it again, Rico, 'cause the next time you'll nail it."

I mean if it wasn't for Gilberto, I probably wouldn't have ever gone anywhere outside the neighborhood, the guy always telling my Moms, who was forever watching my ass, that he would look after me. His eyes were so sincere and warm that she would cut me slack sometimes, as long as I was with him. So I guess we were like brothers, even if we didn't look that way, Gilberto being this dark-skinned Puerto Rican and me being, well, the palest *cubano* who ever existed on the planet. No joke.

In fact, Gilberto was one of the only guys in the neighborhood who didn't rag on me for looking like a whitey. Sometimes he got into the faces of dudes who'd call me a white "Wonder bread" MF, and he even whupped some butts on my behalf.

Now, we just hung out on my stoop, trying to stay cool. And I don't mean cool in the street way, but because it was just so freaking hot. As in pigeons looking dazed while they pecked around the sidewalk. As in sewers stinking like hell.

"My man, I got to be going now," he said, getting up. "Got me a date." And he did this thing with his hands, like he was drawing the shape of a really fly-looking girl in the air. "I'll catch you later, Rico, all right?"

"Sure. Have fun, man," I answered. "And thanks for the bucks, Gilberto," I added, feeling suddenly rich myself. As he went off whistling, all merrily, towards the avenue, I didn't envy his big win, like I might have with someone else. It was just one of those things—like it couldn't have happened to a nicer guy.

For a while I watched that stickball game run its course down the hill, the guys playing it, with just broomsticks and thirty-five-cent pink Spaldings, really cursing up a storm and smoking pot between innings: They didn't give a damn about anything or anybody, like they didn't have any respect. I mean, there was this skinny Puerto Rican kid, named Poppo, jumping up on a car hood to catch a fly ball and leaving his sneaker prints and dents on it, like who the hell cared! And you could even tell which of them was a junkie, like this guy named Bumpy. He just sort of took forever to get his act together at the plate (which was just a manhole cover). With an unlit cigarette dangling between his lips, he was moving real slow as if he were a scuba diver in the ocean, or one of those astronauts walking on the moon.

But waiting for my Moms was getting old, and like I said, it was hot. So freakin' hot that I was tempted to jump in front of the open fire hydrant on the other side of the hill—my stoop was just on top of the street—all these little kids running in and out of its gushing waters to escape the heat. And let me tell you: That spray looked inviting as hell. But I guess I believed I was getting a little too old for that, even if I really wanted to, so I just packed the stoop in and headed upstairs, figuring that my Moms would turn up sooner or later.

two

I ALWAYS FELT good after seeing Gilberto, but once I got up to our fourth-floor walkup apartment, that mood left me. Except for the living room, which faced the street, it was dark, on account of the fact that my Moms was constantly turning the lights off to save on the electric bill. That always spooked me. After I put on the hall light, framed pictures of Jesus holding his own glowing heart were the first things I saw, then a bunch of old family photographs from Cuba, where I'd never been—to me, it was just this crocodile-shaped island, south of Florida, that you saw on maps—then some pictures of yours truly, posed with my family.

My Moms was a brunette with skin somewhere between cinnamon and *café con leche*. Ditto for my chubby little sister, Isabel. And my Pops had wavy dark hair and brown eyes. Then there was me. Hazel eyes, blonde hair, fair skin, and *freckles* for God's sakes! The odd one out—and in glasses! My own cousins used to call me *"blanquito"* and "Pinky," and other things too.

I mean, my looks really got in my face. As I moved along to my room, it was like I could still hear what visitors used to say when they saw me for the first time.

"Oh, what a cute adorable white boy."

"Is he really your son?"

"¿No me digas? But he looks so . . . so . . . different from you!"

On top of that I'd be thinking about something my Moms once told me.

"Mamá," I had asked her. "How come I look so different?"

"¿Qúe?" she asked me, in Spanish.

"Why am I so pale?"

"¡Es nada!" she told me. "It's nothing. You're just lucky, that's all. *Tienes que tener orgullo de ser tan blanco.* You should be proud to be so white."

"But how did that happen?"

"How? What does it matter? You'll have an easier time in life."

"But I want to know."

So she went into a little act. "If you must know, *hijo*, I found you in the garbage can in front of this very building."

"What?"

"*Ríe, es un chiste*," she said. "Come on, laugh. It's a joke!"

Finally, when she saw that I didn't think it was so funny, she gave me the real rundown.

"It's very simple," she told me. "One of your great-grandfathers was an Irishman—*un irlandés*. You have his blood, *me entiendes?*"

I nodded, as it made sense, imagining this blond-haired Irish man, a hundred years ago, stepping off a ship somewhere in Cuba and marrying into my family line. But I still wondered, Why me and no one else?

I thought about that stuff a lot, even when I didn't want to.

Like every time I walked into a bodega in another neighborhood and some Latino kids would give me the evil whammy with their eyes, like I had no business being there. Or I'd be in a department store with my Moms, going through the discount bins, and folks would look us over, as if wondering what that Cuban lady was doing with the white kid, like she was some kind of maid watching over me. And forget about all the times I'd go down into the Harlem park to play softball: I always brought along "get-jumped," money 'cause I attracted both Latino and black takeoff artists who saw my white skin as a kind of flashing neon sign that said "Rob me."

I got jumped so often that I wished I could wear a mask, like a superhero, so that I wouldn't get hassled.

And I had other ghosts to deal with in our own apartment hall. Like every time I walked in, I would think about how my Pops, coming home really plastered, would take forever to open that door with his keys, and how once, he just crashed into this foyer bookcase, bringing all this shit down, all the glass animals and cheap porcelain figures my Moms collected and kept, for some reason, in that hall, and how that made her feel really, really sad.

Then really, really angry.

Anyway, my little dump was at the end of that long and narrow hallway, next to my sister's room. In it I kept my favorite things: my comic books, my beat-up Stella guitar, my transistor radio, and piles of secondhand sci-fi paperbacks and horror magazines.

Man, it was hot in there. I got pliers off my bureau to open the window. Since my room is on a fire escape,

my Moms had the superintendent drill some holes
through the window frames, so that she could put these
big four-inch nails in as locks, in case someone would
try to climb in. She got that way after we'd been broken
into last summer, someone taking the few things we had
worth a damn in the apartment: my Moms's gold chain
and crucifix, a gold ring, a couple of my Pops's Timex
watches, and for some reason, the Hansel and Gretel
weather barometer that one of our neighbors gave us
when she couldn't take the neighborhood anymore and
moved away for good.

My Moms was already freaked about a lot of things,
but that burglary really sent her over the top. She suddenly had a thing about keeping every window shut
whenever we left the apartment, even in the summer:
It drove me crazy. Aside from turning the joint into an
oven, every time I wanted to open my window, I had to
pull those big nails loose with pliers.

Doing so, I leaned my head out to see if my other
buddy, Jimmy, was around.

"Yo Jimmy, you there?" I called down.

Jimmy lived in a basement apartment across the
courtyard in the building behind my own, where his
Pops was the superintendent. It was a dark sanctum,

like where Dracula might be hanging out, and I didn't know how Jimmy put up with living next to a boiler room and ticking electric meters, in an apartment without any windows, but he did. Lately he had been looking especially pasty. I suppose all that stuff was catching up with him, and I could swear that he smelled like a basement—of ashes and electrical wires and heating oil. I never liked going there. So, whenever we hung out, Jimmy usually came up to me.

"Yo Jimmy, you there?" I tried again.

I didn't hear anything at first. I thought that maybe he was somewhere else in the building, sweeping up the floors.

But after a few moments I saw him coming out of the basement passageway. Half Irish and half Puerto Rican, he was a skinny-assed dude, dressed in a sleeveless T-shirt and blue jeans, his hand over his brow, like an Indian scout, his eyes blinking through his glasses from the change of light. He had a thin chain and crucifix around his neck. He was holding a broom.

"Hey, Rico, what's up?" he called.

"You got a second? I got something to run by you!"

"All right, but I'm supposed to be working for my Pops," Jimmy said, like it was a hassle.

While I waited, I took the bills Gilberto had given me and spread them out on my bed. Two hundred smackers! Twenty luscious ten-dollar bills. I stashed a hundred in a sock under my bed for a "rainy day." Then I figured I might give my Pops forty, money being tight since he'd quit one of his two jobs when he'd gotten sick last year. And maybe I'd give my Moms some bucks to buy a dress, and Isabel a ten spot to keep her in the Hershey bars she loved to eat. And that would still leave me enough to buy this nice old Harmony guitar I'd been checking out in a pawnshop window on 125th Street, which was going for fifteen and way better than the cheap Stella guitar I had.

Then I figured I'd throw Jimmy a twenty, so that he could buy himself some first-class artist supplies, like real drawing paper and good ink pens instead of the ballpoints and cheap yellow paper he used to illustrate our homegrown comic-book stories. I wrote them, he drew them up. I mean, the guy could *draw*! And just about anything—from babes in *Playboy*, to scenes from our neighborhood—and it was nothing for him to take characters like Betty and Veronica from the *Archie* comics and show what they would look like without their clothes on. And when it came to copying characters like Spider-Man and the Incredible Hulk, no one could touch him.

He even won some prizes for his drawings in high school. That was before he had to drop out to help his old man around the building—hauling up garbage, and sweeping and mopping them halls for his room and board.

How Jimmy put up with his Pops was beyond me.

Once, I watched Jimmy show his Pops this amazing watercolor drawing he had made in Riverside Park. His Pops hardly glanced at it when he said, "So what's this worth? Ten cents?"

And he threw Jimmy a dime.

Then this other time, Jimmy'd come up with his face covered in bruises, his Pops being the kind of guy who'd slap or punch you just for looking at him the wrong way. I mean, talk about *bad* luck.

But even though his Pops made him feel like crap, when it came to drawing our comics, Jimmy still delivered, holing up in my room for hours and working away. One of our superheroes was called *"El Gato,"* or "The Cat," this dude who could turn himself into a supermuscular feline creature and go anywhere—up walls, down elevator shafts, over rooftops and even fly—in that guise. We did this one eight-page story, in which the Cat falls in love with a dog-woman, and we liked it so much that we printed up forty copies of it on a mimeograph machine at school. Okay, so it came out blue and blurred and smelling inky like school exams, but we were so proud of "The Adventures of *El Gato*!" that we tried to sell copies in front of the subway and on street corners for a dime apiece.

When we sold exactly twelve, that hassled Jimmy, as if all that work had hardly seemed worth the trouble to him.

"Like who would want this stuff anyway?" Jimmy asked me the last time I told him about a new story.

"Like one of the big comic-books companies! That's who!" I said to him. "I mean, Superman was created by two guys our age! And look what happened with that dude, right?" I had to keep reminding Jimmy it was all a part of the learning process. Like, we had to start somewhere.

He just shrugged, as if it didn't matter.

So, each time I got a new idea, I always had to talk him into getting off his butt to work on it.

Now, when I heard Jimmy knocking on the door and I let him in, he was sweating like hell, so much that his glasses, which were held together with Scotch tape, kept slipping down his nose.

"Damn, it's hot, Rico," he said. "I can't believe this shit."

It was so brutal that even the houseflies could barely crawl across the sill, and the linoleum tiles on our floors, the cheap kind, were curling up and buckling like they wanted to get the F out.

"So what's going on?" he asked.

"I got something for you," I said, nodding towards my room.

I was dying to tell him about Gilberto, but I kept it under my hat for the moment.

He plopped down on my bed, and I said, "You know the art supplies you used to talk about buying?"

"Yeah, so what about it?"

"Well, I got the bucks."

"Is that right?"

I gave him two ten-dollar bills.

"Where you'd get this?"

"A little bird gave it to me," I said gleefully.

"Like which little bird?"

"Hey, what's the difference?"

He looked at those bills again. "And I don't have to pay you back?"

"Nah, it's for you, with my blessing, bro," I said.

He folded them up into tiny squares before putting them in his pocket. Then he lit himself up a cigarette. He'd been smoking since he was ten, seven years now.

"But, Jimmy," I said. "I'm giving you this so that you can buy that special kind of paper and stuff."

"Yeah, sure, bristol board and all that shit." He nodded.

"And once we get you hooked up," I went on enthusiastically, "we're gonna put together a real professional comic strip to show the companies. You hear me?" and I slapped him five. "We'll be a real team!"

But he didn't seem too excited.

"No, I mean it. Like, it could be our real chance, right?"

Okay, I didn't expect him to be jumping up and down with joy or kissing my ass over my gift, but to see him so blasé dragged my head.

"Sure, Rico," he said, kind of sighing. "Whatever you say."

"If you want," I told him, "I'll go to the art store with you tomorrow."

It was downtown, on Broadway in the eighties.

"Nah, that's all right," he said, dabbing his sweaty head with part of his T-shirt. "It's too freaking hot anyway. How's about some other time, huh?"

And then he reached into his jeans pocket and pulled out a joint. He was about to light it.

"Jimmy, be cool with that," I said. "My Moms's got a nose like a hound. And believe me, she knows what *yerba* smells like."

"Okay, let's go up to the roof."

Even though I always worried that someone, like the superintendent, Mr. Casey, would catch us, Jimmy couldn't care less. He just loved the Harlem views with all those water towers and church steeples glowing all gold-like in the sun, especially when he was high. But as we were going down the hall, the front door opened and my Moms walked in. "Why hello, Jeemy," she said pleasantly. "How are you?" But with me, she looked cross. "*¿Ay, pero Rico, por qué no me estabas esperando?*"—"Why weren't you waiting for me?" She shook her head. "Why did you make me come up the stairs?"

"Ma," I said, "I was just talking with Jimmy."

"Yes, talking," she said, "but now we go to the A&P."

With that Jimmy took off, and while my Moms used the bathroom, complaining away about me to herself, I started having second thoughts—not about Jimmy, but about spending those bucks on a dress.

three

JIMMY NEVER GOT around to buying those art supplies, but I never got in his face about it. A month went by, and by then the neighborhood had caught wind of Gilberto's bounty. If his lottery win was supposed to be a secret, it didn't stay one for long. Gilberto's mother had started to brag about him at the beauty salon where my Moms worked, boasting that her son had given her enough bucks to buy a little hideaway in Puerto Rico, if she wanted to.

And Gilberto couldn't resist buying all kinds of toys for the little kids on our street, especially pogo sticks— the latest craze. You couldn't walk up the block without seeing all these kids bouncing along the sidewalk and off the curb, or disappearing down a basement stairway, their heads bobbing in and out of sight like basketballs.

I mean they were pogo-stick crazy, thanks to him. But he was a sport about other things too. Like treating the kids to ice cream when the truck came along going *cling*, *cling*, *ding*, *ding*. He even handed out a few twenties to some of the poorer folks on our block who were on welfare.

He seemed so flush with bucks, I half expected him to show up with a brand-new Mustang, or a Harley-Davidson, but he never did.

One day, when I bumped into Gilberto on the street, I just had to come out and ask him what he was planning to do with that money.

"Why, my man, the smartest thing in the world!" he said, putting his arm around my shoulder as we went walking up the hill towards my stoop. "Yes sirree, come late September I'll be starting school at this really sweet little college in the Midwest."

"College? You're going to college? In the Midwest? The *Midwest*? You're jiving me, right?"

"No, I'm not. It's a school in southern Wisconsin."

I nearly gagged. Wisconsin? The first thing that popped into my head was of a fourth-grade project I did for Sister Hillary—or Sister Hillarious as we called the pudgy Sinsenawan nun. I had to make a cardboard model of a Wisconsin farm, with silos, cornfields, and, oh yeah, some Guernseys or Holsteins—I could never remember which was which. Somehow, I couldn't picture Gilberto there—no way.

I scratched my nose.

"But why the hell Wisconsin? Isn't that where all those cows hang out?" I asked.

He shook his head, as if I was crazy to ask. "Look, let me show you something."

Reaching in the back pocket of his jeans, he pulled out a glossy brochure. It was all creased up, like he had folded and unfolded it a million times. We copped a squat on my stoop. When I spread the brochure open on my lap, under the words "Milton College, Where Dreams Come True!" were the prettiest pictures—of green lawns and shady willow trees and wholesome, well-dressed white kids sitting on the manicured grass by a pond, reading books and talking. In the background were all these nice stone churchlike buildings, with arched windows. And in every picture there seemed to be big patches of cheery blue sky, all radiant and shit with sunlight, like the future was shining down on those students.

"So, what do you think?" Gilberto asked me, just as a rat came running out of the basement, past us and into the street.

"What? It's ugly, man," I said, watching the rat's beady little eyes looking out from under a parked car. Gilberto slapped me on the knee.

"No, not that, dummy, the college!"

"Yeah, it looks nice," I said, glancing through the brochure again. "But is that really you? I mean, it looks really boring."

Gilberto started running his fingers through his hair, like he did whenever I started irritating him.

"Boring? How the heck would you know?"

He was right but I couldn't admit it. I guess the idea of him taking off was already bugging me.

"And what are you gonna study out there, anyway?" I asked, glancing at the brochure again. "'Animal husbandry'?"

That was one of the "majors" that was listed in the brochure, along with "horticultural studies," "farming techniques," and "other areas of exciting learning."

He just shook his head.

"Look, Rico, what I end up studying doesn't make a damn bit of difference to me. The thing is, I'll be getting a foot up in life."

Then he grabbed my shoulders.

"Let me ask you something," he said, with this "look

and listen to me, for real" expression. "If you were in my shoes and had a chance to get away from all this crap, wouldn't you want to?"

"Yeah, I guess so," I answered, even if I couldn't imagine living anywhere else.

"I mean, what am I supposed to do, hang around this neighborhood forever?" He got up, started pacing around the sidewalk, checking out the wheels of a parked Oldsmobile, as if for the whereabouts of that rat. "All I know is that I got me a real opportunity. In fact, when I called up those folks out there and told them that I'd been hipped to their school by one of my teachers, and that I didn't want to end up in a community college, they couldn't have been nicer. As long as I had me a high school diploma, I could get in, they said, even on such short notice. On top of that"—he smiled again, stroked his goatee—"they even offered me a partial scholarship on account of the fact that dudes like us are disadvantaged and all."

"I guess that's cool," I conceded.

"I mean, it's a normal place where people do normal things and you don't always have to be watching your back. There are no gangs, no drugs, no muggers, no steamy dirty subways, you hear?"

He was so carried away, he sounded like a preacher.

"So, who in their right mind is gonna turn that chance down?" he continued. "It's an opportunity and a half, a way for this dude to get some *new* electricity in his veins." Then he added, pointing his toothpick at me, "I just want to see something else besides this funky neighborhood and I don't want to end up in Vietnam one day to do it."

Looking down at my shoes, I knew Gilberto was right. I tried smiling, but couldn't.

"What's with the big-assed frown?" Gilberto asked. "You should be happy for me!"

"I am, it's just that—"

"Rico," he said, putting his arm around me, grinning big-time like a brother. "If you're worried that I'm going to go off and forget about my little *cubano* buddy here, get that crazy stuff out of your head, all right?"

But I couldn't help it. I *was* feeling sorry for myself. At the same time I knew that I was being a total jerk and had to lighten up. So I finally squeezed out a smile and told Gilberto that his going away to school was one of the greatest things in the world.

four

ON ANOTHER DAMN hot night, a Saturday, while his Moms was upstate visiting her sister in Albany, Gilberto threw himself a going-away party. I'd spent the afternoon helping him get the cold cuts, chips, sodas, and beer. Afterwards, up in his Moms's apartment, Gilberto decided, of all things, to give me a Latin dance lesson.

"How come?" I asked him.

"Because it's about time. You may not look it, but you are one hundred percent Cuban. And as a good *cubano*, you got to get these moves down, all right?"

I had to nod. After all, Cubans were supposed to be among the best dancers in the whole world.

"Besides it'll be one hell of a party. Okay, bro?"

I nodded again, humbly and shit. The truth was that, for some reason, my Moms and Pops had never bothered to teach me—and so what else was I going to do? Especially since it was going to be my first dance party away from home.

So, I just waited while Gilberto looked through his Moms's collection of mambo and cha-cha records piled on top of the living room phonograph console, and put some old crackly record on the spindle.

He turned some knobs. The radio went on: "Splish splash, I was taking a bath, *bap bap bap pa boom!*" came blaring out. Then he clicked it onto the phonograph setting. The record dropped down the turning spindle, turning with a thunk, the needle settling into the grooves: *scritch, scritch, scratch, scratch*, a piano playing hot chords, more scratches, trumpets wailing, then drums and bongos and a cow bell going crazy, *scritch, scritch, scratch, scratch*, the rhythm in *dat dat dat—dat dat* time, but really fast, and in a way that was already confusing the hell out of me.

"Now, come on, my man," Gilberto said, pulling me up to my feet.

And there I was, standing in front of Gilberto and feeling as demure as hell—(translation: freaking timid and shy and scared of looking like a jerk). We started anyway.

"First thing you got to learn is the basic Latin

shimmy," he said. "Like how to pivot on your hips. And then you do this thing with your feet, putting your right foot forward, like you're bowing to someone, then back, then left foot out, then back, then stepping in place again with your right foot, while rolling on your heels, but to the time, one, two, three, one, two, and always swiveling on your hips. You got that, Rico?"

"I think so," I meekly answered.

"Above all, bro, you got to imagine that you're dancing with the flyest girl in the world. I mean, you got to show off your *huevos*, got that?"

"Okay," I said, shrugging.

Well, I stumbled around a lot, messing up, as if I had sandbags tied to my legs. I knew mostly rock-'n'-roll style, without much grace. But Gilberto kept after me, repeating like a Marine Corps drill instructor, "One, two, three, one, two!" and "Bend your knees and move them hips!" and "Don't be a pussy about it!" and "No! It's not like doing the damn mashed potato!"

We were at it for an hour, and all that time, I kept wondering what people, looking up into Gilberto's window from the street, might be thinking at the sight of an awkward white left-footed galoomp of a kid trying to dance the mambo.

✳   ✳   ✳

Since this was my party debut—if it wasn't at Gilberto's, my Moms would have never let me go—I spent the longest time getting ready in front of the bathroom mirror. Long enough for my little sister to start goofing on me.

"Rico's in love! Rico's in love!" Isabel kept saying, stretching "love" into about ten syllables.

I brushed my teeth three times, drowned my hair with my Pops's Vitalis, and slapped on all kinds of Old Spice, so much that I had a sneezing fit. I put on a new shirt, then the wash-and-wear slacks that never creased, and a pair of black suede shoes, hoping that I would look really cool. But every time I looked in that mirror, I wished that I had a button I could press to make my skin a few tones darker, my hazel eyes brown, and my hair black, like adjusting the brightness on a TV set.

I got to the party around eight, after putting up with the third degree from my Moms.

"I don't want you smoking any cigarettes—or anything else!" she warned me. "And you keep away from the bad boys! And you have to be home by eleven. Later than that, something bad can happen to you."

"But *mamá*, it's just across the street."

"I don't care! If you're not home by eleven, I'll send your Poppy over to get you. *Me prometes*, okay?"

"Okay, okay."

But I really didn't have to worry about that: After coming home from his double shift at the Havana-Seville restaurant, my Pops was dozing on the living room couch, the heat of the day and the two big frosty beers he drank first thing through the door having gotten to him. Even down the hall, and over the sound of our sputtering black-and-white TV set, on some stupid game show, I could hear him snoring away. With luck, he might sleep through the whole night.

In any case, when I walked into Gilberto's apartment, with Jimmy in one of his slo-mo modes by my side, the whole place was jumping and so jammed with people that you could hardly move through the room, let alone see anything clearly, with all the lamps fitted with colored bulbs and everybody already dripping with sweat even though the windows were open and Gilberto had fans blowing all over the place. A mix of soul and Latin music blared from the living room, and some of the finest girls in the neighborhood, and girls I had never seen before, were dancing the Watusi, or the mashed potato, or a Latin-style boogaloo in a crazy mix of bodies, everybody bending to the music and gliding in all directions.

A lot of the neighborhood guys were gathered in little packs, snapping among themselves—telling jokes, slapping each other five, and generally carrying on. They were drinking down Gilberto's special rum and gin and vodka punch like they were camels and it was the only water in the desert. Every other thing you heard was "F—king this" and "F—king that." And if a girl came by, they got even rowdier, trying out their raps. (The guys in military uniforms made out the best.) It was kind of chaotic and exciting at the same time, especially when this guy, Chops, passed out from the heat or the booze and slammed into the living room wall, bringing down some family pictures, everybody laughing at first, then applauding when he pushed himself up from the floor.

Then a whole stream of just Latin records kicked in. With that, Gilberto dragged my ass onto the floor and introduced me to this fine *cubanita* named Alicia, who checked me out suspiciously. She was so fly, the only way I could work up the nerve to hit that dance floor was to drink some of Gilberto's atomic-powered, kick-ass-and-take-no-prisoners mystery punch. I downed a glassful, then another.

And let me tell you, you could have sent a rocket ship

up to the planet Krypton with that stuff. Almost instantly, I felt so loose I was sure I could float across the room. For a few songs I was the greatest dancer in the world, even when I sometimes stepped on that poor Alicia's feet. I tried to be cool, but it just wasn't happening: I mean, with all that punch inside me, I grew elephant legs and couldn't even keep time.

Alicia soon disappeared into the crowd.

But I really didn't care. Mainly I was into that punch. A few sips and I'd be down to the bottom of a plastic cup. Then, like magic, there was always someone there to fill it up again. And man, did that stuff get my tongue loose: I told everybody about how me and Jimmy were going to conquer the comic-book world one day. And about my guitar playing and the way my neighbor, Mr. Lopez, had taught me my first chords when I was just a kid of seven. I bragged about being able to play just about anything—Beatles songs, Dylan, the Temptations—but no one really believed me.

After a while, I lost track of the time. And I didn't always know where Jimmy had gone. One second he was standing beside me, tapping his feet to the music, and the next he was by the window, having a smoke. Then he was out on the dance floor himself, the guy's hips moving like a pendulum, as he did a Latin shimmy even while he was nursing a bottle of beer. He was a zombie one second, and then electrified the next.

It was like a Clark Kent–Superman kind of thing. By my side again, his engine wasn't running too tough. He'd slouch slightly, as if the force of gravity was pulling him down. And then, getting a whiff of the reefer that some folks were smoking out on the fire escape, he'd disappear again.

When I finally caught up with him, Jimmy was climbing back out onto the fire escape. Folks offered me a drag, but I already had enough going on with that punch.

Gilberto made a point of walking over to us just then.

"Well, what's going on with you, James? My boy Rico here tells me you guys are doing comic books together."

"Sort of. Rico's the brains behind the whole thing."

"Ah man," Gilberto replied. "Forget the brains, it's the talent that counts! I've seen some of your stuff. It's freakin' great!"

"Yeah, but that was just copying. . . ."

"All I know is, I couldn't do it!" Gilberto said. "So don't be so frowny-assed about your gift, huh?"

That's when Gilberto got into that older brother mode, pulling me close to his side, nearly crushing me.

"One thing, Jimmy," he said, half strangling me with his arm. "I'll be doffing out of here real soon. And the one thing I got to ask you—and for real—is that you look out for my little buddy here. I mean, I don't want him getting into any kind of trouble, and most of all, I don't want him to be getting caught up with any kind of nonsense—no drugs, no skag, you understand?"

Pushing his glasses towards his brow, Jimmy nodded.

Then Gilberto poked his finger into Jimmy's chest.

"I mean it. 'Cause while I'm gone somebody's got to look out for my boy here."

"Sure," Jimmy said, nearly flinching.

"All right!" Gilberto said.

And he gave Jimmy such a rap in the shoulders, his glasses fell to the floor.

I was there for a few hours more. I danced, the girls glowing pink like helium balloons. I kept hearing *har*, *har*s, all night, Gilberto's friends getting off on watching straight little fifteen-year-old Rico stumbling around.

The room began spinning in all kinds of crazy ways.

I threw up twice.

Finally, looking at a clock, I couldn't tell what time

it was, the little hands wriggling all around like funny animals in the cartoons, even when I squinted. Jimmy had left by then, with ten bucks I had lent him—where to, I didn't know.

Then something crazy happened.

Gilberto's bell started ringing. Not with just *ting*, *ting*, like someone showing up late, but with a constant loud pressing of the *timbre* button. No one reacted. Then there was a pounding at the door. And a shrill female voice: *"¡Abre la puerta!"*—"Open the door!"—again and again in Spanish.

Not having a watch, I asked this guy Eddie for the time.

"One thirty in the a.m."

I thought, Holy shit!

Then the pounding got louder, until someone finally opened the door.

Well, in walked my Moms, holding a broom. And, boy, did she look pissed off. Pushing her way through the crowd, the first thing she did was slap my face, screaming a thousand-words-a-minute Spanish at me. Then she dragged me out by my right ear, even when Gilberto raced over and tried to explain that it was all harmless fun.

"Oh, yes? I should call the police!" she told him.

I left Gilberto's place, hearing more laughter, and on

the street my Moms really let me have it with that broom, whacking me on the back and on my butt, like I'd robbed a bank instead of just hanging out and doing what most of the kids in the neighborhood did. And as she kept hitting me, I wondered about why she was being so hard on my ass. As she screamed and screamed at me in Spanish, I wished I could build myself a spaceship and take off for the moon, or crawl into one of the sidewalk garbage cans to hide, and, oh yeah, mainly just disappear into some other time or place, like the Flash or the Green Lantern.

A few days later, I helped Gilberto bring down his suitcases. A gypsy cab was waiting to take him to the airport, and I watched him kissing his Moms good-bye. It was a weird thing: She was crying and crying like he was going off to war.

And I felt like crying a little too.

So we said good-bye or so long or whatever folks say when they're going off to college. I mean it was a big deal. The *Amsterdam News* had even sent a photographer to snap some shots of Gilberto going off (the next day's newspaper would show a photograph of Gilberto waving from the gypsy cab window, a caption saying, "Lucky Local Lottery Winner off to College").

A lot of folks came over to wish him well, and up and down the street you could see people hanging out their windows, waving good-bye.

It was just so freaking nice and sad at the same time.

"So you're okay, huh?" Gilberto asked me just before he was going to take off.

"Yeah, it's just that . . ."

"What?"

"Don't you be forgetting about me, right?" I said in a quiet voice.

Gilberto cocked his brows, smiled.

"Forget about you? Nah, man. I got you right here," he said, tapping his own chest.

Then he gave me a big embrace.

"You take care, and keep your nose clean, all right?" he said, looking me in the eyes. "'Cause if I hear about you messing up, I will personally come back here and kick your ass to kingdom come."

I smiled because I knew he would.

Then, just like that, he gave his Moms another hug, got into the gypsy cab, and started heading uptown to the Bronx, and east towards JFK, off to catch a plane to this enchanted land of butter and milk and corn called Wisconsin.

five

CRAZY. LOUSY. CROWDED. Jive.

Those words being about my new public high school down on Columbus Avenue, "Jo Mama's," as it had been nicknamed by its students.

I started there that September, having left my Catholic school in the Bronx to spare my Pops the tuition money.

Imagine a big, mustard-colored bowl filled with about five thousand black and brown beans, and then sort through it, to find a few white ones here and there. Just watch most of the beans minding their own business, but a few of them going out of their way to hassle and bump into the white beans. Imagine some of those beans walking around so high that they slip out the bowl, or turn weird putrid colors, and some of the others asking the white beans for money every time they got jostled together. Imagine one of those white beans just staring over the edge, and wishing that he could just hop out of that bowl like a dime-store jumping bean.

Well, that white bean was me.

One night, about two months after Gilberto had left, I was in our kitchen sitting over a plate of *frijoles negros* when that bean thing slipped into my mind.

"Rico," asked my Moms. "*¿Qué te pasa?*"

"Oh, I was just thinking, Mommy."

"Yes, always thinking," she said. "Well, you should think about how hard your Poppy works to put food on the table, and eat!"

"I know, *mamá*," I answered.

"Just look at your sister, finishing everything off her plate!"

She always did. My little *gordita* sister was really going at it with a chicken leg at the time.

"She has the right mentality, doesn't she, Rolando?" my Moms said to my Pops. "Appreciating what we do with the sweat of our brows, not like *El Príncipe*, here"—The Prince—"who has always had it easy."

"Whatever you say, *mi amorcita*," my Pops said, sipping from a glass of beer.

"Yes, my love" was one of his most usual responses to just about anything she ever said. He'd always wink at me, and then nod his head slightly, as if to say, *Don't provoke her.*

And yet I always somehow did. Every freaking night.

"But *mamá*, how can you say that, when I got a job in the mornings, and one after school, and I give you half my money every week?"

"*¿Qué?*" she said, as if she couldn't understand any English, the way she always did whenever I said something she didn't want to hear.

I tried to repeat myself in Spanish, which was half-assed compared to my English.

"What did he say?" she asked my Pops. From her expression I knew what she was thinking: *There he is again, my own son, a born and bred child of Cubans, refusing to speak Spanish, like he's above it.*

My Pops sighed.

"Only that he tries hard to help us," he explained to her.

"Well, that's the least he can do," she said in Spanish,

"after all the burdens he brought to our family."

Oh yeah, the burdens. It always came back to the burdens. Just about every day. Like we would have been rich somehow, if I hadn't gotten sick when I was a little kid. I could hardly remember a thing about that, having been only five years old at the time. Only that my Moms went into the bathroom one day and found blood all over the place; then she had come running into my room to find me sleeping on blood-soaked sheets, the stuff leaking out of me like crazy. Yeah, she freaked, went knocking on a neighbor's door—we had no telephone—begging them to call a doctor. It turned out that something was really messed up inside of me, and just like that, I was shipped off for two freaking years to a bunch of hospitals—that's right, *two!*

I finally got better, but a whole bunch of messed-up things happened along the way.

1. (Or *número uno*) I was lonely and scared as shit forever and ever.
2. I missed my folks, but I didn't see them a whole lot—one of the hospitals being way up in Massachusetts.

3. While I was holed up there, nobody talked to me in Spanish, and when I did get home and heard Spanish again, it sounded weird to me. That's when my Moms started making faces because she couldn't always understand what the freakin' hell I was saying.

4. My Pops blamed my Moms for my sickness, and my Moms blamed me for being such a delicate little pussy. She wouldn't even let me out of the apartment when it rained, like if I got wet or something all that blood would start coming out from me again. That's when I started giving off all these mama's boy, Little Lord Fauntleroy vibrations. (And when I decided to get lost in comic-book science-fiction land and began to make friends with Jimmy and Gilberto.)

But the worst was all those bills—for hospital stays, medicines, and doctors (*los gastos*) that my Pops, even with his two jobs, never really caught up with, a permanent look of worry coming over his face, and my Moms, no matter how much I tried to help out, still acting like my sickness was something I had wished on them.

Yeah, the burdens.

I just looked down at the table. Then I looked a little farther below, where a cockroach was skittering across the linoleum, no doubt going to a cockroach carnival inside the baseboards.

When I didn't answer her, she said, "Didn't you hear what I just said to you?"

I nodded.

"Then, why don't you have the respect to answer me?"

"You didn't ask me anything, *mamá*. What do you want from me?"

"From you? Nothing."

Then she looked at me as if it was all my fault.

I guess she really hated living where we lived. When she met my Pops, years ago in Cuba, and he was this boss, handsome dude courting her, the last thing she expected was to end up in a dump like our apartment. Once upon a time she told me about how she was raised in a nice little house on a farm out in the Cuban countryside, where beautiful flowers and towering palms grew everywhere. I mean, she wasn't rich, but she was happy. But then my Pops came along with all these ideas about coming north to New York City, where even a guy like himself, from the sticks and without much of an education, was supposed to find a better life (that was years before the Cuban revolution, by the way). So without knowing much English, they settled down in New York City, where I was born, and my Pops took whatever jobs he could find. One day he became a waiter and we moved into the half-assed building where we lived. He never made a lot of money, and things were already hard enough on everybody without my coming along and getting sick on them. Somehow, I had become a part of the dark magic that took those old dreams from her.

I think she had some formula going on in her head. Like my Pops taking on an extra job for so many years to pay off our debts equaled the heart attack that almost did him in last winter.

But she was always a little jive with me anyway. Even before my Pops got sick. I couldn't figure why. Sometimes she'd just be staring at me, like she envied my white skin. It made me feel so weird, her looking at me with this puzzled expression on her face, as if I was some rich white kid, slumming it up with the spics in our apartment. It was the look she was giving me now.

"From you, I expect nothing," she said again, collecting my plate.

"You just go and live your happy *la-la-la* life," she

added. "You take all the drugs you want and have a good time. It's nothing to me."

Drugs? That was another of her themes.

"*Mamá*, I don't take drugs."

"No, you are as innocent as a lamb. *Un santo.* That's why I found you at Gilberto's so drunk and *quién sabe más!*"—"who knows what else!"

At that point I could really understand why my Pops always had a pint of rye whiskey around. I could understand why he often headed off to a local watering hole, Mr. Farrentino's bar, on the way home from work.

Even before his heart attack.

Before I went to bed that night, my Pops came over and put his large warm hands on my face. Pulling me close he whispered, *"Sin embargo, Rico, no olvidas que tu mamá es una mujer buena"*—"No matter what, Rico, don't forget that your mother is a good woman."

Maybe. But, man, she was one hard case.

That night I couldn't sleep. So while my folks watched TV—I could hear the theme from *The Beverly Hillbillies* show—I started going through a big pile of stories, all written out on yellow pads in ballpoint pen, looking for a good one.

See, a few days before, I had gotten up the chops to call one of the comic-book companies. DC Comics, the guys who published *Superman*.

It went like this.

Ring, ring, ring, ring.

An operator picked up.

"And with whom do you want to speak?"

I said, "Mr. Julius Schwartz," the name I had seen listed in tiny print on the first page of every DC comic.

"One moment, please."

My stomach was in knots, my legs filling with lead.

Then this guy with a deep voice that sounded like he was a burly, barrel-chested guy answered: "Yes, Julius Schwartz speaking."

And I gave him the whole scoop, mainly that Jimmy and me had all kinds of stories and different characters cooking. Told him about The Mountain, and about Lord Lightning, but when I mentioned the Latin Dagger, he sounded particularly interested.

"The 'Latin Dagger,' you say? I like the ring of that. What's that about?"

"Well sir, like he's a superhero from the ghetto. I mean, he's a Puerto Rican guy or maybe Cuban . . ."

"Yes?"

"But he's like a combination of Zorro and Batman and Zeus. I mean, he is a dark-looking character, but very cool."

He laughed.

"You sound kind of young to me," he said. "Are you?"

I lied.

"I'm eighteen."

"Well, that's young, believe you me."

And I heard this guttural laughter coming up from his chest.

"But however old you are," he said, "I'll tell you what you have to do."

"Okay."

"You get yourself some standard eleven by seventeen bristol pages and send me a fully laid-out story. Doesn't have to be inked, but with good pencils, okay? And you send them along with a self-addressed, postage-paid envelope, understand?"

"Yes, sir."

"Well, good-bye now, and when you send them over, remind me about our conversation, won't you?"

And he hung up.

* * *

I was dying to tell Jimmy about that phone call, but I figured that I should decide which Latin Dagger how-he-got-his-powers story was the best before putting him to work on it.

I read one of them over. And it still seemed all right to me.

It was about a spindly, crippled Latino kid named Ricky Ramirez. His neighborhood was terrible, what with junkies and criminals everywhere, and being a good kid, he just wished he could change all of that. One rainy night, while walking home on his crutches, he comes across this old Spanish dude who's lying out in an alley, some guys having just done a number on him. The old man's been crying for help, but no one has stopped to help him, until Ricky does. The old man has a long white beard and isn't dressed like a normal person at all: He looks like a wise man from a King Arthur tale. Turns out that he's a seven-hundred-year-old wizard from Spain. And so, once Ricky helps him, the old wizard, as a reward for his kindness, promises to give Ricky something that will fix his messed-up legs. And that something is a secret magic spell.

But here's the thing: In exchange for this gift, Ricky must devote himself to good deeds. The wizard tells

Ricky that Destiny has sent him there for a reason. And the reason is that the world needs a new hero to fight the forces of Evil.

In addition to fixing up his legs, that spell will give him the greatest weapons to fight that evil.

A magic dagger and a cape of indestructibility!

Oh, heed my words, young man. Each
time you repeat that spell, for one hour
by day or night, you will be stronger
than any mortal. You will be great,
but with your powers will come much
responsibility!

Then after he instructs Ricky to recite that spell in front of a church where the forces of good are most easily called forth, the old man dies, and as soon as he closes his eyes, he just vanishes.

Poof!

So Ricky does what aspiring superheroes do. He follows the old man's instructions. He heads to a church and begins to recite the spell. Then all these mystic forces come swirling down from the sky upon him. Lifted up, he feels himself changing. His body is no longer weak; his legs are suddenly strong and so is the rest of him. When he lands back on the ground, in a hoary mist, he is no longer wearing his street clothes but a black, skintight outfit, and has a cape draped over his shoulders. The last touch is a glowing dagger that falls from the sky into his hands. It speaks to him, saying:

> I was forged on the battlefields of human
> folly, but with me, thou shalt help stamp
> out the cruelties and injustices you see
> unfolding before you, each day.

His first big battle takes place that very night, with all these stone gargoyles shooting up from Hell—

> For evil wishes to destroy the good before
> it can blossom!

Fighting them, in a spectacular battle, he cuts each one into pieces with his magic dagger, only to see each cut-up gargoyle multiply. But then he figures out how to get rid of them. With his superstrength, he tosses the gargoyles up into space, where they remain, in orbit circling the Earth, petrified and helpless forever.

When the hour passes, he changes back to his former spindly self, and though he can now walk without the crutches, he decides that he must continue to use them as part of his secret identity. Promising himself to use that one hour of superpower each day to carry out good deeds, he heads back home to eat supper with his widowed mother. When she asks him, "What's new?" he tells her, "Not much, Mom. Just another day in my boring ordinary life." But he winks at the reader while saying so.

Okay, so he wasn't Spider-Man, but the idea was pretty good anyway. This was the one. Psyched, I opened my window and stuck my head out, whistling and calling out Jimmy's name into the courtyard. He didn't answer.

Come to think of it, for the past month I hadn't seen much of him at all.

six

IN THE MORNING, after my early shift at Mr. Gordon's laundry, I caught a bus down to school. At about ten to nine I passed through Jo Mama's front gates, where some of the students were getting spot-checked for weapons or drugs. Then I climbed a stairway up to homeroom on the third floor, where my teacher, Mrs. Ernestina Thompson, a black lady, was trying to take attendance. But it wasn't easy: In a classroom where the students were goofing on each other, throwing shit, listening to radios, blowing bubble gum, and generally ignoring her, it was like she almost didn't exist.

Just as the bell was about to ring, commencing the school day officially, and just as Mrs. Thompson was starting up with one of her "You may hate school now but won't regret these circumstances in the future" speeches, three gunshots sounded from the street—*crack, crack, crack*. Then, a minute later, there were two more, louder, closer, and echoing, like they were coming from the downstairs entrance hall.

Telling everybody to stay put, Mrs. Thompson dashed out of the classroom, us kids going crazy with excitement.

"Wuz that a 45? Or a 9 mm?" a kid asked.

"Or a shotgun. That would be cool. What chew think?"

Then a fire alarm went off and an announcement came over the speaker system. The principal, Mr. Myers, informed everybody that "an incident involving gun-play" had taken place and that we should all keep calm. A few of my classmates, these tough-looking black guys, got up, running out into the halls like they had to rescue a buddy, but the rest of us waited.

By then Mrs. Thompson came back with the scoop. She looked so concerned that even the wisest-assed student made no smart remarks. Suddenly not an eraser or crumpled candy wrapper was flying around the room.

"My dear children," she began, her expression serious. "As you've heard, there's been another shooting in our school."

Another shooting? That's just great! I thought.

Sorting through some papers on her desk, and sighing big time, she went on. "Just remember, no matter how often this kind of tragic thing happens, we've got to stay positive, understand?"

"Uh-huh" and "Yes, Mrs. Thompson," said a few of the students, while most—you could feel it—were hoping to get the rest of the day off. Then, just as Mrs. Thompson was about to read aloud to us from a book, that wish came true. A second announcement came over the PA saying that classes were being suspended. As we filed into the hall, a few kids looked really worried, but most were happy, like it was suddenly a holiday.

Pulled along by the crowd, I got down to the first floor, where a part of that hallway had been cordoned off with yellow ropes. Even with guards trying to move everyone out the building, you couldn't help but look. And there he was, a black kid lying in a pool of his own blood, his feet, in Converse sneakers, twitching like crazy. As the school nurse tried to stop his bleeding with these big bandages, his eyes were dazed and wide open with a holy-shit expression of shock in them, and he was trembling. The security guards kept yelling at everybody to move along, but I couldn't stop staring at the poor kid.

Just when a whole bunch of cops burst in, an ambulance crew trailing behind them, this security guard poked my shoulder with a nightstick: "Hey, boy, are you deaf? Clear the hell out, and I mean it, now!"

So, feeling kind of numb, I made my way to the street.

That's when Mrs. Thompson, spotting me in the crowd, made a point of coming over. She had a kind face, mottled over with freckles, her features all soft and sweet except for her eyes, which looked like they had seen all kinds of sad things and got all scrunched up when she spoke to you. Her voice was gentle.

"Guess you're new here, aren't you, son?"

"Yes, ma'am. It's my first semester."

"Well, I wouldn't let this kind of thing upset you. It happens. Some of the kids who come here just don't have any common sense."

"That's for sure," I said, trying to sound cool.

She smiled. "Look, you'll get by, just as long as you keep your nose clean and keep an eye on the goal, which is your education," she said, dragging out the word *ed-you-kay-shun.*

"Yes, ma'am."

"By the way, Rico, anytime you need advice, you can come and find me at my office."

"Thank you, Mrs. Thompson," I answered in my most pious and sincere tone of voice.

Once she left, I got all pensive and stuff, and for some reason I felt like heading over to a nearby stationery store, to check out the latest comic books. There was just something about superheroes that cheered me up; like wouldn't it be great if they existed in the real world instead of just between the covers of comic books? And when I got into that frame of mind and started up with the whole thing about Good versus Evil, I supposed that the Man Upstairs was the biggest freaking superhero of them all. But if He was, I wondered why the Dude wasn't doing a better job about keeping kids from getting popped, you know?

Anyway, I hung around on the street long enough to watch the meds wheeling the kid into that ambulance, a plasma tube stuck in his arm, an oxygen cup over his face, his sneakers still twitching like crazy.

seven

LATER, BACK UPTOWN, I was walking down the hill on Amsterdam Avenue on my way to the 125th Street library. I was reading this really great book for my English class, *The Adventures of Huckleberry Finn,* about this kid who takes off with a slave to find their freedom, a different kind of thing for me. I wanted to see if there were other books by that author, Mark Twain, on those shelves.

That's when I bumped into Jimmy on the corner of 119th Street. He was in a beat-up raincoat and a Yankees baseball hat.

He was as startled as I was.

"So where you been, James? I haven't seen you lately," I said, knocking fists with him.

"You know, uh, just around."

"But it's been, like, a month!"

"Well, man, with my Pops riding me all the time, I said to hell with that and got me a new job—at Mr. F's bar. You know, like helping out in the kitchen."

"No shit?" I said, surprised.

We started walking.

"So what's going on with you?" Jimmy asked. "How come you're not in school?"

I told him about the shooting. Then I told him about how that editor at DC seemed interested in the Latin Dagger.

But it hardly registered on Jimmy's face.

"Isn't that cool?" I pressed him.

He just shrugged, looking impatiently around.

"Look, I don't know if I'm really still into that stuff," he finally said. "I mean, the thing is, sometimes you just got to move on."

He seemed nervous about something, though: He kept pushing his glasses high on his nose, his brow sweating up a storm.

"But Jimmy, wouldn't it be great to be making some bucks from something you like to do?" I asked him, tapping his shoulder. That just made him stop in his tracks.

"Rico, come on," he said. "You really think it would ever come to anything?"

"Maybe not, but what's the harm in trying?"

He took out a cigarette, lighting it even while he caught a blast of bus exhaust. "Listen, I'm in no mood to argue with you, okay?" He rubbed his nose. "I just ain't into that stuff right now."

As he said that, I could see a world of beatings in his eyes. But something else, too: I mean, he looked kind of sickly.

"Come on, what's really up with you lately?" I asked him.

"You really want to know?" he said, crossing over the curb to spit.

"Yeah, I do." Then I added, "I really do."

He fixed a stare on me.

"Then come with me. I can use someone at my back, anyway," he said, hoofing it along the avenue.

With that mysterious message in my head, we went down the hill for a few blocks, coming to the projects on 124th Street and Amsterdam Avenue. They were these big, boxy, red-brick buildings, maybe twenty stories high, with rows and rows of apartments, each one with the same kinds of windows, one looking just like the other. Messed up as living in a tenement walk-up could be, at least our buildings had character — like pillars and sometimes stone-carved angels and stars decorating the stoops. But there was nothing pretty about the projects. I'd never even been inside one before, always passing by them quickly on my way to the shops of 125th Street.

Like you wouldn't want to spend any kind of time there.

Even my Pops had told me, "Whatever you do, never go into places like that."

But that's exactly where we were going, heading along a pathway of cracked pavement towards a playground, where these big — I mean *big* — black kids with bandanas around their heads were hanging out by these scrawny-assed ginkgo trees, off of whose spindly branches dangled pouches of pot.

"Uh, so, what are we doing here?" I asked Jimmy.

"Well, you wanted to know what I'm up to, right?"

"Yeah."

"Well, then check it out. But be cool."

As we approached, I wasn't too happy about the way those black guys were looking at me.

You best believe I was scared.

As we walked over to them, one of those guys slapped Jimmy five — like he'd known him for a while.

"You here to see Clyde?" the same guy said to Jimmy.

"Yeah, that's right."

"Then follow me."

We came to a side entrance; the guy rapped on the metal door. Through a cracked-glass, honeycombed window, a pair of bloodshot eyes peered at us. Then the dude pushed that door open. As he did so, he pulled a .22-caliber pistol out from inside his belt, which he showed us quickly, smiling as he tucked it back in his waistband. Then he swung the door all the way open.

We went inside. Or to put it another way, Jimmy went in first, and I slinked in after him. For a few minutes we waited under these sickly, hepatitis-yellow fluorescent lights, which kept flickering on and off. Leaning against a wall, I just stared down at my penny loafers, anything being better than looking at all the eyes that were on me. And my man, Jimmy? He kept jiggling the loose change in his raincoat pockets, tapping his right foot nervously. Finally a brawny black guy, who wore a patch over his right eye like a pirate, seemed to have popped up from the darkest reaches of the hall.

I guessed he was Clyde.

Giving me a fierce up and down, he looked *really*

pissed off, his mouth all twisted like he was chewing on something bad.

"So who's the pussy-faced *dark dude?*" he shouted, disgusted, at Jimmy, who stepped back into a corner.

I wanted to get the hell out of there.

"Hey, Jimmy, I axed you, what's with the *dark dude?*" and he poked Jimmy in the chest with his index finger.

"His name is Rico. He's a *cubano*," Jimmy finally said, taking out a handkerchief and dabbing his forehead.

"*Cubano?*" And he spit. "What's that supposed to mean to me? He's a white MF."

Then he stared meanly into Jimmy's eyes. Jimmy was shaking.

"Yeah, I know, I know, but I swear he's cool."

"Cool? Why, shit he is," Clyde said, cracking his knuckles, really loud. "Ain't no whitey on Earth who's that!"

Hearing that word said that way, like being a whitey was pure ugliness, I half smiled and shrugged—why I don't know—but then Clyde shot me an even nastier look, like my being there was nothing to joke about.

"Look," Jimmy said, holding his hands up. "He's my man. You think I'd mess with you?"

And suddenly, looking me over again and maybe

judging me harmless, Clyde calmed down and his manner changed. "All right, all right," he said. Like a friendly shopkeeper, he put his arm around Jimmy's shoulder and asked, "Now, what can I do for you today, my brother?"

"Well, like what we talked about, right?"

"Oh yeah," Clyde said, nodding. "I got it ready. But give me that scratch first."

Turning around, Jimmy pulled a wad of bills, wrapped in a rubber band, out of his left raincoat pocket. Somehow the way he wouldn't look at me, while handing it to Clyde, made me tighten up even more.

"Is this three hundred?" he asked.

"Yeah, man. Count it if you want to."

And Clyde did—twice—and when he was done, he headed over to a corner where he kept a metal box behind some pipes, opened it up, and pulled out an envelope, which he handed to Jimmy.

As Jimmy took a quick look into it, Clyde said, "Trust me, my friend. It's all there. And totally, totally fine, the best of the best, and one hundred percent copacetic."

"I know it, man," said Jimmy, giving him a power handshake, Clyde smiling and myself—well, I was nearly pissing in my pants.

"So we're all set, right?" Clyde said.

"Yeah," Jimmy said. "But do me a solid and give me two bags for myself."

"Uh, well, I could have guessed that," Clyde said, laughing. And as Jimmy pulled out two ten-dollar bills from his pocket, Clyde reached into his shirt pocket, coming up with a cigarette package. Only it didn't have cigarettes in it, just a whole bunch of little glassine envelopes, the size of razor blade wrappers, containing white powder. Clyde emptied two packets out onto Jimmy's palm.

They were filled with heroin: I knew it from the little empty wrappings I'd see on the floor of the boys' room at Jo Mama's, and from a film I once saw in the school auditorium about drugs and how to avoid them, half the kids in the audience being high and snickering when it was shown.

But I also knew what it was because I could read it in Jimmy's eyes. He just looked ashamed of himself, but at the same time, like he didn't give a damn.

All I knew was that I wanted to get out of there, but then, Jimmy, having that stuff in hand, asked him, "Okay if I do some now?"

"Here?" and Clyde seemed all annoyed again. But

then he said, "All right, but go over there under the stairs. And you better have your own works!"

"I do."

Then turning to me, Jimmy said, "Come on, Rico. No lectures please—just help me out."

Next thing I knew, I was standing beside Jimmy under a stairwell, still not quite registering what "help me out" could mean. When he pulled out a small leather case and opened it up, I could hardly believe what was in it: a bottle cap, a pair of pincers, a small plastic bottle of water, a lighter, and a thin hypodermic needle, the kind that my auntie uses for her diabetes. "Jessuz, Jimmy," I said. Far as I was concerned he had to be totally *loco* to be doing that stuff. Me? Hell no! I wouldn't jam a needle into my arm for a million dollars. I'd seen enough of them needles in the hospital to last me a lifetime, but that's just what Jimmy was about to do. Anyway, kiddies, this is how he prepared for it: First, he put the powder in the cap, which he held steady with pincers, and then, adding water, cooked it up with his Ronson lighter. After a few moments it began to boil. That's when he took the syringe and started to suck that fluid up into the needle casing. Fishing a piece of rubber tubing out from his pocket, he turned to me.

"Do me a favor—wrap this tube around my forearm. Hold it tight, okay?"

When I hesitated, thinking that it was some bad business, like something out of a horror movie, Jimmy glared at me. "Come on, don't be such a dark dude."

So I did as he asked, even if I thought it sucked, and as the veins rose up plump and darkish blue on his arm, I actually felt a little sick. He was shooting heroin. Smack. Snow. Skag. The white angel. I'd never seen anybody shooting heroin before, let alone my best friend. I mean, when the hell did he start shooting that stuff?

"Rico, untie the tube," Jimmy instructed.

Then he pushed the plunger. To be truthful, it was kind of interesting to see: the heroin, clear as water, pushing out in one direction and Jimmy's blood rushing into the syringe in another, until an eye of red appeared in the center of the casing, floating there. Took about thirty seconds. In that time Jimmy's eyes got this bugged-out look, his pupils getting big as marbles while his cheeks and all his skin began to sag, like his muscles had checked out.

"Oh, but man, I'm feeling nice," he said as that stuff rushed into his system.

Then his head tilted back, and his eyes glossed over like those pictures in our church of Saint Francis in ecstasy.

We walked out, Jimmy in slo-mo, and me, trying to ignore all these looks. When the door closed behind us—thank God!—I took one last glance at Clyde. Nasty as he was, he winked at me with his one good eye, as if to say, *You get strung out too, white boy, and you're welcome here, all right? No hard feelings!*

Out on Amsterdam again, my job became to make sure that Jimmy did not nod out right there on the sidewalk. A few times I saw his head tilting way back, his knees buckling, as if he was about to crumple to the ground, but then, doing some weird kind of exercise, in which he stuck his arms way over his head and stretched them, he started to come around. I don't know what he was feeling or where he had been, but in one moment he was into a zombie thing and in the next he had gotten it all together.

"You all right, Jimmy?" I asked him.

"All right? Why, I feel fine as hell . . . fine as anyone on the face of the Earth."

Yes, "the face of the Earth," he said that.

Then, lighting a cigarette, he said, "Let's go."

We were slowly—and I mean slowly—making our way back up the hill when he decided to stop off at the local A&P. Buying some chewing gum and a big bottle of cherry cream soda, he shoplifted an aerosol can of whipped cream and a package of chocolate Mallomars, just sticking them in his raincoat pockets. I guess shooting H gives you a big-time craving for sweets, because as soon as we stopped off in the park, Jimmy broke open those Mallomars. He gave me one, then proceeded to eat the rest of the package, topping each one with a big glob of whipped cream.

For a while he just sat back, his feet on the railing, like he was at some nice beach.

Then he started scratching himself like crazy.

"What's with all that itching?" I asked him.

"You just get that way," he said. "It's like you got little jelly balls rolling around your body, just under the skin."

"Like the heebie-jeebies?" I asked, trying to be funny, like it all didn't bother the hell out of me.

"Nah, man, it's just part of feeling nice," he said, his eyes closing in a nod.

"How nice?"

"Really nice—like coming all over your body."

"Damn," I said.

He laughed, *har*, *har*, and looked at me like he was drunk.

"But the main thing is, it helps you forget all the nastiness in your life."

"Yeah," I said. Like if I had his Pops I'd be wanting to get that kind of high too.

Then, staring at the sky, he went off into dreamland for a while.

"Okay, so it feels good," I said as he came around again. "But when the hell did you start up with this junk?" I had to ask.

"When?" He laughed. "It was like a miracle!"

"Say what?"

"Yeah, a f—king miracle. About six months ago I was walking up our street and feeling pretty shitty," he said, scratching at his chin. "So shitty I was just looking down at the sidewalk, like I couldn't hold my head up, you know what I'm saying?"

"Uh-huh."

"And what do I see, but a little packet with my name on it laying by the curb. Just laying there! And so I just picked it up. Walked around with it in my wallet for a week, until I decided to try it. I tore that thing open and put it up my nose, and man, it was instant vacationland! So I got me some more, and well"—and he started scratching inside his shirt again.

"That was it. Little by little I just wanted to do more. Not every day, but like when I could afford it, you know?"

"But how could you afford that stuff? I mean, it's expensive, right?"

He laughed again, his head tilting back. A jet was passing above, west over Harlem, on the way from LaGuardia Airport to who knows where.

"Let me ask you something, Rico," he said, getting all sober for a second. "When you look at me, what do you see?"

"I see my man Jimmy—the cool artist."

"Nah," he said, waving his finger at me. "I mean, what do most people see?"

"I don't know."

But I did know. I just didn't want to say.

"What they see is a doofy-looking kid, with messed-up eyeglasses, who looks like he couldn't hurt a fly, right?"

"I guess."

"Well, there you have it." He was scratching himself again. "I'm so damn harmless-looking, I can run all kinds of errands for folks without attracting much attention."

"But like, who would those folks be?" I asked him, imagining that he was mixed up with some hoods.

"Aw, man, I can't tell you, Rico. That would be violating their trust. But it's way better than working for my Pops, you know?"

He lit a cigarette.

"But I thought you said you were working at the bar?"

"Yeah, I'm doing that, too," he told me, blowing one huge, perfect smoke ring.

When I got home, I was in one bad mood.

I mean the Latin Dagger thing would be falling to the wayside, forever maybe.

And now I had Jimmy to worry about.

Believe me, that dragged my head.

I just couldn't stop thinking about how I helped Jimmy tie up his arm with that tube. Or forget about the bloody eye in that needle staring at me. Then I started thinking about some other things. Like this nice black kid, smiling Alvin, flying kites in the park one day and then on another, nodding out on a rooftop and slipping off the edge, all six stories down. Or this Puerto Rican guy, a former Golden Gloves boxer, named Miguel, high as hell, who fell backwards while climbing up a tenement stairway, breaking his neck. Stories you heard, but just didn't want to believe.

Then my mind wouldn't stop.

There were all these guys you once knew found dead in some lousy toilet with a needle still stuck in their arm.

And I couldn't forget that kid I saw at school this morning—his shocked eyes just followed me around, his Converse sneakers still twitching like crazy. . . .

On top of that, when I came in, my Pops was snoring away, right at the kitchen table, his head slumped down, his chin touching his chest, my Moms circling around him.

Man, things were messed up.

But one thing happened to save the day: A letter from Gilberto was waiting for me on the living room table.

When I tore it open, I swore that I could smell corn and fresh air coming out the envelope.

Hey Rico,

Just a holler to let you know that I'm in one piece and to tell you something about this place.

For one thing, the school really does look like it did in that brochure, and the town is pretty cool too. It's got this big park with a lake, and on the weekends everybody and their mother turns up to barbecue and go out on these motorboats to fish and water ski. There are farms all over the freaking place, and the air is something else too. And the girls! Hey, talk about being in a candy shop, man! They're friendly as hell, and even the finest of them don't have any stuck-up attitudes. Best of all, I get me a lot of attention for just being so different from them all—like I'm probably the only New York City dude out there, and definitely the only P. R., maybe in the whole freaking white bread state!

I've been staying on campus in a dorm with this quiet guy named Chuck, and while I don't mind that, I've been thinking about getting my own place, maybe a farm—they're so cheap to rent around here.

As for my classes—Well, what can I say: School is school. The same old, same old. The main thing is that I'm giving it a shot. Hey, what do I have to lose, right?

Anyway, I don't really have a whole lot more
to say right now, so this is to be continued.
I hope you're all right, and keeping your nose
clean. But just one thing: Do me a favor and
check in on my Moms when you can, if only to
say hello. I don't want her to be getting lonely
and all.

I'll catch you later, my Cubano bro.

G.

I read that letter three times, grateful to be hearing
that something good was happening to someone else,
even if it wasn't me.

eight

SOON ENOUGH, I figured out Jimmy's setup. Like he said, he was working as a dishwasher in Mr. Farrentino's bar, my Pops's local hangout. I'd see Jimmy in the back while looking for my Pops when he was late for dinner, my Moms always sending me out to bring him home. But man, sometimes that wasn't easy. There was always some funky rock-'n'-roll or soul music blaring out of a big, lit-up jukebox, and all these pretty waitresses doting on my Pops. To them he was known as "that nice Cuban guy, Rolando, who always leaves good tips."

My Pops, I have to say, was a good-looking man, a little heavy, about six foot two like Gilberto, but very immense and with these dark, killer-diller soulful eyes. I'd walk in sometimes and see him, with his hands folded under his chin, checking a particular waitress out. But

I made no big thing about that—all the guys in that bar did that.

"So Poppy, come on home," I'd say.

"In a moment," he would answer.

Raising an index finger to the bartender, he'd call for another rye whiskey with a beer chaser.

Sometimes he left easily, and sometimes nothing would get him moving off that bar stool.

"Okay, Poppy," I would say. "But you know how Mommy will get crazy."

My Pops would just shrug, calmly.

And I'd wait and wait and wait.

On one of those nights, while my Pops was lingering, I thought I would just slip back behind the bar, to say hello to Jimmy. He was washing dishes over a giant sink, but down the hall and through an open door, I saw Mr. Farrentino, sitting in his office. He was this beefy bald Italian guy, said to be "nice Mafia." I always liked him. My first job, when I was ten, had been in an ice cream parlor he ran. Then he had bought himself a corner grocery store, working there until he had enough money to open that bar.

He had these super rosy Santa Claus cheeks, like he was the picture of health, and those cheeks were as rosy as ever when I went down the hall to say hello.

But when I peeked in, I did a double take and a half. For one thing, this Latina, her hair dyed platinum blonde, in a silvery miniskirt, was sitting beside him, and for another, he was jamming a needle into his arm. I just froze. Then I began to turn around when I heard him saying, "Come on in, Rico."

It was like nothing was unusual. He shot the stuff up, and as his eyes got all glazed over, he asked me, "So Rico, my boy, how are things going with you?"

Then he pulled the needle out from his thick forearm and dabbed the spot with a piece of cotton dipped in rubbing alcohol.

"Okay," I said. "And by you?"

"Beyoooteefool," he said just as he was really getting off.

That Latina lady was holding her own works, and when he was done, she started to shoot up herself, but being a lady, she turned her back to me.

I mean it was weird, like in a *Twilight Zone* episode.

Anyway, as I started to walk away, it landed on me: So that's who Jimmy was buying the stuff for.

"So Rico," Mr. Farrentino called out. "What you seen me just doing is between us, right?"

"Yeah," I said.

"Well, you've always been a good kid," he said gratefully. "Now come over here."

At first I thought he was going to offer me some smack, but instead, he reached into his pocket and pulled out a bunch of bills, all twenties, maybe a couple of hundred dollars' worth, and tried to slip them into my shirt pocket.

"Nah," I said, backing away. "You don't have to do that for me."

He laughed.

"Ain't for you, but for your father. I've heard he's been going through hard times."

With my Pops spending all kinds of bucks in that place, I figured he'd be getting all that money back anyway. But I said, "Yeah, but I can't, Mr. Farrentino. You're just high."

And then I went back out into the smoky bar.

My Pops was laying some superdrunk rap on an even drunker guy.

"Poppy," I said. "We have to go."

He must have sensed something in my voice. For once, he said, "All right," and began to peel some one-dollar bills out his wallet, leaving them on the bar. He left five, but I took back three.

He didn't even notice.

And then our three-block journey began. Farrentino's bar was down a basement, and just getting my Pops up the stairs was a trip. He must have weighed two hundred and fifty pounds, and with his balance way off, for every few steps up, he would suddenly slip back some steps like he was being pulled down by the famous forces of gravity. But I kept on trying to get him up those stairs, with my hands pressing against his back and getting nowhere, when Jimmy came out, in a long apron, to help. With both of us pushing, we finally made it.

"Well, I owe you one," I called to Jimmy, as he went back into the bar.

"Nah, man, you don't," he called back. "Believe me, you don't."

Once we were out on the sidewalk, it took me about twenty minutes to get my Pops to our apartment building. Then with four flights of stairs awaiting us, the same hassle began again. Up six steps, down two. Up five steps, down three. And on and on. By then he was weighing a thousand pounds, and it was only because Mr. Lopez, our third-floor neighbor, heard me struggling with him and came out to help that I could get my Pops home at all.

nine

THE REST OF that year went by like a slow boat to China, mainly because of school. I hated going there. Just taking a leak in the crowded bathrooms, where guys were getting high, was a trip. A lot of the time, I'd wish that I was invisible, but that wish never came true.

And I couldn't even grow my hair long; my Moms insisting that I get it cut at least once a month.

("Rico, you're starting to look like a girl," she'd say.)

That was particularly jive in terms of that school. For one thing, the white kids who never seemed to get hassled were the hippies. Somehow, they were accepted by the hoods and junkies and takeoff artists. They were mostly Jewish kids, from better neighborhoods than my own—why they were at that school was a mystery to me—but I got to know them from their after-school jam sessions. A lot of them were aspiring musicians, and they'd show up sometimes with guitars and flutes, harmonicas—one guy even played the violin—and stage impromptu sessions out on the street when classes let out.

And some of them were dealers—selling pot and hashish and LSD, their music and drugs going down well with the more rowdy students.

Bringing my old crummy Stella to school (I didn't want to risk my sweet Harmony getting ripped off), I liked playing with those guys. I mean, I wasn't the greatest guitarist in the world, but I wasn't too bad, either.

And at least those hippie guys tried to be nice to my sorry ass. Not so with some of the other folks who hung around Jo Mama's.

Like one afternoon, I left the school late. I'd just tried to join the ASPIRA club, which was for Latino students, but as soon as I had walked in, it took me about thirty seconds to change my mind. The kid behind the desk gave me an up and down that said, *What are* you *doing here?*

And so I walked right out, not wanting to explain a single thing about myself. Why should I have to?

Then as I was heading to the bus stop, three black kids came up to me, like out of nowhere.

Now, up to that time, I had been approached by a lot of black kids who had a thing against whitey. Some just shot me a dirty look, and some smiled like they were cats checking out a mouse, and some, if they were in a pissy mood, like they'd had a lousy day, showed a knife and asked for money. If you didn't turn it over or tried to run away, then it might become nasty, with someone shoving you and maybe slapping your face. But generally once I put my hands up, like in those cowboy movies when the bad guys rob the good guys, I was left alone, as long as I gave up my big one dollar and thirty-eight cents. My attitude was *Okay* and *You got me*. If you were cool enough, people just doffed out. I'd even seen one of the guys who'd ripped me off smiling my way as he ran off, as if he had liked my attitude, or as if we could have been friends in some other life.

But these three guys were different. They just wanted to take their shit out on me.

"You got some money for us, chump?" one of them asked. And when I didn't answer and tried to keep on walking, he punched me in the side of my head. A hate punch. Then a second guy knocked me down, and while I was lying on the sidewalk, a third started kicking me in the ribs, like he was trying to break them. Then one of them went through my pockets, taking my wallet, which had my bus pass, my school ID, and four dollars in it.

Finally, like it was the funniest thing in the world, one of them stomped my eyeglasses into little pieces. Then, slapping each other five, and hooting and laughing, they disappeared down the avenue, the whole thing taking about two really long minutes.

Cussing myself for turning off my nasty-persons radar, I picked up what was left of my glasses and, dragging my ass off the ground, started walking home, my nose bleeding, my ribs aching, both my head and ego hurting like hell. You can tell yourself all kinds of things when something like that happens, like it was just bad luck, that you were stupid for not looking around. But those guys were just out to mess with someone: I mean, it happened so fast I couldn't even remember what they looked like, except that they were black or, as my Moms and Pops would have put it, that they were *negritos americanos*—to be avoided at all times—which, of course, in my school and New York City was a joke.

I just felt bad—like, what did I ever do to deserve that kind of beating? Nothing. So I ended up telling myself it was just a freak accident, like getting hit by a car or something. But, man, it was tough to be walking uptown past the playgrounds and the projects where all these other black guys were hanging out, their radios blasting, without wishing they could all disappear.

So, feeling like that kind of thinking wasn't right either, I told myself over and over again that I had to be way more careful (as if that would have made a difference!).

And not to get hung up about all blacks just because of a few means ones.

And to practice what the priests used to talk about in church—forgiveness: to turn the other cheek and all that crap, like Jesus would have.

Yeah, right.

I'll tell you, though: When it rains, it pours, as the saying goes.

Not twenty minutes later, as I passed by 108th Street, a Latino kid tossed a soda bottle at me, and later, as I was walking up my block, Irish Eddie was duking it out with this skinny Puerto Rican kid, Fernando. A two-hundred-pounder against a flyweight, they were really going at it on the street. A circle of about twenty guys, most of them Eddie's friends, surrounded them and chanted, "Fight, fight!" and shouted things like "Kick that spic's ass!" That was no easy thing, though. One bad, fleet-footed dude, little Fernando was cutting the bigger guy's face up with these lightning-fast punches. But that only made Eddie, one of the meaner guys around, madder. Talk about being pissed off! As much as he was outclassed, out-moved, and outpunched, Eddie kept going forward, and every time he got hit, he'd smile, wipe the spit and blood off his mug, and say, "Come on. Is that all you got, ya ugly *spic*!"

It was kind of exciting at first, any fight being cool as long you aren't the one getting your ass kicked in, and I enjoyed seeing the little guy messing up the big guy. A Good-versus-Evil thing. And it took my mind off the BS I'd just been through. For a little while anyway. But something was bugging me. Like hearing the word "spic" over and over again, and just feeling the hatred that Eddie had for Fernando and vice versa. That word hit my ears like a fist, 'cause it made me think about my Moms and Pops, and all the stories I used to hear about how bad some white folks treated them when they first came to New York and how they were laughed at because they couldn't speak English and just looked different—the skin thing. So naturally I was rooting for Fernando but feeling weird at the same time, because when it came down to it, I looked more like Eddie than Fernando and that made me feel ashamed as hell.

But suddenly the fight turned dirty: Eddie, tired of getting hit, picked up a garbage can lid and punched Fernando in the face with it. Two of his teeth went flying, his lip split open, and the poor guy finally got knocked to the ground. Then Eddie started kicking at his ribs and head, muttering, "So you like this, spic?" It was like watching a replay of what had just happened to me, the nastiness of it so churning up my guts that I felt like throwing up.

I don't know what the heck I was thinking, but I went up to Eddie and tried to pull him off the guy. Like in one of those comic-book stories when the sickly kid suddenly gets superpowers and decides to do the right thing. But real life isn't like that. As soon as I grabbed Eddie by the arm, he jammed his elbow back, slamming me on the shoulder and almost sending me flying: I would've fallen to the sidewalk if some guys hadn't caught me and pushed me back towards him. Eddie, laying off of Fernando, now gave me the dirtiest look.

"You mind your own business, huh?" he said to me. "Or you'll be next!"

Scared as I was feeling, I had to open my big mouth anyway.

"Just leave the guy alone," I said. "What'd he do to you, anyway?"

That just made Eddie angrier.

"And what do you care about the spic?"

"It's just not right," I said, shaking. "And why are you calling him a spic anyway?"

And then he stepped closer and started poking me in the chest.

"Oh yeah . . . I forgot . . . Ain't you a spic too?"

And that's when I was worse than a doubting St. Thomas, 'cause instead of saying, *Yeah, I am*, I just turned red, not because I was scared, but because I really didn't know how to answer him.

"So just get the F out of here," he said to me.

And maybe he was about to throw a punch my way anyway, when, of all people, my Pops, having watched this shit from our window, came downstairs with a baseball bat. Pushing through the other guys, he stepped between me and Eddie. Then like some bad-assed macho, my Pops, stone-cold sober and looking like he meant it *big-time*, told Eddie, "You leave my son alone, understand?" And then, he just put his arm around my shoulder and walked me up to the stoop.

The kicker was that my Pops thought my bruised face *was* Eddie's fault. But I told him the truth—about the black kids jumping me.

"You just have to be more careful," he told me. "There're a lot of *sinvergüenzas* out there." He meant low-life louses. "Just stay away from them, huh?"

"Sure, Pop," I said, as if I had a choice.

"And from *mierdas* like that guy Eddie. We all have to live together, right?"

"Yeah, Pop, but that guy is bad news. He was calling Fernando a spic, and—"

But my Pops cut me off, putting a finger to my lips.

"Never, never use that word, my boy," he said. "And besides," he added, cutting into me like a knife, "that word will never apply to you. You're an americano, and never forget that."

So we sat for a while watching as the cops—*Irish* cops—screeched over in a squad car, telling the crowd to take a long walk and asking no questions about who started what or why. Eddie got off scot-free, and Fernando, with his messed-up face, went limping off to the emergency ward to get his fifty stitches. Finally, I got upstairs—to deal with my Moms, who just freaked over what had happened to me, not 'cause I got jumped, but because replacing my glasses was going to cost ten bucks.

ten

AFTER THAT, I began to cut classes. First a few here and there. Then entire days when I would just go walking all over the city. Visiting the Central Park Zoo was very cool, especially the northern exhibit with its waddling penguins, and just hanging out by the skating rink watching people going around in circles, I could kill hours. Then I'd bop through the nice neighborhoods, on the East Side, seeing how rich people lived, with all them butlers opening doors and chauffeurs shining and waxing their cars. Sometimes I visited my hippie classmates, who were also skipping classes like crazy. All that time I didn't think anyone would really notice or even care, but the school authorities—that is, my homeroom teacher, Mrs. Thompson—did.

✳ ✳ ✳

One day—it was in February—as I was sitting in an art appreciation class and my teacher was talking about Michelangelo, Mrs. Thompson walked into the room with a very serious expression on her face, like she was on a special mission.

"Rico," she said, after speaking to my teacher and coming over to me, "gather up your books and come along."

On our way down to the principal's office on the second floor, she only said, "Rico, lately I've been very disappointed in you."

Inside the office, about five people sat by a long table. I recognized the principal, Mr. Myers, from his pictures in the hall. But the others—two men and two women looking sternly at me—I had never seen before.

The principal spoke up first, standing: He wanted to shake my hand. His hand was plump and warm and soft, not like my Pops's.

"Rico," he began, "if you are wondering why we've brought you here . . ." *Blah, blah, blah* . . . "If you will recall," he continued. *Blah, blah, blah*.

Next thing I knew, someone else was boring the shit out of me: a social worker. He was flipping through some papers.

"You were given an intelligence test last fall. Do you remember it?"

I didn't answer. Just breathed deeply and tapped my fingers against the table.

"*Reeeko*," another one of them said, testily. "Are you paying attention?" He made a face when I didn't answer right away.

"I asked you a question, young man," he tried again.

"Yeah," I said, finally giving in.

"Well, you scored remarkably high. In the top percentile."

I had no idea what he was talking about: All I knew was, that test was stupid.

"Okay, so?" I said, without looking at him.

He began to read over some records about me.

"And you seem to do well in your exams."

So what else was new? I just shrugged.

Blah, blah, blah some more.

And then I tuned in again.

"Young man, the point is that you have the *potential* of being one of the finest students in our school," this guy said. "Does that *register* with you at all?"

"Not particularly," I said, those high-class words bugging me.

Ignoring my response, he barreled on. "But the fact is, you haven't been holding up your end of the bargain."

"What do you mean?" I asked, offended. "Ain't it enough for me to ace those dumb exams?"

He had been smiling until then but became very serious.

"That's not the point. According to Mrs. Thompson's attendance records, you've been cutting classes left and right lately. Is that correct?" His eyebrows got all screwed up.

"Yeah, so what?" I said.

"Can you tell us why?"

I shrugged.

"I don't know. I just feel hassled coming here."

"I see," he said. "And, this feeling you have—would that have to do with the *diversity* of the student body?"

"What do you mean?" I asked.

"Are you bothered by the fact that the majority of our students are black?"

They were looking at each other, nodding, like he had asked the greatest question in the world.

"Not particularly," I said. "It's just that some of them just don't like white kids, that's all."

He sighed.

"And you consider yourself white, then?"

"I don't consider myself anything, if you want to know."

"I understand that you come from a Cuban family, is that so?" He had an unlit pipe, which he began sucking on.

"Yeah, I do."

"Then I would think that you would try harder to fit in with your fellow Hispanic students here." He stood up, pointing his pipe at me. "We have several clubs in this school for Hispanic youths like yourself."

Like myself? Who was the guy kidding?

"I know about that stuff," I told him. "But that's not exactly my thing."

They started whispering among themselves.

Then the principal introduced me to someone else. He was this nervous, thin guy in a pin-striped shirt, who wore his bifocal glasses really low on his nose. Dr. Fein, the school shrink. He had a terrible rash on his wrists and had just been staring and staring at me.

"Well, Rico, can you tell me something?" Dr. Fein asked.

"Sure."

"Just what do you want to do with your life, really?"

I thought about it for a while.

"Like, write comic books, and maybe science-fiction stories one day. But I don't know. Some kind of books, anyway." Man, that perked them up big-time. "But I also think I'd like to be a guitar player with a band like the Stones, or doing the serious stuff like that Spanish guy Segovia—I can read notes, you know." They all nodded, seemingly impressed. "Otherwise, I don't have the slightest idea." I shrugged my shoulders again.

That's when I heard a *chug-chug-chug*, the boring-assed question express coming closer down the tracks. *Woo, woo!* 'Cause just then they started nosing around even more.

Was my home life happy? ("Yeah," I said, thinking it wasn't anybody's business.)

Did my Pops or Moms ever hit me? ("No way," I answered, even if they sometimes did.)

Did I have pride in my Cuban roots? ("You best believe it," I told them, actually having never thought about it.)

And was I aware that cutting classes could affect my chances for going to college, even if I aced the almighty Regents exams? ("Uh-uh," I answered, truly surprised.)

Then the school shrink, looking me over carefully

and scratching his wrist raw, said I had to start showing up again, or else, they, the authorities, would be siccing their truant officers on me.

Well, even if I knew they were kind of right, I had to pull their coats as to the truth about school.

"Know what? You crowd, like, forty kids into a dinky classroom, right? And some of them are telling the teachers to go screw themselves, and some are nodding out. I mean, I was in a class when a kid started beating off in the back! How can anybody really learn a goddamn thing with all that going on?"

They muttered among themselves again for a while. And then Mrs. Thompson, being so kindly and all, said, "Rico, you have to understand that we're only trying to help you."

"Uh-huh," I said, shrugging.

"I don't want you to be hurting your future, just because some of your classes don't sit well with you, understand?" she said, looking at me with those damn kindly eyes.

But, *don't sit well with me?*

I nodded, even if it wasn't just about that.

With her hands in front of her, Mrs. Thompson just stared at me. And then all of them started staring at me, waiting for an answer. I felt like I was this insect being looked at through a microscope.

Thinking about how my Pops and Moms would feel if I really screwed up, I finally said, "Okay, okay, I get the message."

And then it was like the sun swept into the room. All of them smiling.

Afterwards, Mrs. Thompson went walking with me. The next-period bell had rung, and while the halls swarmed with students, I told her I had best be getting on to my American history class. But once she was out of sight, I ducked down a stairway and followed the hall to the street and practically ran uptown.

For my folks' sake, I tried to stay in school. I went at least two, sometimes three times a week, for most of that spring. Even so, one evening, while we were sitting at dinner, two truancy officers came knocking on our door. I mean, with all the kids who never, ever showed up, they must have been busy as hell, but that was when they finally caught up to me.

My Pops was about to devour a platter of fried pork chops with onions and fries when my Moms, answering the door, came running down the hall.

"*Ay, ay, ay*, we have trouble," she said.

These two truant officers walked in behind her. One was this tall, worn-out-looking white guy in a hat and rumpled suit, who seemed just fed up with his job, and the other was this prim, nicely dressed black lady—I liked her instantly because of her pretty dark eyes—clutching some folders against her chest.

"We hate to interrupt your dinner," she said. "But we're here to inform you that your son, Rico Fuentes, has been a truant for some time, and is, therefore, in danger of permanent *suspension*."

My Pops, all sober and caught in the middle of a chew, just looked at the lady.

"Not my boy."

"Yes, your boy."

And for some reason she smiled at me.

"What is a truant?" my Pops asked.

"A student who does not go to school."

My Pops turned his head, gave me a fierce look.

"That can't be," he said. "My son, Rico, I know, always goes to school."

"Uh-uh," she said. "That's just not the case, according to our records."

Then they hung around for about another fifteen minutes, explaining how serious my situation was.

When they left, my Moms who, I think, sort of followed things in English, started carrying on about the arrogance of a Negro woman trespassing into our home. But she still came after me, slapping my face again and again until my Pops told her to calm down. Then he called me into the living room for a talk. Isabel was sitting in front of the TV watching *The Three Stooges*. My Pops sent her away, pouting.

Even if I knew what was coming, I was sort of happy that he wasn't drunk. His face wasn't sagging; his eyes weren't bloodshot. I mean he was looking like the Pops who used to come home from his downtown job with a comic book always stuck in his pocket to give me. For some reason, the comics he picked out featured either *Flash*—the fastest man on Earth—or *Adam Strange*, adventurer in another world. I guess 'cause they both wore bright red costumes, that being one of his favorite colors.

He wasn't one for a lot of words.

"Rico," he said, shaking his head. *"Tengo una pregunta para ti.*—I have a question for you.—Why you being so bad? I don't understand," he asked me, switching into English, his eyes all sad. "Do you want to shame our family?"

"No," I answered.

"Do you want to drive your mother into misery?"

I shook my head.

"Then why are you not at school?"

I really had no answer except that I thought it sucked. But then, when I looked into his eyes, I just couldn't say that.

"Poppy, if you saw that place you might understand."

He had lit a cigarette, a Kent, blowing the fumes towards me and nodding, without any idea what that school was like other than that it was an *escuela pública.*

"Look," he finally said. "I know you don't like that school. I see that every day on your face. But what you must remember, my son, is that if you don't graduate, you might end up being one of those guys riding up and down in elevators all day or worse—in the gutter. Do you want that?"

"No, Poppy," I answered sincerely.

"Then you know what you must do," he said gently. "Okay, *mi hijo?*"

I nodded.

"Because if you don't, there's only one thing we can do." He was shaking his head again. "And that is to send you to stay with your *tío* Pepe in Florida."

Tío Pepe, Pops's older brother, was a former Marine and a veteran of the Bay of Pigs invasion of Cuba, and he ran a military academy in Tampa. Oh, that would be just great, I kept thinking, trying to picture myself in a cadet's uniform doing drills.

"Aw, c'mon. You wouldn't do *that*!"

"To be honest, Rico," my Pops said, "you've seemed so unhappy lately that your *mamá* and I have been talking about it."

Yeah, like when they weren't screaming at each other.

"I know your *tío* isn't the easiest-going guy, but it would be good for you." Then, as if the news would somehow cheer me up, he added, "We could even send you down there early for the summer, to work for him. Would that make you happy?"

Then he reached over to touch my face.

"That, my boy, is what we will do, if you continue on your way. You understand?"

"All right, Poppy," I said, the very thought of spending the next year down there with the Mussolini of my family scaring the hell out of me. "I'll do my best."

"*¿Me prometes?* You promise me?"

"Sure, Pop," I said.

Then while my Pops stretched out in his easy chair, I went back into my room, and feeling trapped and way pissed off at the way things were playing out, I punched a wall, the skin of my knuckles peeling off.

Later, I pulled the nails out of my window, snuck down the fire escape to the courtyard and street, and went looking for Jimmy. He had moved out of his basement and was staying in a little room of his own in the back of Mr. Farrentino's bar: I guess the guy had a thing for darkness, as that place didn't have any windows either. When I found him, I could hardly breathe. With my stomach in knots, all this stuff was jamming up in my guts.

Like I was a bad guy.

And like I didn't care about anybody else.

And like I was just an uptight whitey, in the end.

And not really a Latino at all.

Like people jumped me because I was a dope.

And deserved it.

Truly deserved it.

'Cause I couldn't help my Pops.

And 'cause my Moms was down on me.

And because that Latino thing was starting to make me feel weird.

Like you can't be, 'cause you don't look it.

And your Spanish is half-assed.

And you don't belong.

Not to the Irish, even if you have their blood in your veins, 'cause they hate "spics."

And not to the "spics," 'cause they think you're Irish.

As for the black folks, they just hate whitey. Not all of them, but enough of them to hassle you to death.

Man, was my head dragged.

I mean, talk about growing up with people shoving sticks up your butt!

That was me.

That night I wanted out from all that shit.

Really *out*, *out*, *out*.

Jimmy was lying on a cot in this dingy room, with stacks of liquor cases and all kinds of titty magazines spread on the floor around him; he was smoking, a cigarette already burned down to its filter in his yellow-tinged hand, which dangled off the side of that cot. I guess he was feeling too "nice" to be bothered by anything.

"Yo Rico, what's up?" he said, rubbing his eyes.

He was in a pair of boxers and a T-shirt. His body looked stringy, like in those movies about prisoners of war. I think he had been dreaming about something. I mean, before he noticed me, he had just been staring and staring at this lightbulb, hanging down from the ceiling on a crooked wire.

"So what's going on with you?" I asked him.

"Not much, my man," he told me. "What brings you here to my palatial crib?"

"Uh, I was just looking for my Pops. You seen him?"

"Nah, man. I just been here."

Then he looked at me closely: I must have still looked as angry as I felt.

"So, what do you really want?"

Embarrassed as hell, I could barely say what I wanted to say. But then I finally did: "Jimmy, you got any smack you can spare?"

"What?" and he sat bolt upright.

"Like, would you sell me some?" I asked, avoiding his eyes. I mean, I never thought Mr. Righteous here would *ever* do that stuff. Then I looked around the room. Alongside some Bacardi rum ads, featuring these really chesty girls in bikinis, Jimmy had tacked some of his old beaucoup drawings to the wall.

"Say that again?"

"You heard me," I said, staring at the floor.

With that, he got an expression on his face that I'd never seen before.

"You kidding me, right?"

"No, I mean it, man. I'd like to try it."

I did: I wanted out, to escape everything, even for a few hours, like to crawl out of my own skin.

He thought about it for a moment.

"Nah, man. No way!" he said, shaking his head, like that was the last thing he'd ever do. He was definitely upset.

"But why not? You love that stuff!"

"Uh-uh, I don't love anything! Besides"—he was rubbing a knuckle against his nose—"that's me, not you. Rico, you just don't want to go there, you understand?"

"Aw, come on, Jimmy," I tried again.

Then he got all composed suddenly, straightening out his glasses, pulling on a pair of jeans.

"I know you don't want to hear it. But it's not for you."

That hit me like an insult.

"Yeah, so it's cool with everybody else but me, is that what you're saying?" I said, feeling even more pissed off.

"Aw, man," Jimmy said. "You're just too straight." He was standing up now. "And you know what else?"

"What?"

"I just don't want you getting that kind of high, that's all."

"But you—"

"And like what the F do I have to lose?" he said, cutting me off.

Then he looked me straight in the eyes. Something was happening to him, like he was almost crying.

"Rico, man, it's one thing if I'm screwing up, but if something was to happen to you—Well, I'd just never get over that shit. So the answer is *no*!"

I tried one more time.

"But I thought you were my friend!"

"I am! And that's why I'm telling you no. Period. End of story. *¿Me entiendes, hombre?*"

"Damn, Jimmy," I said, breathing deeply, fuming.

"Look, if you really want it, you can just walk over to 108th Street, where there are dudes selling it all over the place." He started wiping his glasses clean with a piece of his T-shirt. "Whatever you do, I ain't gonna be the one to give it to you. No way." And then as a friendly gesture he reached into a box and pulled out a joint, which he lit and offered to me.

"Here, maybe this will chill you out."

But after a single toke, I just gave it back. Curled up again on his cot, like he was crawling into a cocoon, Jimmy said in a softer voice, "Rico, whatever you were thinking, it's just not for you, okay?"

"Yeah, I get it, I get it," I answered, still steamed.

"Look, I know something's hassling you," he said, tapping tight the filter end of a Tareyton cigarette. "I mean, *you look hassled*, but I never want to hear you asking me about that stuff again, all right?"

When I left Jimmy, still feeling like the walls were closing in on me everywhere—at home, at school, on the streets—like no matter where I hung out I'd have problems, I sat on a park bench checking out the moon. It was glowing so big and crazy and happily that night that I would have punched it in the mug if I could have reached that far. But what could I do? You could daydream forever, I told myself, without changing a single thing. And getting high was like signing on to a dream cruise, and I figured Jimmy was right after all, at least maybe about me. As pissed off as I felt at first, I figured that I was just blowing off steam.

I mean, I realized that I had to get real.

But the craziest thing is that after I thought about it, once I was back in my little room, I somehow began trusting Jimmy again.

Now, even if my Pops had given me the ultimate lowdown, I just couldn't go back to Jo Mama's on a regular basis. It was like an antimagnetic thing, and I was a piece of metal. I would get up, gather my books, look in the mirror, get dressed, start heading down to the Amsterdam Avenue bus stop, get on that bus, and walk into school, and sometimes I lasted till noon. But I wouldn't even bother to make it through lunch, when kids would just grab your package of Ring Dings and baloney sandwich off your tray and slap you in the back of your head. No way was I putting up with that shit anymore.

The only class I always tried to make was Mrs. Grable's late-morning English class because no matter how messed up I was feeling, I still liked books. The best ones, in my opinion, were written by Walt Whitman and that guy Mark Twain: I must have read that *Huckleberry Finn* book three times over that semester, just because I loved that stuff about the white kid helping the slave to get away. I started to like that book maybe even more than my favorite John Carter of Mars novels. I mean, the way that John Carter dude was always getting zapped off by cosmic rays to another planet was definitely cool. But Huck's and Jim's journey while trying to find their freedom just spoke to me, and big-time, that idea always drumming in my head.

Once I got done with Mrs. Grable's class, I would just doff for the day.

I started to hang with Jimmy again, mainly to look out for him, like he had for me that night. And it was a good thing that I did.

Come this nice spring afternoon, Jimmy and I were lying out on the lawn of Riverside Park under a shady oak tree. Off in dreamland, he was staring at the sky, and I asked him, "So Jimmy, are you ever gonna cut that stuff loose?"

Some pretty college girls were playing volleyball on the lawn, and in the distance a white Good Humor truck was stopping every now and then to sell ice cream.

Instead of answering me, he sat up, pulled a ciggie out of his shirt pocket. He was so spaced that after lighting a match, he just kept staring at the flame until it almost burned down to his fingers, his eyes closing.

"Hey, Jimmy," I said, nudging him.

"What?"

"Are you gonna light your smoke or what?"

"Oh yeah."

He did and then began to nod, his eyes closing, his lips slightly parting, the cigarette still burning away.

I felt like shaking him just then, the way I wanted to shake my Pops when I'd see him dozing off at the kitchen table. But where my Pops, his cheeks and nose flushed, looked almost peaceful, Jimmy looked halfway dead, his skin pale and the guy hardly breathing. I also knew that, sick as he seemed, he'd be popping his eyes open soon enough, like he always did. And so, feeling a little bored, I decided to walk over to this promenade wall with its panoramic views of the Hudson River, wondering just where all the barges and sailboats were going.

And wishing I was on one of them.

I was watching this Circle Line ferry coming north on the river when I suddenly heard Jimmy screaming, "Uh! Uh! Uh!" and "Help me!"

When I get over to him, Jimmy's writhing on the lawn, his cheap-assed shirt completely in flames. So completely I could smell his skin burning. My heart going like a thousand beats a minutes, I started to roll him around on the ground. But that shirt just wouldn't go out. Jimmy kept crying, "Oh man, I'm gonna die! I'm gonna die!" I grabbed a handful of dirt and threw it on the flames, but that shirt, maybe rayon, just kept burning on.

Then I started shouting "Help" at the top of my lungs.

All of these other folks came running over, the college girls pouring bottles of soda over him, but the flames wouldn't go out. I even tried to rip his shirt loose, singeing the hell out of my hands, goddamn it, but it just kept on burning, Jimmy screaming in pain like I never heard before. Just then, thank the Lord, this Parks Department guy, a black dude with rasta braids, riding by on a cart, raced over to us. He had a pair of gardener's gloves on, and kneeling down before Jimmy, took out some shears and began to cut his shirt up, pulling shreds of it off. With those pieces came most of the skin on the top part of Jimmy's chest, just under his neck. What was left was all red like a raw steak, oozing pink liquids and little bubbles that, popping, gave off a kind of steam. I mean, it was one of the most horrible things I had ever seen.

* * *

When the ambulance finally arrived—took about half
an hour—Jimmy was shivering like crazy, all this frothy
stuff coming out of his mouth. His eyes were tearing
big-time but were also looking just straight out at
nothing in particular. By then some cops had screeched
onto the scene in their squad car, and man, did they
have a lot of questions for me. Fortunately, Jimmy didn't
have anything on him, so I didn't have to worry about
that. But I really had no answers for them when one
of these cops, checking out my ID, asked me what
I was doing in that park when I should've been in
school. So while Jimmy was taken to the hospital emergency room on 114th Street, I ended up at the precinct
house on 127th.

The cops called my Pops at his job downtown, and it
took him a few hours to come and get me. Sitting there, in
a holding pen, my mind kept racing ahead to the moment
when I would be walking into our apartment and all the
crap I would be going through: my Moms hitting and
yelling at me, like I was the worst son in the whole world.
At the same time I tried not to make eye contact with
the other guys being held there, some looking like they
would just love to kick my ass.

Finally, my Pops walked in, his hat in hand. He wasn't angry like I expected. He just had the saddest look on his face. Once he was done talking with the desk sergeant and we got out of that place, he didn't say a word to me. He just kept walking on in silence, shaking his head.

But when we came to our block, he turned to me: "Rico, I'm too upset to talk to you right now. But just so that you know, I'm sending you to live with your *tío* Pepe this summer."

That night was a bitch. I couldn't even begin to sleep. Tossing and turning, I just kept thinking about how I had really blown everything and, at the same time, about how Jimmy's face looked when he was burning up, or wondering if he was even still alive; and how my Pops looked like his heart was breaking over having to send me away, my mind racing in all kinds of directions. I just didn't want to go, but I couldn't stay, either. It wasn't like I had anything against Pepe. It's just that he was one cold dude, not a bad guy but nowhere as warm as my Pops could be. The few times we met, the man never once hugged me, just gave me a hard handshake and looked me up and down like I was too soft and mild for his taste. Just thinking about being cooped up with him for a whole year—marching, drilling, wearing uniforms, and whatever the heck military school kids did—freaked me out big-time.

Anyway, that's when I began wondering what Gilberto was up to in Wisconsin.

As for Jimmy? I went to the hospital every day for two weeks trying to visit him before they finally allowed me into the burn ward. It was not a happy place. He was in this room with about twenty other people, their beds in a row, but he seemed miserably alone, like not even his Pops was there to keep him company. All these tubes were hooked up to him, and his upper chest was wrapped in some kind of white mesh, like bandages, but not so heavy. His blistered face was covered in Vaseline.

"Aw man, Jimmy," I said, walking up to him. "You are one ugly mo'!"

He was on something, that's for sure, but still it must have hurt like hell. There were tears in his eyes.

"Yo Rico, my man."

And he tried to give me his hand, but winced when he moved it.

"How you doing?" I asked.

"Not so tough. This shit hurts like a MF."

"I bet it does." Seeing him in such pain, I wasn't sure

what to say. I wondered if he even remembered how it happened. So I asked him if he did.

"What do you think?" he said, closing his eyes for a moment. "That damn cigarette set my shirt on fire."

"You were nodding something fierce," I reminded him.

"Yeah," he admitted.

I didn't have to say the obvious, like next time it could be much worse. So I just decided to go for it and tell him what was really on my mind.

"So what are you gonna do when you get out?"

"How the F should I know?" He opened his eyes.

"You gonna still mess with that stuff?"

"Who the hell knows?" and he almost got angry.

But I needed to tell him. "Jimmy, I want you to cut it loose, all right?"

He turned his head slightly and frowned. Whether from the pain or because of what I said, I didn't know.

"Rico, do me a favor?" he asked suddenly, changing the subject. "Can you get me a smoke?"

"What, are you crazy?" I said, gawking at him. And he almost smiled, this "guess I am a crazy MF" look in his eyes.

"When you're right, Rico, you're right."

A nurse came by with a cup of orange juice for him to sip through a bending straw. As he drank it down, making all those sucking noises, I told him about my plans.

"Look, I wanna talk to you about something. Because I've been messing up at school, my Pops wants to send me off to this military academy down in Florida. But no way do I want that to happen, you following?"

Jimmy kind of nodded.

"Anyway," I went on, "come this summer, I'm gonna get the hell out of here."

"Like, to where?" he asked, suddenly more alert than he'd been since I got there.

"I don't really know, but I'm hoping that I can go stay with Gilberto on this farm he has out in Wisconsin."

"He got himself a farm?"

"Yeah, he rented himself a corn farm. Can you believe that? He's as crazy as you!"

"Really? That's a pisser!"

"Yeah. But I haven't run it by him yet."

"Okay, so what's that got to do with me?"

"Well, what do you think? If I do it, you're my man. I want you to come along."

He tried to look like he wasn't interested.

"Jimmy, I mean it. It's bad enough that I got my

Pops to worry about, but I can't leave if I'm worrying about you, too."

I wasn't being completely up front: I also didn't want to make the trip alone. "And if you stay here, everybody and their mothers, from Mr. Farrentino to those guys in the projects, will be trying to hook you up again!"

I watched this shapely nurse go by: She was attending to this guy who just moaned and moaned. He was wrapped up like a mummy—his nose was just this metal cap.

"Am I right?" I asked him.

"Yeah, okay, okay, you're right," he said, trying to sit up a little. "But, really, what's it to you?"

"What's it to me?" I slapped my forehead. "You're my partner! My main man! And one day, we are gonna end up selling our shit to one of those comic companies."

"You really think so? You *really* think that could happen?"

"Hell yeah, I do! I've been reading that stuff my whole life. I know what's good. *We're* good!" And I crossed my heart. "Anyway, I don't know what Gilberto will say, but I'm gonna run it by him."

"You would do that for me?"

And when I nodded, Jimmy reached over and, even though it made his face wince up, again he squeezed my hand.

By the time Jimmy got out of the hospital, wearing a red bandana around his neck to hide the burn scars, I had everything arranged with Gilberto: It was all cool with him. Not that he approved of my running away, but he absolutely hated that my Pops was planning to send me to Florida. And when it came to my bringing Jimmy along, that was okay too, since he had a lot of room in the house—as long as Jimmy didn't turn out to be a pain in the ass.

Part 2 **CUTTING OUT**

eleven

IT WAS ABOUT nine thirty on a Friday morning in late June. School had been out for a few weeks, and my Moms had gone to work. And there I was, slinking out of the apartment with my Harmony guitar, a half-filled duffel bag, and a cardboard sign I'd made on the sly, the word WISCONSIN in giant letters written out in thick blue Magic Marker. And let me tell you, it was just in the nick of time, as I was supposed to be leaving for Florida the very next day. Only Gilberto and Jimmy knew about my plans, no one else, and my parents didn't suspect a thing. I had been pretending, for their sake, that I was actually looking forward to spending the year with Pepe.

Okay, I didn't feel good about it, but what was I supposed to do?

Before I took off, though, I had to at least leave a few notes.

For Mr. Gordon at the laundry and Mr. Ramirez at the bookstore, apologizing for quitting my part-time jobs so suddenly. And I wrote one to my little sister, saying that I had to be going and I'd miss her a lot and that she shouldn't be worried about me and not to cry at night, 'cause I'd always be thinking about her. I almost told her in person, but I just couldn't; she wouldn't have been able to keep it under her hat. The hardest note was for my Moms and Pops. Not because of what I wrote—like about how they wouldn't have to worry about me making trouble for them anymore—but because, while writing it down, I kept thinking about how they would react: my Pops getting all sad, my Moms, maybe sad too, but mainly worried and freaking out enough that she'd go to the windows screaming, "Police! Police!"

Leaving that note on the kitchen table, I snuck out my building, then cut through a couple of basements until I came out on the other side of the block without anyone spotting me, unless you counted this German shepherd, Rusty, who started barking at me. Then I cut west to the park and from there went downhill to the

125th Street pier, where Jimmy was waiting for me under the trestles of the West Side Highway.

He was in his raincoat and pacing around, watching the scummy garbage-filled water slapping the timbers, a smell of tar and chemicals and sewage in the air. He was looking way better by then. Since he had gotten out of the hospital, he'd put on about ten pounds, mainly from drinking beer I think, but his eyes and skin had started to lose that sickly look.

And best of all, it was like the old Jimmy was back again. A few days before, when he had come up to hang out in my room and I showed him what I was planning to bring along in my duffel bag, he just couldn't help but goof on me. I mean, even though I knew that Wisconsin was only a thousand miles away, I felt like I was getting ready for an interplanetary space mission.

"Rico, where the hell do you think we're going to, northern Siberia?" he asked me. "You got so much junk in there, you could open a store!"

Then he tried lifting it up.

"Uh-uh," he said, shaking his head. "No way am I gonna be helping you drag that thing around! They got stores in Wisconsin, you know."

"Okay, okay!" I said.

"So let's give it another look, huh?" he said, emptying that bag out on my bed.

First thing he picked up was a flashlight.

"This I can see bringing along maybe," he said. "But that's only a maybe. And I can see bringing this water bottle, but why the three Cokes?" And he set down the bottles on the floor. "I mean, Rico, do you really think there ain't no Cokes once you get out of New York?"

"You never know."

"And what's going on with this jive yo-yo?"

He was talking about my favorite Duncan Expert Award Butterfly yo-yo—the one I could do "around the world" with.

"Uh, 'cause my sister gave me that," I told him. "Besides, what if we get bored while we're hitchhiking? We could play with it, right?"

"Nah, nah, nah, nah," he said, tossing that into a reject pile. "I think we can skip the yo-yo, okay?"

"I guess."

Then he picked out a magnifying glass.

"And unless you're planning to jerk off *a lot* out there," he said to me, "and I know you probably *are*, we can ditch this magnifying glass, right?"

And he put that aside.

"Har, har," I said. "Very funny."

Then there were all the paperbacks I had thrown in, about twenty of them, mostly science fiction, except for a *Huckleberry Finn* paperback I'd picked up.

"And what you gonna be doing with all of these? I mean, this stuff weighs a ton! Don't you know we got to travel light?"

"Yeah, yeah," I admitted.

Once Jimmy stopped smirking over every damn thing I'd packed, this is how it broke down:

Laminated prayer card of the Holy Virgin
   Mother shown rising to Heaven: no.
Mr. Baldy roll the balls into his eyes game: no.
   ("Say what?")
Small bag of green rubber toy soldiers: no.
   ("Say what?" again.)
Notebooks and those other books: yes.
Ditto a couple of my Latin Dagger scripts.
Picture of my family, nearly weightless: yes.
A blanket: no.
Three *Daredevil* comics: yes, but the others
   were out.
One *Mad* magazine: yes.

Toothbrush, toothpaste: yes.

Transistor radio: yes.

Two combs: yes.

Mickey Mouse T-shirt: yes.

Pack of Famous Monsters collector cards: no.

Extra pack of strings to go along with my
    guitar: yes.

A bag of pens and pencils: yes.

An umbrella: no.

A gyroscope: no.

One baseball cap: yes.

A sweater and other practical clothes: yes.

Three just-in-case rubbers: yes, even if they
    were a thousand years old.

But Jimmy? The only thing he had with him the morning we left was a bottom-heavy bowling bag. "Yo Jimmy," I said. "You still up for this?"

For an answer he adjusted the bandana around his neck. "You know it, man."

As we headed up a long-ass ramp to the actual highway above, I asked Jimmy what he had brought along.

"Some underpants and what-have-you," he said. "Just what I could pack without the boss noticing."

"But what's clinking in the bag?" I asked him.

"Oh, you know, just a few brewskies, in case we get thirsty."

We?

"But you didn't bring any pot, right? Like the last thing we need is to get picked up," I said, already starting to feel the heat of the day.

"No way," he said. "You think I'm that dumb?"

"Just asking," I said in relief.

He reached into his pocket and took out another cigarette, lighting it with the burning end of an old one. Going uphill, along that ramp, he was breathing hard.

"So, you're really okay with all this?" I asked him.

And he stopped. After he caught his breath, he said, "Man, I already told you!" He was stomping out his old smoke with his Converse sneakers. "I got no choice."

I nodded.

"You were right, man. Like even last night," he began, while spitting over the side of the railing, "when I was over at the projects to cop for Mr. F one last time, that guy Clyde just kept asking me over and over if I wanted some for myself, and when I told him I couldn't—like

I was on other medications and stuff, because of the burns—he told me I was plain full of shit and to get out of his face."

"Well, what did you expect?" I said. "The dude's not exactly Saint Peter."

"Yeah." He was quiet for a minute, looking towards the river. Then he turned to me. "But I'll tell you, Rico, it wasn't easy for me to turn him down."

"What do you mean?" I asked, this uneasy feeling creeping into me.

"Like, no matter how much you swear to your mother that it's the worst thing, you still want to do it again, like twenty-four hours a day. Hell, I still dream about getting high sometimes."

Damn, I thought. So that's what having a jones is like.

We kept walking along and not five minutes had gone by when he stopped again and said, "Man, but I'm thirsty, Rico."

Then he went into his bag, took out a bottle of beer, and fizzed it open.

"You mind?"

"Knock yourself out."

✳ ✳ ✳

Once we got up to the entry ramp, we just started waiting by the highway shoulder, inhaling traffic fumes. I was the front man: In my little plaid shirt and with my hair nicely combed, I stuck out my thumb while Jimmy stood next to me holding up that cardboard sign saying WISCONSIN. But most folks wouldn't even bother to look our way, cars and trucks zooming by. The few wise guys who did usually gave us the finger or shouted "F-off!"; one fatso, driving a van, tossed a Styrofoam cup filled with coffee and cigarette butts at our feet, and another guy actually swerved his car our way as if he wanted to run us over. Man, I thought, people can be mean.

By about noon, just when we were beginning to feel discouraged and Jimmy, a hangdog expression on his face, could barely hold up that sign, a blue Cadillac pulled over. A black man with a thick neck like a boxer's, and wearing a white captain's hat, rolled down his window. A welcome breeze of air-conditioning flowed out in cooling waves.

"I'm driving over to Newark," he said, smiling. "Okay by you boys?"

I looked at Jimmy, he shrugged, and so we got in. It was kind of thrilling, that being the first time I'd ever hitched a ride—or actually gone anywhere on my own.

Jimmy, at least, had visited his family down in P. R. once or twice, but I had never been farther away from New York City than Bear Mountain, a couple hours upstate, where my Poppy had taken me when I was little. And to those hospitals when I was sick—but they didn't count.

The driver had a pair of dice hanging off his front mirror, and on his dashboard sat a plastic black Jesus, the sort I'd seen in the religious shops in Harlem.

As we headed north towards the George Washington Bridge on our way to New Jersey, the driver asked cheerfully enough, "So you boys are going to Wisconsin, huh?"

"Yes sir," I answered.

"Ain't been there myself, but I hear it's as white bread as any place. Why the hell you going there?"

I told him to visit a friend, and that made him laugh. Then his tone changed.

"Well, you boys will be very comfortable there. The white man rules in those parts, the evil hand of God, the white devils who are the ruination of this Earth. That's where they live."

Great, I thought, nudging Jimmy, but he just kept looking out the window as if to catch one last view of the skyline we were leaving behind.

Anyway, the driver had a little wicked beard, which he stroked when amused by his own thoughts, and he laughed in a clipped kind of way, with "heh-hehs," and as we were crossing the bridge, in slow traffic, the city behind us, he started to go on and on about the nastiness of the white race.

"If you boys read the histories of this world, you will discover that there hasn't been a single war that wasn't started by some white devil or another," he said, his voice deep and gravelly. "God knows, my people were tormented by yours—and don't pretend that it ain't so!"

And he smashed his fist against the dashboard.

I glanced quickly at Jimmy again and cleared my throat, but Jimmy just shrugged, like to say, *Forget it*.

The guy went on.

"You itty-bitty boys should know that slavery, the most evil thing in the world, was invented by *your people*."

When I didn't say anything, I could see his thick eyebrows shifting fiercely in the mirror. And that he was staring at me.

"Are you listening?"

"Who, me?" I said, wishing we were not in that car.

"Who the hell do you think I'm talking to?"

"All right, I'm listening," I said.

Then he started up again.

"I am, like most every other nigger in this country, descended from slaves! And being so, and please don't take this personally, I hate your people."

That's when Jimmy glanced at me, as if to say, *Man, this is jive.*

And while I thought about telling our driver that I had cousins in Cuba who were as black as himself, with all shades of color running through the past generations of my family, and that I knew all kinds of nice black folks back home—even if I had my share of hassles, too—I doubted that he would have believed me. Then, as he went on some more about the white devils, it hit me that the only reason he had picked us up was to torture us with his nasty feelings.

Like that was my kind of luck.

"Anyway, you boys wouldn't know suffering. And being ignorant of *actual history*, as most white devils are, you should be grateful for what I'm going to instruct you in now."

And he went into this rambling thing about the history of Africa, and how the Europeans, in cahoots with the Arabs, started the whole slavery thing. I mean, he was just shouting and shouting about that stuff, his lightning-bolt eyes all crazy through the mirror, and while I had no choice but to listen, I did my best to tune him out, looking at all the blighted highway scenery along the New Jersey interstate, refineries pumping out clouds of smoke everywhere you looked, the sky a murky haze.

When we finally pulled into a service area parking lot near Newark, I swore I would kiss the ground. But before we could get out, he had a few other things to tell us.

"Now," he said, turning to us, "you boys just remember everything I told you about the evil and corruption of the blood that flows through your veins, you hear?"

"All right, we will," I said, with my white-ass stomach in knots.

"And if you was to be at all decent and grateful," he added, "you might give me something for my trouble."

"What do you mean, something?" I asked, sensing we were about to get ripped off.

"Uh, like some money. I mean, I ain't a charity bus service for spoiled-rotten white kids after all."

That surprised me: Jimmy was a lot darker than me, having almost an olive complexion.

"Like how much?" I asked him.

"You got a twenty?"

"Twenty? I don't have that," I said lying.

"Oh, is that right?" he said. "Do you think I'm some kind of fool? You're too soft-looking to be broke. That one," he said, pointing to Jimmy. "I'd bet he's got nothing, but you, no way."

"No man, I'm telling you the truth."

"'Man'? What gives you the right to address me like that? I ain't your 'man'! Like who the hell are you to me?"

And just like that, he reached down under his front seat and pulled out a billy club. "How about if I drive you boys off to a quiet spot and give you a good whipping? What do you say to that, since you don't seem to appreciate the cordiality I've shown you?"

And he smashed that billy club hard against the seat beside him.

"Yes sirree, I wouldn't mind using this at all."

Suddenly, I could see him driving us over to the far end of that parking lot, where nobody was around and the cars were lined up in steamy silence. I could see him taking all his shit out on us and getting away with it. I could hardly talk, and my ding-dong had started to shrivel up.

"But you can thank your lucky stars that I'm in a good mood today and ain't no thief," he said, pronouncing that word as *teef*. "So just give me the twenty dollars, and we'll leave it at that. All right?"

"All right, all right," I said, my face all turned red.

I had about forty dollars in one of my pockets, another two hundred or so stuck inside my shoe, savings from my jobs and some of Gilberto's rainy day money. I didn't want to give him a dime, but I really didn't want to get the crap beaten out of us, so I fished out two tens from my pocket, which he snatched away.

"Now get the hell out of here, before I change my mind."

As we tumbled out into the steaming afternoon, he was still mumbling all kinds of foul things under his breath, ending with "Now you boys have a good day." Then his car screeched out of the parking lot.

"Well, that sucked," I said to Jimmy.

"Indeed it did," he answered, reaching into his pocket for a smoke.

The service station asphalt was covered with grease puddles; seedy-looking attendants were feeding gas into these enormous trucks. We washed up in the grimy men's room, and then I joined Jimmy in a beer. I mean, we drank bottles two and three really fast in that men's room, and because I hadn't eaten anything, it sort of went to my head, in a slightly buzzing kind of way, enough for me to pretend that we hadn't just been hustled. Then we stood out by the service area exit ramp, taking turns holding up our pathetic sign, watching truck after truck and just as many cars passing by.

Finally Jimmy dropped the sign and sat on the railing.

"Hey, Rico," he said. "This is definitely a drag."

"I know. But you aren't about to quit on me, just because of one asshole?"

"Nah, but man, it's hot."

After a while, I took a paperback out of my pack—an Edgar Rice Burroughs novel—and began to read it, holding the book with one hand and sticking out my thumb with the other.

"What's that shit?" Jimmy asked.

"You know, one of my John Carter of Mars books," I told him.

He gave me a crazy look, shaking his head, like he was wondering what he had gotten himself into.

Turned out that my reading a book was a good thing,

because as we were sitting along the railing, baking and forlorn, we heard a *beep-beep*. Our second ride had come along. This time, the driver wasn't an angry black man, but a blond lady in dark sunglasses. She was sitting behind the wheel of a white Ford Mustang convertible and must have felt sorry for us, or maybe she was put at ease by the fact that I seemed studious.

In any case, she pulled over and told us to hop in.

When we took off, the engine cylinders blasting, her hair was waving like a flag behind her head. That car, with its shining chrome and dimpled hood, reminded me of the kinds of cars my Pops used to check out when they passed by on the street, like they weren't cars at all but shapely women—the kind of car he would whistle over and would have driven if he had ever learned how to, or could have afforded one. Like it was a Cuban thing to do.

And there I was, sitting on those nice plump seats in that convertible, that pretty lady behind the wheel.

"So, just what are you boys going to do in Wisconsin?" she asked most pleasantly.

I told her about Gilberto.

"A farm?" she said. "Sounds like you boys will have some fun!"

And she clicked on the radio. Surfing music came on.

"I'll be going as far as a little town, Tylerville, in central Pennsylvania. If you don't mind a detour, I can take you along a nicer route than this interstate. You guys okay with that?"

"No problem, but . . . are we going to have to pay you?" I asked her, feeling totally embarrassed, but needing to know.

"What? Pay me! Don't be silly," she said, laughing.

So I told her about how we had gotten beat for twenty dollars.

"Well, all some people can think about is money," she said. "But I assure you boys that I'm not one of them." And she laughed again. "Anyway, my name's Jocelyn."

"I'm Rico and my friend, he's Jimmy."

And I gave Jimmy a glance and said to him, "See? They're not all going to be wackos."

"Now, you boys just relax," she said as she jammed on the accelerator, and we raced off along the interstate of New Jersey.

It was a few hours before Jimmy and me started feeling like we were really going somewhere. Watching the scenery and shooting through underpasses, with town exits and billboards going by in a blur was definitely cool, and if I closed my eyes and felt the rushing wind against my face, it was as if we were flying. But I became really excited when we finally got off the highway and came to this road and a sign said WELCOME TO PENNSYLVANIA.

A new state! Why, I was feeling like Columbus scoping out the shores of America for the first time!

Then the countryside really started to get all lush and green, like it was an enchanted fairyland of beautiful woods and meadows and sprawling farms. There were little vegetable stands, and pretty barns and silos in every direction we looked, and freakin' cows checking us out as we passed by—the kind of crap I had only seen in magazine ads and movies. Just the way the air smelled, of trees, soil, and water—not faucet water, or sprinkler water, or even rain water, but like the clear waters that run in brooks and streams. All of that just made you feel good.

And you could hear all kinds of little birdies singing in the woods and even the wind rustling through the treetops. It was so different from what me and Jimmy were used to, I kept jostling him whenever he began

to doze, mainly to point out the cows, and that made
the lady laugh, but in a kind way, like my pointing was
making her happy.

I found just about everything I saw thrilling. Even if
we were only a couple of hundred miles or so from New
York, we may as well have been on another planet.

Like take the farmer dudes. The lady told me they
were called Amish, and just to look at them made you
feel like you were in some old-time movie. A lot of them
had long beards and wore hats and black jackets with
vests and frilly bow ties, and they drove around in horse-
drawn carriages instead of cars.

I mean, I never seen anything like them before.

With all that crowding into my head, I kept thinking
about my man John Carter of Mars and a little bit about
Huckleberry Finn and the slave Jim taking off together,
and you know what else?

I felt me and my man Jimmy were on an adventure too.

I mean, it was like whatever we had been about didn't
matter anymore.

On top of all that, the lady was just too nice. So nice, in
fact, we wondered if she was crazy. She kept asking us if
we were hungry, stopping once at a burger joint, where

we ate our hearts out, and then at an old-fashioned ice cream stand, where she bought us ice cream sundaes and stuff. She never even blinked an eye about paying, like she was rich and just wanted to look out after us.

And when she had finally dropped us off at some truck stop, just before six, when the sun was still cooking up a storm, she called me over.

"Rico, take this so you and your friend can have something to eat later."

And she gave me a twenty-dollar bill.

I stared at the bill, and then at her. "You kidding?"

"It's nothing, really," she said. "I just don't want you boys to think that life is always going to be unfair to you."

And then without making a big deal out of it, she drove off to her home, which was somewhere around there.

So we waited again. All kinds of trucks came pulling in and out, to get gas or diesel fuel, but they were mostly doing local hauls. With Jimmy watching our stuff, each time I saw a truck come in, I'd run up to the driver and ask in my most polite manner, "Mister, any chance you're heading out to Route 80 west?"

And almost every time, the driver would sort of shake his head and say something like "That's some distance south. Maybe sixty or seventy miles."

All Jimmy and me could do was hang around and hope for the best, but come sunset the gas station owner closed up shop. He was turning off all the lights when he saw us sitting near the restrooms on a bench, swatting at these little green bugs that just seemed to come oozing out of the ground, trying to figure out what to do next. Jimmy was not in a good mood. He wasn't saying much to me at that point and feeling pissy because he had almost finished off all the beers he had brought along. The gas station guy walked over with a sort of limp. He was this stringy dude, and his face was all gnarly and sunburned.

"You boys can't be spending the night here," he said, shining a flashlight on our faces.

Jimmy just said, "Uh-huh," and scratched his head.

He must have felt sorry for us too, because he said he knew about a cheap motel nearby where we could spend the night for three dollars apiece. He'd even drive us over if we wanted. Since we really didn't have much choice—like, it was getting darker and darker—I told him sure, thanks.

He drove us a few miles down this road where there were no lights, no traffic signs, no nothing, just this endless darkness around us. I guess that's what forests turn into at night, but I was sort of creeped out. I was used to the different darkness of the city: Messed up and scary as that could be, at least you saw people, and apartments all lit up, and streetlights.

The motel itself, some joint called Gertie's, was just this series of rooms in a long shed. When we walked into our room and I took a look at the two little beds, one old fan, and just a beat-up black-and-white TV sitting on a stool, my heart sank. What kind of adventure was this? But Jimmy plopped down on his bed, the mattress sinking under him, and reached into his bag, pulling out a bottle of pills, a new one on me. He tapped a few onto his palm and was popping them into his mouth when he noticed the way I was staring at him.

His mood got all crazy.

"Rico, what the F you looking at me that way for? These are for my burns."

"What are they?"

"They're for 'tissue' pain."

"Say what?"

"Yeah, all kinds of inner pain, man. And anyways

these are legitimate. One hundred percent legal. I got the prescriptions in my pocket."

"Okay, okay, don't get bent out of shape."

Then he offered me one, but I turned him down.

Jimmy, mellowing out, curled up on the bed and was soon sleeping away. But me? I just kept thinking and thinking.

First about the smell in that room, really musty and lemony at the same time, from Lysol.

Then I wondered how many people had fooled around on my bed. That completely skeeved me out.

Later, I tried to sleep but couldn't. Every time I closed my eyes, I saw my Pops and Moms freaking: my Pops walking around the neighborhood asking people if they knew anything about where I might have gone. Then I saw the police coming to the door and imagined all the gossip that would spread around the block because a police car had pulled up to the curb.

I got out of bed and started playing around with the TV set, adjusting its rabbit ears antennae and changing the channels. I kept hoping something good would come in, but most stations were either hokey or just static. Finally, I tuned in a movie—which I could kind of watch despite the rolling screen. It was about this cool monster,

Godzilla, tearing up Tokyo, but that didn't help me much either. Just seeing all these apartment houses tumbling down, as the monster crushed them, I kept thinking of my own building and my Pops standing in front of the stoop, looking worried as hell.

The rest of our days on the road, well, they kind of melted together in a stew of other rides, with some folks who were nice, and some who weren't.

A few high points and things I learned:

You can go a hundred miles sometimes without seeing any black folks. And if there are Latinos around, they must be hiding somewhere, for you don't see any of them, either.

And you learn that teenage boys are like meat pies to some. On our second day, we were in the middle of nowhere Ohio, when this guy picked us up in this fancy German car. When we jumped into the back, though, he insisted we sit in the front seat with him. So we did, Jimmy and me just shrugging at each other. Seeming nice enough, he asked us all the usual questions, and as we drove along these pretty roads, while the most boring-assed classical music was playing on his radio, he just kept looking our way and smiling.

Then, out of the blue, he said to Jimmy, who was sitting next to him, "So what's your name?"

"Jimmy," he answered.

"Oh, Jimmy? I got a friend named Jimmy who's a conductor. Would you like to meet him?"

"Uhhhh, not really."

"No, but you must."

And then, even as he was driving along, he unzipped his fly and pulled his stiffy out, and started waving it around as if in time to the music.

"This is my Jimmy!" he said all happy. "Isn't he a dilly?"

With that, Jimmy, about the gentlest guy in the universe, turned purple and said, "Put that away, Mister, or I will kick your ass to kingdom come!"

And he held up his fist and started trembling, like he would really put a hurting on the man.

"Okay, okay," the man said. "I was just hoping you boys might like to have some fun."

And even though the guy's thing went into hiding, Jimmy said to him, "Now pull the F over, and now!"

He did, and in about a minute we were stuck in the middle of nowhere again, our stuff sitting by the side of the road.

* * *

But all in all it wasn't a bad trip.

We could always catch a few hours' sleep in the rest stations along the way, and bit by bit, whether we were going along local roads or on the interstate, which was faster, we seemed to be making progress.

Now, some rest stops were really bad, and some were kind of pleasant, with the kids who worked in the fast food places and diners looking rosy-cheeked and wholesome, like they were happy in their lives. Both Pennsylvania and Ohio hit me that way, and the farther west we went, the more polite folks seemed, few having that nasty, don't-get-in-my-face expression that you see in New York City.

And I have to say that at first, I kind of liked being around those white folks. I mean I didn't feel that anyone was judging me in any way. I could already see how being in a nice place sort of calmed people down, though I did notice how some of the kids working behind the counters—that is, the ones who weren't smiling all the time—looked stone-cold bored.

You'd hear a radio in one of those burger joints, and not one line of a Spanish song coming from it. Only the twangs of guitars or hokey cowboy voices singing about *"purtee"* girls and sunshine, or syrupy Musak, instead. And if you went into a food shop, no way would you find a bunch of plantains or some nice chorizos or a Cuban sandwich—you know, the kind made with pork and cheese and sweet pickles and grilled bread—to chow down on. As I said to Jimmy, "We're not in New York anymore."

On the other hand, even when you saw the same kinds of places over and over again, McDonald's and Burger King mainly, in such small towns, there were a lot of pretty libraries and churches and schools with big playing fields. I mean, even the cemeteries looked nice and comfortable.

It was like a whole new world.

Like Jimmy and me had just landed in a spaceship.

Or come onto one of those places in a raft.

Bit by bit, we somehow made our way to Chicago. And from Chicago, a map told me, it wasn't all that far to southern Wisconsin and a town called Janesville, which was the closest one to where Gilberto lived.

We caught our last ride at about eleven in the morning, with some Hell's Angel kind of dude, his skin completely covered over with blue and purple dragon tattoos. A big, burly, bearded guy, tough-looking in leather, he had the image down pat, but if he was a Hell's Angel, he wasn't anything like the ones I used to see in

Greenwich Village—he did not act at all like the kind of guy to brawl over nothing, like the New York angels. In fact he was listening to the Beatles on the radio, and when me and Jimmy climbed into his van, he couldn't have been friendlier. And that van smelled sweet from pot. *Hallelujah!* was written all over Jimmy's face. I mean the driver was so cool about it, and so unconcerned about the cops, that buzzed as he was and speeding along, he just kept laughing and laughing, while offering me and Jimmy some.

Anyway, at sometime around half past noon, four days after we had left the city, that Hell's Angel guy dropped us off at a gas station on the outskirts of Janesville.

Getting to a pay telephone, I dropped a dime in and called Gilberto.

Part 3 **ALL KINDS OF FUN ON THE FARM**

twelve

WHEN GILBERTO BEEPED at us from his pickup truck and pulled over, I couldn't believe how much he had changed. Was it really him?

He was wearing a lacquered straw hat and coveralls, a sort of corny-looking shirt with all kinds of little stars on it, and while he still had his goatee, he'd grown his sideburns really long, like truckers do, but had cut back on his Afro. Chewing on a toothpick, as always, with the brim of his hat pulled down low over his longish face, which was half-covered in shadow, he looked as much like a farmer as any Puerto Rican dude from New York could.

Parking his truck, he jumped out, flashing the friendliest grin.

"Well, you crazy dudes made it, huh?" he said, giving

me a whopping slap five and Jimmy a handshake. Then he looked us over, half smiling.

"What's so funny?" I asked him.

"It's just that you guys look so New York!"

"What do you mean?" I said, looking down at myself. "Is it the way we're dressed or something?" I asked, thinking so what if both me and Jimmy were wearing Converse sneakers, which were the rage in Harlem.

"Uh-uh," Gilberto said, cocking his head to the side. "It's the look on your faces! Like you're expecting someone to take you off! Hey, guys, I got news for you: This ain't New York."

"I know, I know," I said.

"So lighten up! And smile. You guys have officially arrived in the land of milk and honey!"

And he threw our stuff into the back of his truck and told us to get in.

From town we drove out to this sleepy road, seeing hardly any other cars, just fields and fields and the occasional tractor, one of those farmers waving at us in a most friendly manner, as if he was Gilberto's friend.

"You know that dude?" I asked him.

"Nah, it's just their way," and he waved back.

In no hurry—he wasn't going any faster than fifteen miles an hour and drove with his elbow out the window—he would occasionally take in a deep breath of the country air, a mix of cow manure, corn cuttings, and fertilizer—and smile as if it was the sweetest perfume. Then a breeze would come along, all so fresh, as if it had flowed out of a garden. And with the sky so blue and without a whiff of the big city around us, and birds chirping like they were having a wild party in the trees, you just started to feel lazy and relaxed, like you were finally away at the outdoor summer camp you'd never attended as a kid.

A land of milk and honey? I can't say. But it was a truly different place, all pretty and peaceful, and not a discarded syringe anywhere in sight.

Going along, Gilberto chattered away.

"See that farmhouse over there, with the red roof?" he said, pointing. "This very fine-looking girl lives there. I've been trying to figure out how to get a date with her, but her old man is one of the few people around here who won't even say hello to me, on account of this."

And Gilberto pulled up his sleeve, tapping his own darkish skin.

"It kills me, because now and then when I've seen

her standing by the fence, I've pulled over to talk to her, and she's always seemed interested in knowing me better. Anyways, I have my eye on her, even if I bet her Poppy's probably a Klan member."

I stared at him. "KKK? You're kidding, right?"

"Nope," Gilberto said. "Heard they've held rallies around here in years past. I mean, most folks are really nice and not prejudiced at all, but, you know, some still think a certain way."

Then he scratched his chin.

"I mean, whenever that farmer's around and sees my pickup going by, he just stares and stares." Then Gilberto shrugged. "But what are you gonna do?"

And then he slapped me on the knee.

"And see that place there?" he continued.

He pointed to a log cabin lodge at the side of the road.

"That's called the 'Hunter's Barn.' If you get the munchies and want to chow down, that's where you can go. For two bucks you can buy yourself a platter of steak and eggs or hot cakes with sausages and syrup. And next door to that is a grocery store—only they call it a 'general store' out here. They sell all kinds of neat stuff you can't find back east, like beef and venison jerky, and maple syrup and shit."

Damn, was I imagining things, or did Gilberto really use the word "neat"?

"You know how much a case of Milwaukee beer costs out here?" And before I could guess, he said, "Two twenty-five for twenty-four cans. And stuff like milk, butter, and cheese, that costs almost nothing. It's wild—this is where it all comes from."

I was looking forward to checking those new places out, but Jimmy didn't exactly seem enchanted. "Sounds just dandy," he said with this bored look on his face.

I wondered what he was thinking.

"Anyway, my farm isn't too far from here," Gilberto went on. "With you guys, there'll be seven of us altogether."

"Seven? You running a commune or something?" I asked.

"Nah, I just rent out some rooms," Gilberto said. "It's a big-assed place, and easy enough to get along in. But there's one thing about it that might not thrill you all."

I braced myself before saying, "Uh-huh. And what's that?"

"See, I only pay about two hundred dollars a month rent. That's for a big ol' house, a barn, and fifteen acres of land."

I never whistled, but I did then, like he was big-time.

"We've got electricity and a telephone, and I have running water that we pump up from a well, for washing and cooking. But the thing is, bathroomwise, we use an outhouse. That's the only really funky hassle about the place."

Outhouse? I never even heard the word. "Uh, hate to sound *dumb-erino*, but what the hell's an outhouse?"

He laughed.

"Let me put it to you this way, Rico. Like, what do you think people used to do before they had flush toilets?"

"I don't know. Maybe go in their backyards behind a bush or something."

He snapped his fingers.

"Almost! What they used to do is dig a deep hole in the ground and then put a little shed over it—where folks could do their business."

Wow, that was nice. Even Jimmy, who was half dozing, gave me a look.

"You mean you don't have a regular toilet?" I asked. How couldn't there be a regular toilet? And he won a lottery?

"Nope," Gilberto said, pulling out the toothpick from his mouth and smiling big-time. "But it's nothing to sweat over. You can always sneak out to take a leak if you don't want to deal with it, but for anything more complicated, you use the outhouse."

Jimmy now had a "whoopy do" look in his eyes.

"That's the main reason why I don't pay much rent," Gilberto explained. "It's like a throwback to the old days and, because of that, not up to snuff for most folks, especially when it comes time to clean it out."

Say what?

"You got to clean all that stuff *out*?"

"Yep," Gilberto said, nodding, this sly enjoying-the-heck-out-of-himself smile on his lips. "Someone's gotta. Once every few months, depending, of course, on the traffic."

"Wow," I said, imagining what my Moms and Pops, who'd come from farms in Cuba, would have thought about me ending up at one without a working toilet. I could hear them laughing across the good old U. S. of A., see them shaking their heads.

Gilberto lived about a quarter of a mile off a road that cut through some neglected cornfields, where crows and other birds were feasting away on row after row of blackened husks. Beeping his horn to scatter them, he grinned as all these black birds shot up from the field like arrows.

"All that rotting corn," he said, laughing, "is mine. Obviously, I'm not too much of a farmer."

"You grew corn?"

"Tried to," Gilberto said, chuckling. "Started in the spring. But I was too stingy on the pesticides. And boy, that cracked the local farmers up," he said, honking at a passing truck. "Somehow, I thought if you used half as much as you needed, then at least half the corn would grow. And so I've mainly been raising insects— cutworms, corn flea beetles, and little hungry aphids, you name it. Man, have they been chowing down."

"Sounds like you've got it figured out, though," I said.

"Yup. Like what you think might be easy, ain't always so."

We went up a slight hill, along a dirt road, past an old barn and piles of rusted equipment—rakes, hoes, a wheel-less wagon, wheelbarrows, and all kinds of milk crates and broken chairs, even a sofa that had seen better days. Then we came to the house itself, a big, crooked, rickety-looking, A-framed sort of thing, half the paint peeling off. Along one side of the house, a makeshift scaffold had been put up, paint cans strewn about on the ground below. Gilberto parked, and as we got out, he saw me looking at the scaffolding. "Hey," he said. "You guys know anything about painting?"

"I guess so." I nodded. How hard could it be?

"Good, 'cause I could use some help."

I didn't mind—we had to be doing something.

"Sure. Like when?"

"Later, after you settle in."

"You okay with that, Jimmy?"

He was adjusting his bandana and looking around. "No *problema*," he said, his posture in a slouch.

But I could see that Jimmy was wondering what the heck he had gotten himself into.

Inside, there was as much clutter and junk as there'd been outside. Everything in the house, old rocking chairs and trunks, even what looked like a witch's spinning wheel, along with all kinds of other stuff, either had been left behind by the owners, or had been picked up by Gilberto from the side of the road. Tattered rugs covered the wood floor, and there was a potbellied stove in a corner, and yellowing magazines in stacks along the walls.

The place smelled kind of musty and funky, too, and

that got worse when we climbed up to the second floor. Gilberto showed us to our rooms; they were just off this drafty hallway, maybe twenty feet long, leading, Gilberto told us, to the outhouse, which was set off from the rest of the building.

"Aw, man," I said as I lugged my stuff, this strong odor of ammonia and you-know-what hitting me right away. "Is it always like that?" I asked.

"Not always," Gilberto said, smiling. "Some days are worse than others. It can be really horrible on hot days, but you'll get used to it."

"I guess. But why's it up *here*?" I asked him.

"'Cause of the winters when nobody wants to go out. It gets cold—and I mean *cold*—around here."

I looked at Jimmy, and he made a face, as if to say "Terrific!"

"Go ahead and look," Gilberto encouraged me.

I had to take a leak anyway. Going down that hallway, the floors creaking under me, I pushed open that door and nearly gagged from the fumes. There were pails of ashes in a row along the floor and a couple of signs on the wall.

One of them said, IF CRAP WERE MONEY, POOR PEOPLE WOULD HAVE BEEN BORN WITHOUT BUTTS.

"And there's nothing downstairs?" I asked Gilberto when I came out, not wanting to sleep in stinkville each night.

"Afraid not. The downstairs rooms are all taken. But like I said, you'll get used to it."

Then he gave me an encouraging rap on the back.

"Now, you settle in," he said. "Come down for a beer and some eats when you're done."

My room was pretty nice even if there wasn't much to it, basically a mattress, a table, a lamp and a chair, a speckled mirror, a creaky floor. But the one thing about it was the view. Its window looked west, and because the land was flat, you could see a long way to other farms—their barns, silos, and houses casting shadows—and fields that fit the description of "rolling," like something out of a pretty movie, or from one of those Jolly Green Giant ads on the TV. You could even make out tractors, like tiny toys, off in the distance, doing whatever tractors do.

Oh yeah, hoeing, plowing, I guess.

Just looking out that window made me feel that I was a million miles from what used to bug me in the city. Like standing on a dark subway platform or walking by the projects at night and knowing that somebody, somewhere, out to rip you off, was watching your every move. It was great to think that there was no way that would happen here. Those wide-open spaces seemed one thousand percent more peaceful than anywhere in New York, even the parks.

I really liked that: It made me feel calm in a way I didn't remember ever feeling before. Looking up at the sky and the few wisps of clouds that floated by, I just drank up that beautiful blueness, an amazing blueness like you'd find in another world.

thirteen

AFTER LUNCH, GILBERTO threw me and Jimmy some coveralls, and the next thing we knew, we were out in the yard trying to get our lazy asses geared up to work. Neither of us was thrilled. An afternoon off would have been nice after being on the road, but I told Jimmy that it would be really jive if we didn't help out, considering how Gilberto had been so cool about our staying with him. The problem was that we were slightly buzzed from drinking beers with our baloney sandwiches.

Which brings me to a rule of thumb: Do not drink three bottles of beer and climb a scaffold two stories up in the hot afternoon sun to paint a house.

For one thing, when Jimmy started climbing the ladder, his foot slipped, and he would have fallen ass-backwards, with his bucket of paint and all, if Gilberto, up on the scaffold, hadn't grabbed him in time. I had been below holding the rickety scaffold steady, and so I switched jobs with Jimmy. And soon enough I was twenty feet up, with a bucket of paint and a couple of brushes and scrapers.

"So what you gotta do, Rico," Gilberto said, taking a scraper, "is just go at the old paint like this, right?"

And he showed me, hacking away, all those flakes coming down like snow.

"But be careful about walking on these planks," Gilberto warned me. "Like, you don't want to be moving too suddenly."

That wasn't too hard, and when we were finished scraping clean that section of the wall, Gilberto handed me an open can of white paint.

"Now, there ain't nothing to this," he said, stirring the brush in that paint until it looked like whipped cream. "Just slop it on, all nice and even, okay? I mean, this ain't the Taj Mahal."

"Got it," I said.

So, we were painting and painting, Jimmy hanging in there down below and Gilberto whistling happily away like he used to when we delivered newspapers together.

Talking about the folks who were staying with him, Gilberto told us that one of them, this Colorado girl, eighteen and fine, was his current squeeze.

"You'll meet Wendy later," he said. "She'll be back from Madison tonight."

I was telling him about our hitchhiking trip, and that I was happy as hell to see him again, when out of nowhere, as he was dipping a brush in the can, he turned to me and said, "Rico, I got to ask you something."

"Uh, yeah?"

"Like, how long you planning to stay?"

I was surprised that he asked, so I thought about it.

"As long as it's cool with you," I said after a moment. "Is that all right?"

"Yeah," he said. "But you ever gonna let your Moms and Pops know you're here?"

Uh-oh, I was thinking, feeling my face go all red.

"I don't know how I can," I said. "I mean if I do, you best believe that my ass will end up in Florida."

"But you're gonna have to sooner or later, right?" he asked like he was my Jiminy Cricket conscience.

"Yeah," I said, but I couldn't even begin to imagine what I could say to them, and I just didn't really want to think about it yet. Because we just got here. And because once I did, I'd start feeling bad. Gilberto, knowing me so well, must have sensed it.

"Look, I didn't mean to blow your head, but it's something to think about. That's all I'm saying. You only got one Moms and Pops, right?"

I just nodded and Gilberto, having spoken his mind, started whistling again, even if I could tell that my attitude kind of bothered him.

That afternoon I learned that the same way some thoughts can suddenly bug you—

Did I do the right thing?

Am I a bad guy for having run away?

—so can other things.

See, after a while I started to get a little careless. Slopping down that paint as quickly as I could, I was working on a stretch of the roof called an eave, which I could barely reach, even on my tiptoes, when I came to a big, baggy-looking sack hanging stuck to a corner. I slapped at it a few times with my paintbrush, to knock it off the ledge. But as soon as I did, that bag started buzzing. Then this wicked-assed black wasp with a mean-looking helmet head and a stinger and a half sticking out its butt came crawling out this hole and, taking off like a jet fighter, started zipping in circles around me.

"Holy shit!" I shouted, swinging my brush at it.

Luckily, I smashed it against the wall with my paint-brush. But then more of those suckers started exploding out of that bag, like maybe twenty or thirty of them, and I swear it was like they had something against me. Maybe it was the heat or those beers I drank, but for a second I could swear that they were wearing my Moms's and Pops's faces, all of them going crazy and trying to sting my ass. All I could do was flail at them, and while I was jerking around, that scaffold started wobbling like crazy.

"Get the hell down!" Gilberto called, climbing onto the ladder. I was moving along the planks towards the ladder myself, going "Whoa!" and "Be nice!" to them wasps, when I kicked my can of paint over and all that shit went spilling over the side, half soaking Jimmy's head in white.

It was kind of funny and painful to see. By the time I scrambled down the ladder, poor Jimmy was standing there, just wiping that gook off his face.

"You okay?" I asked him.

"Yeah, great, Rico. I just love it!" he said.

Then we all started laughing, Jimmy included.

"Stand still for a second," Gilberto told Jimmy. And taking a garden hose, he just started spraying water on him, trying to get that paint off and saying, "I baptize you in the name of the jive wasps, and the summer and motherf—king nature!"

"Keep going," Jimmy said.

And Gilberto did, not only spraying Jimmy, but pointing that nozzle at his own head, drenching it, and then, what the heck, he turned it on me. And I can tell you, not only did that cool water feel good, but a rainbow came shimmering through the spray.

But then I felt an ache on my head, and touching it, a lump rising. My arm began to hurt and so did my leg, and then my neck started bothering me. I had been stung four times, that nasty stuff aching like crazy.

fourteen

THAT EVENING ME and Jimmy met everybody. There was Polly, an art student from Gilberto's school, and Bonnie and Curt, a hippie couple. Fine as fine could be, Bonnie resembled the girl on the red Sun-Maid raisin boxes, but with a body and a half, while her guy reminded me of the singer James Taylor, being really thin and having real long hair, too, and sideburns that curled around his jaw. Polly was this quiet sort, with a pretty, spoon-shaped face and wire-rimmed glasses, hair flowing down to her waist.

The biggest surprise was Gilberto's girl. She came in sometime after eight, when we were all sitting around with plates on our laps and eating some weird vegetable dish made with okra and radishes, carrots and eggplant, that Bonnie served up with brown rice—the most tasteless thing I'd ever tried. (But I still ate the whole plate up, telling her, "Man, is this good!")

Since Gilberto had told me that Wendy was from Colorado, I expected an all-American cowgirl, but Wendy was as black as black could be. Tall and thin, with a huge Afro, she came stomping into the room in high boots and a suede miniskirt.

After Gilberto introduced us, she smiled and with a little wave of her long-fingered hands said, "Howdy!," loopy bracelets jangling off her wrists. Then: "My goodness, but I'm famished! Gilly, what do we have for eats?"

Gilly? I thought. *Gilly?* Gee freaking whiz.

When she found out, she said, "Oh goody! I love vegetables!" And while she started to eat, she said, no joke, "Yum, yum."

At that point, Jimmy looked at me, mystified. And I knew exactly what he was thinking. We'd heard of black girls who acted white, but had never met any before. And there she was, sitting across from me in a big stuffed chair, just chattering away, cheerful as hell.

Done with her dinner, she waved around a piece of paper. "Just finished writing my latest poem. You all want to hear it?" she asked.

Everybody said they did.

Leaning his lanky frame against a doorway, a beer in hand, Gilberto just winked my way, then rolled his eyes.

"I call this," Wendy said, the tone of her voice suddenly serious, "'Who am I?'"

Clearing her throat, she began.

> *Who am I?*
> *But a someone.*
> *A someone*
> *Made of bones*
> *Sinews,*
> *Of neurons*
> *Of synapses*
> *And luscious*
> *Deserving Black flesh. . . .*

And that went on for about ten minutes, the poem sounding pretty good, especially when she started getting heavy-duty about certain parts of her body. I never heard anything like it before. When she finished and we clapped, she took all these bows, like a ballerina, just beaming.

By then, Jimmy and me were beat, trying not to yawn.

And I was still aching from those stings. I mean, it had been a long day. But then just as Jimmy, who still had some paint flecks sticking to his skin, started to head up the stairs behind me, Curt pulled out a joint and Jimmy just changed his mind, hanging back.

"Catch you later," he said to me.

I went up to my room, not minding leaving those folks behind. I just wanted to read something—that night it was *Huckleberry Finn* again, a book that always made me feel all right. Like that guy Huck Finn was in the room with me, telling me his story, the way he put things, sticking in my head. Even while everybody else was laughing down below and I could hear the music and their footsteps in the hall as they came up the stairs to use the outhouse, and crickets, which were like a million voices talking all at once, sounding from the fields, Huck's book kept me company until I started to get drowsy.

The best thing was that from my bed I could see the sky through the window. All those freaking stars—in the way you never can see them from New York City, like salt spilled on a black table, zillions of them—and with little streaks cutting across the horizon now and then, all pretty and sad at the same time, like the sky was crying. I don't know exactly when, but sometime in the middle of the night, while everybody else was sleeping, I just had to go down into the yard to check those stars out in all their glory. Lying down on my back in the grass, I looked up, picking out a few of the constellations and planets I had learned about in school—Venus and Mars maybe, Hercules, the Big and Little Dippers, the North Star gleaming like a silver Christmas ornament.

Like Cassiopeia, a lady sitting, not on a subway, worried about her purse, but up in heaven.

And horny Capricorn.

And Cygnus the swan . . .

After a while, I saw all kinds of other things as well. Like horses bounding through the galaxies, rocket ships shooting past the moon, even angels plucking at a guitar or two; then I made out a map of the world, spreading across space. In that I saw a little island, shaped like a crocodile, and I remembered my Pops showing me a map and saying, "See this island, boy, that's Cuba, and never forget it, okay?" I saw beer bottles, and garbage cans too, but then that faded.

Then—and I wasn't even high—I felt like I was swimming in the Milky Way. I'd never seen it so clearly

before, not even from my tenement rooftop, that endless stream of stars, like a river in its way, all graceful
and shit, stretching like an Aladdin's carpet across the
farthest reaches of outer space.

Like I said before, it was a whole different world.

———

fifteen

WELL, IT TOOK me and Gilberto and Jimmy two weeks to finish painting the house, a job that left my right hand covered with blisters, and Jimmy getting sunburned in a way he wasn't used to, except where he kept that kerchief around his neck. He complained a lot. He would get on the scaffold beside me and, while splashing down the paint, say things like "Rico, this is almost cool, but we ain't being paid for anything."

"It's our room and board, okay?" I'd say.

"I know, but it seems jive," Jimmy would say, sulking.

At first I didn't get it, but then it hit me that he was probably still hurting from the way his Pops used to work him for nothing.

"Listen, Jimmy," I told him one day. "Gilberto's

looking out for us, you know? I mean, he's been paying the rent, buying the food, right?"

"Uh-huh," Jimmy said, like he didn't want to hear it.

"So this is the least we can do."

"Yeah, I know," he said. "But after a while this shit gets boring."

"Well, we got to do what we got to do. So just be cool, huh?"

"All right," Jimmy said sticking his brush in a paint bucket, in slo-mo.

Still, for all his complaining, one thing I noticed was the way Jimmy would just stare and stare whenever this girl Polly left the house and started walking across the fields, hauling along an easel, a folding chair, and a wooden box filled with watercolors and oil paints or whatever she used—I didn't know. Wearing a straw sun hat and finding a place she liked, with a nice view of the surrounding farms, or maybe in a field of wildflowers, she would plop her stuff down and sit before her easel, quietly making drawings.

Up on the scaffold, Jimmy could not take his eyes off of her.

"So, Jimmy, what's up with you?" I asked him one day, nodding towards Polly in the field.

"Nothing, man, I'm just trying to paint this crap."

"But you keep checking out that girl Polly. What's with that?"

"Ain't but nothing. I'm just curious, that's all. I mean, like, she draws, right?"

He wiped some sweat off his forehead, his glasses all steamed up.

"So why don't you just walk up to her and tell her that you have the artistic wares too?" I said.

"Aw, forget that. Like, what would she do with a freak like me?" he said, slapping paint against that wall like he was punching it. "I've seen the way she—and everybody else—looks at me because I'm always covering my neck up."

"You're imagining things," I said. But at the same time I thought about how, my room being next door to Jimmy's, I sometimes heard him yelping at night while he dreamed, like he was on fire all over again. "You can't be thinking freaky things like that. You're one hell of a beaucoup artist! I bet your best stuff would blow her away."

"It ain't that," he said. "Like, what would she even

begin to think after seeing this nasty stuff?" And he touched his chest below his neck. "Like, who would ever want to hang out with this?" Then he pulled off his bandana and showed me his scars for the first time. They looked like something from the moon, with craters and weird crests and waves, and the skin was really different—not white, not black, not even in-between, but something strange, like the wild pink of a fried-up sea crab that had been stomped on.

I was startled.

"You want to touch it?" he said with a crazy smile.

"No way!"

"Well, man, if you think that's ugly," Jimmy said, "imagine how I feel having to walk around like this!" And he covered up again. "So, Rico, any time I start thinking about getting next to someone, I just look at this shit in the mirror or feel it with my hand and tell myself 'Uh-uh!'"

What could I say? His scars *were* nasty. But somehow out of my mouth came "Hey, even Frankenstein's monster was kind of lovable, you hear? And Dracula too!"

"Har, har. Thanks a lot!"

"No, I mean it, just talk to the girl!" I said, trying to stir him up. "What you got to lose?"

And Jimmy just sighed, like that would never happen.

Once we finished painting the house, I figured we could just loaf for a while. And we did. Mainly hanging around the farm and trying to find things to do. I had my books, my music, my comic stories, but it wasn't the same for Jimmy. He was restless, chain-smoking up a storm, circling around the living room, or else copping a squat on the couch to watch daytime TV, until boredom drove him upstairs to his bed in the middle of the day, a half case of beer, a pack of cigarettes, and a transistor radio in hand. He'd chill on his mattress, sometimes on his floor, without a care. He was great at that. For five days straight, if you happened by his doorway, you'd find Jimmy zoning out from the world. I can't tell you all the times I tried to get him off his ass—he was starting to look a little pale and zombie-like to me—but no matter what I said to him—"Hey, James, you want to go exploring the back woods with me?" or "Like, Gilberto told me about this nice pond, underneath a waterfall, where we can check out hippie chicks skinny-dipping"—he'd just look at me like I was one insane MF and mumble, "Nah, Rico, you just do your own thing. I'm feeling fine as hell."

Then, being a genius, I put two and two together and it hit me that Jimmy was still getting through his days with painkillers and beer. I wasn't imagining things. I'd see him passed out on his mattress in the middle of the day, his clothes still on, the beautiful blue sky reflecting off his glasses.

It drove me crazy. What killed me was that my Pops did the exact same thing. On weekends, usually the late afternoon, he would be dozing by the kitchen table all torn up, my Moms being out with some friends. As soon as I heard her coming into the apartment, I'd start shaking him, slapping his cheeks and splashing water on his face, so my Moms wouldn't flip totally out.

I wanted to do the same for Jimmy.

But seeing him looking so peaceful, even if his mouth was half open, I decided not to mess with his vibes.

After all, Jimmy, with his chest burns and messed-up glasses, was Jimmy.

So I just closed the door.

One morning, about a week after we had finished up our painting job, Gilberto had something new for us to do—cleaning out the receptacle bin under what he called the "throne room."

The outhouse.

"Oh, golly gee," I said to Gilberto sarcastically. "What a thrill!"

"Sorry, guy," said Gilberto, "but it's something we gotta do."

I was sitting on the porch in the coveralls he'd given me: I wore nothing else, staying mainly on the farm. I had slipped into a new look, and loved it. Like I was really a farm boy. But as for cleaning out an outhouse? It was not on my top-ten list of things to do.

"Are you being for real?"

"Yup, but think about it this way," he said. "You'll know what them pioneers had to go through for hundreds of years. It'll be like participating in a history lesson."

"Wowee," I said, making a face.

Gilberto laughed.

"Looky here, it won't be so bad," he said, slapping me on the back. "And it has to be done."

"Fine, fine," I said, getting up.

"So go haul your pal Jimmy out of bed. He's got to do his thing too."

Yes, swami, I thought. And yes, swami, baloney, and salami, I hear and obey—but getting Jimmy up wasn't so easy. I knocked on his door, but he didn't answer, and when I pushed it open, he was off in dreamland. A pill bottle was sitting on the floor, next to a couple of empty beer cans.

His glasses were still on his face.

"Yo Jimmy, come on. Get up, man!" I said, shaking him until he finally opened his eyes.

"So what time is it?" he asked out of some sleepy depth.

"It's past ten," I told him.

"That's nice. How about giving me another fifteen minutes, huh?"

"No, man, we got things to do!"

"Like what sort of things?" he said, sitting up and rubbing his eyes.

"Like cleaning up the outhouse!"

"What?"

"Yeah, today's the day," I said, trying to sound cheerful.

"No way." He fell back on the bed. I tugged on his arm and even shook him a few times to let him know that I wasn't kidding. Finally, he sat up, saying, "Rico, why do you have to be hassling me? I was just having me the nicest dream."

"Come on, man," I said impatiently. "We just got to do right by Gilberto, okay?"

"All right. I'll be down there in a few minutes, but damn"—he was groggily shaking his head—"what is this, a boot camp?"

In fact, I started thinking that maybe my *tío* Pepe's academy in Florida wouldn't have been all that bad. After all, how many cadets cleaned outhouses?

Here's how it's done, in case you're interested.

First, you put a plasterer's mask over your mouth and nose and march out like you're on your way to a firing squad. Then, from the yard, you enter what looks like a little barn. Clicking on a light, you see that all the stuff, mixed with lime or ashes, has been dropping down the outhouse shaft into a thick, circular, wooden bin about six feet across and four feet deep.

Then you get up on a stepladder and begin to dig it out with some very long shovels, transferring the gook into a wheelbarrow. And while you're doing this, and everyone involved is saying things like "Gross," "Grody," "Jessuz freaking Christ," "Funkee," "Uhhhh!," and "Dag!," and "Watch where you're tossing that!," "Oh this is for real!," and "Holy mama mia!," you can't help but have an appreciation for how very special and wonderful modern flushing toilets—"*inodoros*" my mother called them—really are.

You drink a lot of beer, while each of you waits to take a turn with the shovel.

You see all kinds of stuff in that murkiness: Kotex, pens, pencils, even paperback novels and comic books, all having somehow fallen in. Some money too, a dollar bill popping out now and then, with George Washington looking a little embarrassed. But no way do you want to even think about fishing anything out.

Each time a wheelbarrow gets full—we had three to work with—you push it towards a ditch at the far end of a rotting cornfield, and dump its contents down the slope. Along the way, a thousand black flies go swarming around you, and it's surprising to see just how many spiders and worms have made that stuff their home.

And all kinds of birds come floating down to investigate the heap.

We were all miserable.

But Rex, Gilberto's hound, was really happy. Circling around, sniffing like crazy, his tail was wagging, like he was the special guest at a party.

Took about fifty or so trips, maybe three hours of going back and forth with the wheelbarrows.

"*Mierda,*" I said to myself.

The Spanish word for you-know-what.

Once we'd hauled it all out, we all pitched in to cover the slimy mound over with dirt, along with some just-in-case lime. If Gilberto had been interested in keeping it as a fertilizer, as some farmers did, we could have just left it to dry up in the sun, but thank God, he wasn't.

Jimmy was standing next to me by that *delightful* mound, having a smoke.

"Damn, man." I nudged him with my elbow. "Just look at all that! And it's just from one house!"

"Yeah, it's kind of scary, that's for sure," he said, nodding.

"Well, just think about it," I said, doing some numbers in my head. "If that was just from one house and there are millions of houses all over the world, not to mention apartment and office buildings, department stores, and all kinds of little villages with huts and even people who live in caves, man, that comes to one hell of a pile, doesn't it?"

"Yeah," Jimmy said. "But let's not dwell too much on that shit, okay?"

I didn't know if he was joking or not, but I dropped the subject, just feeling glad that Jimmy was on his feet again.

Back by the house, all the wheelbarrows were hosed down and everyone trudged back inside, sniffing at their clothes. I was dying to take a shower. But that was another makeshift thing: the shower being just some hoses running up into a little closet-sized room from a faulty heater in the cellar, the water always a bit cold.

I showered anyway; had to.

Later, when everyone had cleaned up, Gilberto offered to make a run over to the McDonald's on Route 26 in thanks for the job we had done.

"How about it, guys, huh? Juicy cheeseburgers and french fries on me!"

Curt, a vegetarian, said another midwestern word: "Yuck!"

"Hey, come on, guys. Don't you deserve a break today?"

But a hamburger?

"Qué carajo," as my father would say.

Never thought I'd turn down a free meal, but once you've done that kind of work, putting two and two together, your appetite isn't quite the same, not for a few days at least.

I just ate some Ritz crackers and jelly. Curt lit up a joint and put some Allman Brothers on the phonograph.

Jimmy, fresh from his own shower, with his hair all combed and looking "spiffy"—another of the words I'd started to pick up out there—was reading a *Life* magazine from 1943, with stories about the Second World War. Every now and then, he'd get up to look out the window, then sit down again. I couldn't figure out what was going on with him until Polly pulled up and parked her Volkswagen van by the barn. While we had been digging out the outhouse, she had been over to Gilberto's college, taking some kind of summer art class, and as soon as she started unloading, Jimmy got up instantly and, as fast as the Flash, was suddenly beside her, helping her carry her things into the house.

She walked in holding a big paper pad. She'd let anybody look at it, and anybody included Jimmy. It was filled with charcoal drawings of nudes, posed like they were just statues in a museum.

"These are smoking," he said to her, turning the pages. "They kick ass!"

She actually blushed. I'm not sure if it was from his language—like, nobody talked that way out there—or if she believed him at all.

"You really think so?" she asked, smiling.

Then: "Yeah, they're really *chévere*."

"What's *chévere*?" she asked, all amused.

"That's like when something's cool, or boss, or dynamite," Jimmy told her, being both jive and suave at the same time. "It's not only hip but has a side to it that's really swift or elegant—like yourself, you know?"

"Really?" she asked, glancing at him.

I started thinking to myself, Tell her, Jimmy. Tell her!

And, just like he could read my mind, Jimmy said, "Look, I know they're really good 'cause I can draw myself."

"You can?" Polly said, like she was genuinely interested. "Can you show me something?"

"All right," he told her, looking at her carefully. "Sit down."

"Now?"

"Yeah," he said. "Why not? I'll show you."

So she sat down in her *Beverly Hillbillies* granny dress, tucking her knees together, and took off her wire-rimmed glasses, twirling her long wavy hair back, waiting.

Taking up her pad and a few pencils, Jimmy lit a smoke and asked me to get him a beer. Then he held up a thumb and started lining her up like he was looking through a gun sight. Adjusting his bandana to keep it in place, he began gliding his hand over the page, his head dropping low, so that his face seemed rimmed by jowls. It reminded me of when he would practice drawing my face, up on my roof, his eyes getting all serious, or like when we were in my little room, Jimmy knocking himself out trying to illustrate our comics.

He drew real fast: Curt was turning over that Allman Brothers record just as Jimmy, working like a maniac, had filled that page up with Polly. I know because I was standing behind him, feeling proud as hell, watching.

Lighting up a new smoke, he looked it over, shrugged, and handed that pad to her.

"It ain't much," he said, as she took it. "But I'll finish it up later."

It was a good likeness. In fact, he made her look finer than she was. She wasn't all that built, but he gave her grand and heroic boobies, like Wonder Woman's, and without her glasses on, she had this blank look in her eyes like Mr. Magoo, but he made her eyes seem alert and alive.

Putting a hand to her neck, her glasses back on, she studied that drawing carefully. And really slowly, like she was trying to figure out how he had done it so quickly. She just looked and looked, without saying a thing, and for some reason that bugged Jimmy big-time. He got up and, having killed his beer, went over to the fridge for another.

"Like I said, I'll finish it later," he told her when he came back. "But what do you think?"

"It's really good," she finally said, smiling. "You have a real gift!"

When I heard that, I thought *Hallelujah!* like my comic-book dreams would come alive again. But Jimmy being Jimmy, and able to switch moods in a second, suddenly slumped down into a chair. His eyes rolled up in his head, and he looked like he was suddenly being carried away in some kind of rush, like when he got high on H.

And then he started telling Polly all kinds of crazy stuff, most of it about how he just wasn't any good.

"Well, thanks, Polly, but my drawings are BS—anyone can do them," he said. "I mean I got a long-assed way to go, but it's not like it really means anything to me, anyway. . . . Like, you don't have to be stroking me to be nice. I know the truth, you hear?"

And she seemed flustered, saying, "But I just—"

That didn't stop him.

"Even if you're a pretty chick who don't want to be mean, I know what's really happening with this crap. Like it's not even worth a piss, you know? Like I ain't no artist asshole, you hear, 'cause being a man ain't got nothing to do with that and . . ."

To my horror, Jimmy went on and on, talking the kind of trash his Pops used to lay on him, and she got up, thanking him again, but it wasn't like he heard her. Then I suddenly realized what was going on: He must have taken a whole bunch of those damn painkiller pills.

Jimmy didn't even bother with dinner that night. He just sat in a corner rocking chair, drinking beer and chain-smoking, working that drawing over, erasing things, one after the other, then scribbling all over that page like he was possessed.

Then he'd get up and go to the fridge again.

"Yo Rico?" he called to me, when he finally finished the drawing.

I was sitting beside Wendy.

"So what do you think?" he said, his voice all low and cracked, showing me the drawing.

I was amazed by how Jimmy had ruined the thing. It was now a crazy version of Polly, with so many zig-zagging lines, in wild beehivelike clusters, that she looked like a hundred-year-old ghoul from some horror movie.

"Uh . . . well . . . ," I said. "It's cool. But I wouldn't show it to Polly just now, all right?"

He got all offended.

"Something wrong with it?" he asked, his voice loud.

"Nah, it's great! But you should wait before showing it to her," I said, sitting up.

"So you're saying it's bullshit, right?"

"Nah, nah, Jimmy, I'm not—" But before I could say another word, he ripped that page out the pad and tore it up. Then he tossed the pad behind him.

"All right," he said, "I get you."

And he started rocking back and forth in that chair, really sucking up a cigarette.

"Damn, Jimmy," I said.

It wasn't like people weren't noticing. Stopping what they were doing, Gilberto, Wendy, Bonnie, and Polly were staring our way. Only Curt, off by the record player, pretending to be Jimi Hendrix, wasn't.

"Jimmy," I said, in my most respectful voice. "You got to be cool, all right?"

But it was like he couldn't hear me. A few minutes later he was asleep.

It wasn't even half past nine.

The next morning Gilberto called me into the kitchen. He was putting Jimmy's discarded beer bottles into a case.

"I know that cleaning the outhouse was a drag," he said. "But what's going on with your boy Jimmy?"

"I don't know," I said, feeling embarrassed as hell.

"I mean, I love you, my bro, but is he gonna be a problem?"

"No, Gilberto," I said, shaking my head. "It's just that

he's been kind of messed up since he had his burning accident, you know?"

"Uh-huh, so what's that mean?" Gilberto asked, giving my right shoulder a death squeeze. "Is he on something?"

"Nothing I know about," I said, my face turning red like it did whenever I told a lie.

"Come outside with me," Gilberto said. As he pushed open the screen door with his boot and carried out the case of empties into the yard, a concerned look on his face, I was thinking, Uh-oh.

"Look, Rico," he said, putting the case down. "I've been around the block enough to tell when somebody's getting high. So don't BS me, all right?"

"I wouldn't," I said. "I swear."

"So what's he taking?"

"Painkillers—but he has to, because of those burns I told you about," I finally admitted. "Otherwise he can't even sleep."

"Uh-huh," he said. This vein—a vein I'd never seen before—stood out on his forehead. "Look, I got to be honest with you, Rico," he began. "I don't mind that you came out here, and I don't even mind that you brought Jimmy. But I *do mind* if that shit is going on in my house. I came out here to get away from that junkie mentality. I don't need it, you understand?"

Stopping, he reached through his pockets, pulling out a pouch of Bull Durham tobacco and some rolling papers. As upset as I was, I still found it an elegant thing to watch: It took him about a minute to roll a cigarette, the strings of that pouch dangling from his lips, the cigarette coming out as full and round and nicely packed as a Marlboro. Then, striking a kitchen match off the heel of his boot and lighting the thing, Gilberto went on: "Look, I feel bad for the guy. I'm sorry he got burned up and stuff, but that's not my problem. All I can say is that you best be having a talk with him about straightening out, 'cause otherwise both of you will be out on your asses. Like, I don't want that negative energy in my house, you hear me?"

"Yeah, Gilberto, I hear you," I said, thinking how unfair it was, that you can have a good intention and it will come back on you in a bad way.

Then he rapped me a few times on my shoulder, but gently.

"I mean it, Rico," he said, heading back inside, the screen door slapping against the frame about four or five times before finally closing.

*　*　*

After that I sat on the porch, watching the sun rising higher in the east and worrying about Jimmy. Then I figured that there was only one thing I could do, since no amount of talking to my man James would make a difference. Heading back into the house, I slinked up to his room. Seeing Jimmy in wonderland, I looked around for his bowling bag.

In it, I found a picture of Jimmy's last girlfriend, from before he had started messing around with drugs, this fly and angelic-looking *dominicana*, Carmen. Then a picture of me and Jimmy, taken a few years back, on the stoop: I had a wise-guy smirk on my face, and I was holding up two fingers behind Jimmy's head, giving him rabbit ears. A tube of cortisone cream, a packet of moistened gauze, a bottle of cologne, then some underpants, ten packets of gum, a bottle opener, three pencils, and a small pad of paper.

Then, down at the very bottom, with a sock rolled around them, I found two bottles of pills.

When Jimmy woke up that afternoon, he came pounding on my door, all agitated.

"Rico," he said. "Did you take my stuff?"

He was trembling with anger.

"Yep," I said. "For your own good."

"Aw, man," he said, smacking the door frame. "How could you be so lame?"

I shrugged.

Then he just pushed his way past me into my room and started looking through my bag, then in my closet.

"What did you do with them?" he demanded.

"I ain't telling you," I said.

"Why you busting my chops?" he asked, glaring at me. "Like, what did I do to you?"

"Jimmy, I did it because I'm your friend, you understand?"

"Yeah, right, like a friend does that, huh?" he said, even looking inside a pair of my sneakers. When he saw they were empty, he threw them against the wall.

"Jimmy, they're not here."

"Well, then where the F are they?"

I decided to tell him, if only to get him off my back.

"If you got to know, I dumped them down the outhouse."

And like it wasn't even two minutes later when Jimmy was down in the yard opening the outhouse shed door. I can't imagine what he saw in that bin: I mean people had been using it since the afternoon before and human stuff is mostly made of acids—uric acids, I knew from biology classes—dissolving everything in their wake. But Jimmy actually tried to find them, staring down into that bin and putting up with the stink, for nothing.

After that, he wouldn't talk to me. He started disappearing, doing no work around the farm and walking to town along the cornfield roads until someone would come driving by and give him a lift. It was Wendy who told me she saw Jimmy coming out of one of the pharmacies with a really pissed-off expression on his face—like he had been trying to refill his prescription and had been turned down.

Probably over and over again.

Every time I saw him, I'd say, "Come on, I was only looking out for you, man!"

And he'd just give me this get-out-of-my-face look.

Or turn his back to me when I walked into a room.

Come the late afternoon, he couldn't wait for Curt to drive up with Bonnie, so that he could hit him up for a joint. Otherwise, he just hung around drinking beer after beer on the porch or stalked around the field, pissed off out of his brains and tossing his empties into a ditch or at an old scarecrow as if it were me.

The whole thing was jive: He was being jive, but you know what?

After a few weeks, I just couldn't take it anymore. Coming home from a fence-mending job for a nearby farmer who I had met on the road—paid me ten dollars for the afternoon's work—and finding Jimmy still sulking away on the porch, I said to him, "Look, if you're going to let this mess us up for good, then you should just go back to New York, all right?" Then, "I'll even give you the bucks for the bus fare, if you're that miserable."

At first he just pretended that I wasn't there.

"Hey, Jimmy," I said, almost shouting, "I'm talking to you!"

Finally, he turned and looked at me.

"Let me pull your coat to something—what you did really sucked," he said. "If you did that to somebody in New York, they would have kicked your ass, or worse. You know that, right?"

"Yeah," I said, slapping at a black fly that had landed on my arm. "But this ain't New York."

"That's for sure," he said, looking out at the field.

Then he didn't say anything for a while.

"Like I said, Jimmy, if you don't like it here, I'll give you the bucks to go, okay?"

But even Jimmy, deep down, must have thought that there was something special about that farm, and the fresh air, and being away from all the hassles of the city.

"I didn't say I wanted to leave," he told me finally. "It's just that you really pissed me off."

Like I didn't know that, right?

"But you know what? I'm gonna forgive you anyway."

Forgive me for what? For trying to save him from getting a really bad jones for those pills? But I kept my trap shut.

"You mean, we're cool?" I asked him.

"Yeah, I guess so," he said, bumping me gently with his shoulder. "Now give me a solid."

We shook hands the normal way, and then with one hand sideways on the other, knocked our knuckles together.

So I guess we were friends again.

And man, did that feel good.

Almost as good as what I saw a few days later.

I was looking out my window when I saw Jimmy coming out of the house with Polly. I don't know what kind of raps he had laid on her, but he was carrying her easel and two chairs. She was carrying a pad and a sleek wooden box. Walking a long way out into the field, towards this one spot where there were all these shady trees, the ground around them all white with dandelions, the kind you can just blow away, they set up their chairs and Jimmy sat with her as she began to draw. Then he took up his own pad, sketching beside her, until the sun started to set.

Part 4 **THE GAS STATION**

sixteen

BY AUGUST, DOING not much more than just hanging around the farm on all those dead quiet days got real
old for me. I can't say that I was missing New York—hell
no! But I missed some things about it: like walking
down to Jack's stationery store to look over the latest
comic books, or having an egg cream soda and ketchup-
smothered french fries at its counter. And I missed those
stickball games, with those guys jiving on the street. And
other stuff like running into the ladies from the beauty
salon where my Moms worked, and all the cheek pinching
they would lay on me.

I even kind of missed my part-time jobs—at the
morning laundry with Mr. Gordon and at Mr. Ramirez's
used-bookstore, in the afternoons, where I could sit
behind the counter and read for hours—and then,

heading home, messed up as things could be sometimes, just bumping into my Pops on the street and walking up the block with him, my Pops offering me some Chiclets to chew, his arm around my shoulder, the two of us, just being together.

Once I'd start thinking about home, all kinds of stuff—Cuban stuff—would come into my head. Like the little altar to the *Virgen de Cobre*, patron saint to Cuba, that my Moms kept in the corner of her bedroom, then the dartboard with Fidel Castro's picture on it that my Pops used to bring out for his friends' amusement, the games of dominoes they'd play in the kitchen, my Pops's pals—plumbers, superintendents, shoe salesmen—compatriots he called them, drinking rum until early in the morning and getting so wrecked I'd hear them singing Cuban songs as they went home along the street, dogs barking, people closing their windows or shouting complaints in their wake.

Then, out of nowhere, I saw my *mamá* hemming my trousers, me squirming and her telling me in Spanish how *cubanos* were good dressers, and *had* to be, and how special Cubans were, in her snooty opinion, as opposed to other Latinos. Puerto Ricans were really great, she'd say—*nearly* Cuban; Mexicans and Dominicans were good souls too, like all Latinos, but as far as she was concerned Cubans were in their own category.

That got me into remembering this presentation I had to do before my seventh-grade class in grammar school when I tried to explain to Sister Horrendous (yep, all the nuns got nicknames) and my fellow students what being Cuban was about to me. I'd kind of poked around in the school encyclopedia, but what I talked about mainly came off the top of my head. Barely able to stop stuttering because so many eyes were watching me, and because I was shy as hell and a wise-ass at the same time, my list/explanations went something like this:

1. Being Cuban was the best because the town of Santiago, in the eastern province near where my Moms and Pops were born, was one of the first capitals of the Caribbean. Christopher Columbus first discovered its bay in 1492, or so, after he had sailed the ocean blue without falling off the edge of the world. (Solid, right?)

2. Cuba was cool because lots of exotic flowers and beautiful trees, of rarest woods, grow all

over the island and . . . because Cubans have the best and *biggest plátanos* anywhere.

3. Havana, its modern capital, was one mother of a city, even if it got ransacked and looted by pirates a lot, and the British admiral dude went there and set the place on fire in sixteen hundred and something.

4. And like my Moms told me, the whole place was so beautiful that mermaids like living near its beaches. Anyway, Havana was known as "the Paris of the Caribbean" while the whole island of Cuba was nicknamed the "Pearl of the Antilles."

5. And, like, its women had the most *supremo* butts in the universe (but I couldn't say that).

6. Lots of sugar and cigars came from Cuba, at least until the, uh, nasty Cuban revolution and that bearded guy Fidel Castro came in and took everybody's freedom away. That's why lots of Cubans living over here have big balls, work hard, and absolutely hate Communism.

7. Way before the revolution that took place

in 1959, when I was a little baby, there were thousands of Cubans already here in this country, like my Pops. But after that stuff went down, Cubans went crazy wanting to get out, big-time, all kinds of cousins of mine, coming to the States on rafts, by boats, and airplane because they wanted to be free.

8. And, as my Pops told me, having to work so freaking hard to make something of yourself from scratch develops your character, which is why Cubans don't have a hell of a lot of patience for people who don't work.

9. And Cubans are really proud of being Cuban: Yep, Cubans are the cream of the coffee.

10. Oh yeah, and we gave the world Desi Arnaz, also known as Ricky Ricardo. (Thank you, thank you.)

Then that faded, as quickly and strangely as it had come.

Sitting on Gilberto's porch, with our 100 percent genuinely American fields spreading out endlessly before me, I'd wonder just what the F I was about. Oh yeah, a *white* runaway son of Cubans, hanging out at his Puerto Rican pal's farm in the middle of corn country Wisconsin. Figure that. It was crazy.

Most days I didn't think much of anything at all. I got dead in my head. I mean, there wasn't even a movie house or a stationery store or music shop anywhere within walking distance. Still, the air was fresh, nice breezes often blowing, but even with that shit going on, what with little birds hopping around on the lawn and the occasional squirrel scampering down a tree to hustle me, I still got a little restless.

Sometimes I got so bored sitting on the porch that my mind would run away with me. I actually believed that the birds—the larks, bobolinks, blackbirds, and swallows that Bonnie, a nature buff, once pointed out as they bopped around in the trees—were talking up a storm. And I could swear that I had made friends with an insect, this praying mantis that landed by my side one morning, hopping or flying in from who knows where, just to hang out with me. It was regal, like an alien king, always cleaning its mandibles. It had these eyes on the side of its head, black like beads, a thick and long torso, its back looking like the outer skin of corn, all green.

The next day, it was back. And the next. I didn't know what that thing ate, but in town one day, I bought it some bird seed. Sprinkling those seeds on the ground only attracted birds, though, a whole flock of them, scarfing those grains down like there was no tomorrow.

One afternoon when that praying mantis showed up again, and I started talking to it, like it was a pet, saying, "What can I get for you, little bro?" Gilberto came along and howled. "Okay, you've lost it, Rico. You're talking to an *insect*, aren't you?"

"I guess I am," I said, feeling like a doofus.

"Damn, you need to get yourself a girlfriend!" he said, shaking his head.

He squatted down beside me, the praying mantis flying off into the trees.

"Anyway, Rico, I got good news for you." I knew that he had just started a pretty good part-time job at a brewery in Milwaukee and that he had been talking to a sign-shop owner in town about getting Jimmy something there, but I had no idea that he had been asking around for me.

"What's that?" I asked him.

"Well, I got you a job!" he announced happily.

"Doing what?"

"Pumping gas, at the Clark's service station."

"Pumping gas?" I asked, frowning. It was something I never thought I'd ever do.

"Yep. The night shift. It goes from eight at night until eight in the morning, and it pays a buck fifty an hour." Gilberto was clearly proud of himself. "I know the dude who runs it—he's cool."

"But from eight to eight?" I said.

"Yeah, but don't sweat it," Gilberto said cheerfully. "It's only four or five nights a week, and it's dead most of the time. Hardly anyone comes along after eleven, just truckers mainly."

He rapped me on my back.

"Busy time doesn't last long at all. You'll be collecting money just for hanging around. How about it?"

That didn't sound so bad. "Okay," I said, "but how will I get there?"

"You can take my bicycle while the weather's still warm. Otherwise, I'll drop you off or you can borrow the truck."

"Hey, but I can't drive," I said.

"Maybe not yet, but we'll get you a permit and you'll learn, right?" Gilberto said, being his super positive self.

Then as Gilberto got up and headed into the house, that praying mantis flew back down onto the porch.

My imaginary conversation with the praying mantis:

"So, my little bro, what do you think?"

"About?" that wise-looking creature asked.

"The gas station job. You think that'll be cool?"

"Yeah, as far as jobs go," he said, chomping down on a fly.

"But all the rest?"

"You mean about cutting things loose with your family? It's on you, man!" His mandibles worked like crazy.

"But I can't be just going back to that, you under-stand?"

"I know what you're saying," the praying mantis said. "But the thing is, you just best put that stuff from your mind. 'Cause if you don't, you'll drive yourself crazy."

And maybe I already was. I mean, what was I doing talking to an insect like that, even if it was in my head?

seventeen

THREE DAYS LATER Gilberto drove me to the Clark's station and introduced me to the owner. An island of gas pumps and glaring yellow fluorescent lights, it stood at the outskirts of Janesville and just across from the interstate juncture that ran north to Madison. Its owner was a tall, sandy-haired fellow named Mr. Jenkins. He was all business; he never once smiled while asking me all these questions.

"So your name is Rico?"

"Yeah."

"But your last name is Fuentes. What's that?" he said, pronouncing it *fraw-ny-tuss*.

"Well, sir," I said, trying to be cool as possible. "It's a Spanish name. My folks are Cuban."

"Cuban?" he said, looking startled. "I wouldn't have

guessed that in a million years from looking at you." Then, giving me an up and down, he added, "You don't look anything like the wetbacks I see from time to time."

I cringed. Here we go again, I thought. The midwestern version of a spic.

"And you're a high school graduate?"

"I am," I said, lying.

"Well, Rico, I'll take you on. You look like a bright kid to me. Here, I should show you a few things."

The first was how to operate a gas pump—no big deal. The second was the way some motor oils, costing more than others, had their own shelves ("Do not mix them up"). The third was a cigarette rack, at thirty-five cents a pack, the inventory of which I had to keep strict tabs on, and the fourth was a floor safe, which you opened with a special set of keys every morning, to deposit whatever bucks had come in.

"You got that?"

"Yes, I think so."

He went on.

"Now, when someone comes in you say, 'How can I help you, sir?' And really politely, like that driver is the most important person in the world. Got that?"

"Sure."

"Now say it."

What? But he was being serious. So I repeated, half-heartedly, "'Can I help you, sir?'"

Mr. Jenkins wasn't satisfied. He was wringing his hands.

"Not like that, Rico. Say it like you mean it."

I did, pretending that I was really interested.

"Then while you're filling up their tank, you give their windshield a quick spray with a cleaner, and then you wipe it down with a rag. A lot of them will come in gummed up with insects, you know?"

"Okay."

"And then you always ask them if they want you to check their oil. You know how to?"

My Pops didn't have a car, so I didn't.

"Oh brother," he said, showing me how to use a dipstick.

"Above all, no slacking off, okay? When it's slow, I expect you to keep busy, sweep up. And you've got to mop down the restrooms at least once a night and make sure they have enough toilet paper and stuff. Got it?"

"Uh-huh."

Wow, I was thinking, first an outhouse and now I have to clean toilets, too.

Then he gave me a blue Clark station shirt, which he said he'd have to charge me five dollars for, and a metal change maker, filled with twenty dollars' worth of coins, to wear on a belt.

"One more thing," he said. "I know you're from New York City, so you probably have this idea that everybody's honest out here. And that's true most of the time, but sometimes it's not. Trust no one, understand?"

"Sure," I said, kind of smugly. After all, I was from New York.

"You don't sell a single thing on credit, understand? You'll hear a lot of cock-and-bull stories meant to tug on your heart. But just remember, if you get ripped off, it comes out of your pocket. Got that?"

"Uh-huh."

"And if you have any problems with anybody, you call the state police. The number's posted on the wall," and he pointed to this corkboard above the desk.

I nodded, wondering what he meant by "problems."

"Anyway, it's not rocket science," he said before taking off. "But I expect you to do a good job, you hear?"

"Yes, sir."

Then he made a final little speech.

"By leaving you in charge, Rico, I hope you will understand that I am entrusting you with my business. I have a wife and two kids to look after, and my franchise here is everything to me. You mess up, and I'll fire your ass. You understand?"

"Yep," I answered, with another midwestern word creeping into my vocabulary.

Then, just before he drove away, I could see the gears in his brain turning with doubts about whether he had made a mistake by trusting a kid with such a job.

A new lesson:

Somehow, even when you're told not to trust anybody, and you think that you're a slick dude from the big city, just being in such a nice-seeming place, with your radar turned off, will fool you.

It was my third night at the Clark's station. After I'd gassed up about a zillion cars, this earnest-seeming guy pulled into the station at about eleven to fill his tank. He was on his way to Madison, where his wife was in a hospital about to deliver a baby, he told me.

"Wow, that's really nice," I said.

"Yes sirree, I can't wait!" he said, clapping his hands. "Hey, where you from anyway, buddy?"

"New York City."

"Well, Mr. New York, do me a favor," he said, his arm dangling over the side. "While you're at it, could you put in a few quarts of oil? I like the sixty weight."

"No problem," I said, going to the pump.

"And, uh, how about a couple of packs of Marlboros?"

"All right."

So I filled his tank, put in a couple of quarts of oil, gave him the smokes.

And when I was done, I told him, "That comes to eleven twenty-five."

"Okeydokey," he said, reaching into his pocket for his wallet. But when he pulled it out and looked inside it, he looked really surprised.

"You're not going to believe this, buddy," he said with a bewildered expression on his face, "but with my wife expecting and all, I forgot to bring my dang money along." He smacked the side of his head. "Boy, am I stupid."

"You're kidding me, right?" I said.

"Kid you! No way!" he said, with his hands folded up, like he was about to pray. "But I swear I'm good for it. I'll drop the money off tomorrow night."

"Uh-huh," I said, feeling like I shouldn't believe him.

"Look, you can ask your boss about me, if you want to."

"You know Mr. Jenkins?"

"Sure, we go a long way back. Go right ahead and call him," he insisted. "Tell him Skip Hamsun is a little short on the cash, and he'll tell you that it's all right."

"And you don't have a credit card?" I pressed him.

"Nope, never bother with them. But like I said, just call him up. I'll be waiting right here."

"Skip Hamsun, right?" I said, turning towards the station office.

"That's right. Or better yet, tell him 'Skip from Beloit.' He'll know," he added, nodding his head in an encouraging way. "But hurry up, will you. I gotta get to the hospital."

I had the boss's number up on the corkboard next to the number for the state police. But even as I started to dial the telephone, I heard the *vroom, vroom* of his engine starting. Next thing I know, the guy had taken off, north onto the interstate and into the darkness of night.

Okay, I told myself. So you got ripped off, so what? Just be alert the next time, and not so trusting, okay?

* * *

But that same week brought the bad check that some lady wrote out to pay for her tank of gas. Because she was so pretty, I believed everything she said about not having had a chance to cash her paycheck. So I let her write out a check for ten dollars more than what the gas cost.

Well, to make a long story short, Mr. Slicky here had to swallow that check.

And then there was the friendly trucker on a cross-country haul who had come along at about four in the morning and, finding me half asleep at my desk inside the station, gave me, as a tip, a handful of little white pills to help me stay awake. After I'd filled up his big tanks with about a hundred or so gallons of gas, he paid me with two crisp twenty-dollar bills. He was so nice that he told me to keep the three dollars or so in change.

Anyway, the twenties turned out to be counterfeit, both of the bills having identical serial numbers. The boss circled the numbers with a red marker and posted the bills on the wall over the desk, and I came out minus sixty-five dollars for the week.

Mr. Jenkins's lecture number 2:

"Well, I'm sorry to tell you this, but you'll have to pay that money back, Rico," he said, shaking his head like I was the dumbest guy who ever worked there.

"But at least I hope you learned a lesson and won't be so stupid in the future. Next time, anyone tries to shortchange you, or writes out a check, you better make sure to get their info off their driver's license. Or if they take off in a hurry, you make sure to jot down their license plate number, so at least you can give the troopers something to work with."

He looked at me long and hard.

"As for those bills, that's a new one on me, and I don't know what to tell you except that you should always check out their numbers, particularly when they're so crisp and fresh. So remember: If I told you once, I'll tell you again. *Do not trust anyone*, understand?"

"Yeah, all right."

And he walked away, still shaking his head.

Gilberto laughed really hard when I walked into the kitchen the next morning and told him about what happened. "What's the sweat? Just think of it as an education."

Then, popping up some bread from a toaster and slathering it with butter and jelly, he pulled up a chair and said, "Let me ask you something."

"Yeah?" I said, still feeling like a jerk.

"Having been ripped off the way you were, are you ever going to let that happen again?"

"Nope."

"And what did it cost you?"

"A few bucks, I guess," I said.

"So, like, that's the kind of thing you can't learn anywhere, not even in college, where you have to pay all kinds of money for an education, right?"

"I guess so." I nodded.

"Look at it this way," he said, not able to resist smirking. "Even if you got beat, at least you'll save yourself a lot of grief in the future. Right, my man?"

That almost cheered me up, except that I was still feeling embarrassed.

"But, Gilberto, how the hell could I—a guy from New York City—get hustled by some hicks?"

"Like I've told you, Rico," he continued. "It's just different out here in Wonder bread land. It takes a while to read people. I mean, they're different."

I nodded.

He took another bite of that crunchy bread, wiped some jelly off his mustache.

"Rico, there's a fundamental fact to existing that you should be hipped to."

"What's that?"

"It's like this," he said, switching into his primo big brother mode. "Let's say you're a really beautiful girl, like Wendy."

"That's a stretch, but okay."

"Well, here's the thing. Even if you are superfly, you best better believe that there'll always be another girl out there more fly than yourself."

That seemed weird, but okay.

"Or let me put it this way. No matter how slick you might be, at any given moment there's someone out there who's even slicker than you. And that slicker one, if he is truly slick, has got to face the fact that there's someone even slicker than him. In other words," he paused, dusting some crumbs off his hand, "you can't get down on yourself for the way the world is." Then he flashed me a toothy grin. "I mean, Rico, as you go through life, you got to define your advantages and limitations and try to figure out the best way you can get along."

"I'm trying," I said, shrugging.

"Okay, but just look at yourself." He gave me an up and down. "You may not be the best-looking dude, or the slickest, but you are one bright MF, right?"

"I guess," I said.

"But when it comes to street smarts, you just ain't got them. Never have and never will. Which isn't a bad thing. It's just who you are, right?"

Wow, that was like getting a kick in the butt.

But I guess it was true.

"Thing is," he said, taking a sip from his mug, "how could it be otherwise? When you were little, your Moms wouldn't even let you out on the street without her getting on your ass."

That was another embarrassing thing to be reminded about: Like, she wouldn't let me play with the other kids, except in front of my stoop, and if I strayed she would come after me and make a big scene.

I nodded.

"Take me. I am totally cool when it comes to people and hooking up with chicks, but when it comes to the stuff that really counts, like school, I'm a stiff."

"But you're smart as hell."

"Yeah, but not like you. Why, if I hadn't hit that lottery, I would have ended up in some community college in the Bronx or Brooklyn instead of going away to a real school. But you—you got some kind of brain in your head. I've known that since you were a little kid."

He sipped some more coffee.

"And on top of that, you got a good heart, like your Pops. That's something to be proud about!"

Just hearing him mention my Pops that way made me feel good.

"The main thing is that you shouldn't let every little thing mess you up. Just let that shit roll off your back, all right?" he said, reaching over and squeezing my shoulder.

We slapped five, and I smiled, grateful for Gilberto's free life philosophy lesson.

eighteen

ANYWAY, WORKING AT the gas station turned my days upside down. It was hard to get used to. What felt truly weird, after spending a boring-as-hell night at the station, was coming back to the farm before everyone was getting up. If you turned on the TV, there wasn't much to look at, most of the stations were just static, and the one show I'd watch—*The Farmer's News*, featuring this guy who talked about the latest corn prices—was as exciting as watching paint dry. But I'd still hang around waiting.

Wendy, wearing a long dashiki, was usually the first to stomp into the kitchen. She was nice to me, occasionally preparing my late-night/early-morning dinner-breakfast of fried bacon throw-offs with some fried eggs. Nothing was better than that meal, even if it was sometimes delivered with poetry.

"Just yesterday, a beautiful poem, like some bright stallion, came rushing towards me," Wendy would say, giving me a plate. "Do you want to hear it?"

And I would nod, listening to her, and mostly continuing to nod at the sound of her pretty words, like it was music. But when she would finish up, and I had finished my plate of food, I was glad to be making my way back upstairs.

The bitch of it was that while I was trying to catch some z's, the sunlight flowing in through my window, I could hear the whole household's day unfolding. The floor creaking below, Gilberto getting ready to go off to his job. Wendy with her typewriter clacking away. Polly and Jimmy heading off together to art classes at Milton College—yes, Jimmy!—and Bonnie and Curt, who had this whole puppet theater and music thing going on in Madison, disappearing by noon. From my room I would hear every car or van pulling out, and by one in the afternoon, I was left alone with my thoughts.

You know that movie *The Wizard of Oz*? When that girl Dorothy gets whisked away by a tornado to Munchkinland? And all she thinks about is getting back home to Kansas? And she goes looking into a magic globe and sees her Auntie Em crying and stuff? Well, that was a little bit like me. Lots of times, when I tried to sleep, I'd see my Moms and Pops in my head. And they were always crying, like I had broken their hearts, even if I didn't mean to. On those nights, I would have loved to possess a magic globe that I could toss out the window; as if that would change things, like whisk me to my real home, wherever that may be. Let me hip you, if I may, *just thinking about it doesn't make it happen.*

But more about my gas station job.

I worked there four or five nights a week, depending on how much Mr. Jenkins needed me, and sometimes I worked during the daytime when someone didn't show up. That shift was much busier, but it had its perks, like sunlight, and Mr. Jenkins buying me lunch some days, and sometimes taking me out to the back where he was always tinkering with the zillion-horsepower engine of his stock car, a souped-up Thunderbird that he would race on the weekends.

"This baby will go one forty plus when you floor it."

"No kidding?" I said.

"Play your cards right," he said to me, "and I'll take you out with me one day."

Turned out that he wasn't a bad guy, just a real stickler

about money: I mean, after my shift I'd have to give an accounting of every pack of cigarettes, can of oil, and even the number of gallons of gas sold.

Among the many things I learned was that I did not want to pump gas for a living.

I was doing all right on the job and, after a while, even began to look forward to my nights at the station, where two or three hours could go by without anyone pulling in. Even after I'd made my rounds, cleaning up the place, I always had time on my hands. I'd sit by a desk inside the office reading or else fooling around with my guitar. The hardest thing was to stay alert and not doze off, the *ding ding* that sounded when a car or truck came into the station and tripped a wire hitting me like a fire alarm.

Mainly, I'd think and think, and I couldn't keep my family from popping into my head.

I felt like writing them. Almost sent my Moms a birthday card that September to say that I was all right, but I didn't, convincing myself that a Wisconsin postmark would give me away.

Listening to the radio seemed to help me pass the time, even if most of those stations were a real drag.

Just preachers talking and talking about how if you sent them some money, they would help you get to Heaven. Or all these violins and guys like Perry Como singing away. And like, almost every other station playing bouncy polka music—the kind of stuff that I would never normally listen to unless a gun was put to my head. I was always dialing around, not just for rock-'n'-roll, but looking for the old-fashioned junk my father loved to play on the radio. It used to drive me nuts, but out here, finding it became a mission. Some conga drums or Latin-style flutes, or a voice speaking in Spanish through a blizzard of radio snow, somehow comforted me, even if it sounded chopped up, as if from another world.

On those nights, drifting off in the doldrums of the midnight shift, I became Captain Cubano, interplanetary explorer—and I would knock out stories on a yellow pad about my celestial travels—the universe being my plum.

Just the same, once that kind of thing played out, things got real slow.

But I'll tell you about the night when a Buick station wagon pulled in and I did a double take—because for a few seconds I swore that my Poppy was sitting behind the wheel. It wasn't him, but the driver's sad face, heavy with jowls, and his quiet demeanor, and his burly body, and the way he was slouching sort of reminded me of him. Like my Pops, the driver was dark-featured. He looked like he might be a *cubano*.

And so I couldn't help myself. I had to talk to him.

"So where you off to?" I asked the man.

Somehow I thought he would say something to me in Spanish, but he didn't.

"Ann Arbor, Michigan," he told me. "To a peachy country music festival they hold there."

"You play an instrument?" I asked, wanting to keep him talking.

"Why, yes I do. A good old pedal steel guitar. She's my 'pretty Lily,' right there in the back," he said, patting the seat behind him. "And yourself?"

"Just some guitar," I said, kind of sloughing that off.

"Oh, do you? Beatles stuff, I betcha. Just like about every young person I meet these days. Anyway, kid, a piece of advice—"

Boy, it seemed like I was getting all kinds of advice those days.

"Whatever you might be fantasizing, being a musician is no easy way to make a living."

Then he sighed, lit up a smoke.

"Now fill 'er up, will you?"

Even if that was all, just talking to him made me feel good.

It was like an equation: The man who looked sort of like my Pops + imagination = my Pops for 2 seconds x 10 = being better than no Pops at all.

On another night, a truck filled with migrant workers, Mexicans I supposed, pulled into the station. I guess they were driving back south after working on the corn harvests. When their boss got out, he told them they had ten minutes to use the facilities and to stretch their legs. Most of them were compact muscular guys, very cautious in their movements. While I was putting gas in their truck, I couldn't help but notice how one of them seemed so miserably alone. I mean, he just stood out by the side of the road with his arms pulled back behind his head, like when you do sit-ups, stretching a bit but mainly just looking up at the sky and day-dreaming.

My Spanish wasn't what it should have been, but I was so starved to hear it again that I walked over to the guy and offered him a cigarette.

"*¿Oye, quieres un cigarillo?*" I said, remembering how my Pops used to offer people smokes.

"*Sí, cómo no. Gracias,*" the worker said, accepting one.

But then, because my accent wasn't great, he broke into English.

"Ah, I see you are learning Spanish. Is that so?" he said, taking a drag.

"Oh yeah, in school," I said, ashamed to admit the truth.

"*Bueno,*" he said. "It's good for you to practice, no?"

I took a deep breath.

"*Sí, cómo no,*" I answered, wanting to hear him speaking more Spanish.

Right then, he turned away, blowing a plume of smoke, but I stayed with him.

"*¿A dónde vas?*" I tried again, asking him where he was headed.

But he stuck to English.

"Oh, to a little pueblo, near Veracruz. You ever been there?"

"No."

"Is beautiful, the people are happy," he said. "But *el problema es*, there is no so much work there. That's why I come here, for six months sometimes." And he looked off at this fluorescent lamp, around which all these bugs were swirling. Then he said, "But I miss my family very much.

"*Muchísimo,*" he added. "*Mucho, mucho.*"

Then he excused himself, in a most formal manner: "*Con permiso,*" he said as he went off to join his friends. "*Y gracias por el cigarillo.*"

It was a strange thing. As much as hearing Spanish being spoken at home used to bug me out—like those words were hornets stinging my heart—way out there in Wisconsin, it felt comforting. And warm. And oh so f—king familiar.

It turned out that he was the first and last Spanish-speaking dude I'd see for months at the station. Otherwise it was the usual traffic.

Friday and Saturday nights were the busiest, all kinds of folks driving in. Carloads of teenagers on their way to a drive-in movie, or off to an amusement park; dads with their kids, off for a weekend of camping, tents tied to their car roofs, all kinds of fishing gear stuffed into the back; ministers and their choirs, after a church social; or cheerleaders with their pom-poms and smokin' outfits on their way to a sporting meet. And sometimes farm boys would come along after a night of drinking and whooping it up, friendly types who'd give you a six-pack of beer just because they were buzzed, and swearing that you were their best friend in the world.

And truckers and truckers.

And yes, the state troopers, who came along in the middle of the night to shoot the breeze.

Man, it was a different place.

After a while, I got so used to seeing only white folks that one night, in the late summer, when this Cadillac with Michigan plates pulled up, and I saw that there were four black men sitting inside, my inner radar suddenly went crazy.

It didn't help that the radio had been broadcasting stories about a gang of black men who were traveling the Midwest robbing service stations and sometimes shooting the attendants dead.

"Yes sir, what can I do for you?" I asked nervously, walking up to the driver's window.

"Just fill the tank, will you? With regular." He didn't even look at me, just kept staring straight ahead.

"Sure."

"And your facilities?" the driver asked me.

"Over there," I said, pointing to the back.

This stiletto-thin man with conked-up hair got out first. Then the others, all big and towering over me, followed after him. All were dressed in dark suits and white shirts and black ties, and they gave me the once over as they filed out of the car.

"You got sufficient soap and such? We'd like to wash up, if you don't mind."

"No problem."

And as they sauntered over to the restrooms, I could swear they were checking the place out.

Man, did I hope someone else would drive in, but when I looked down the road in both directions, I couldn't see a single pair of headlights. And the state troopers only came around once a night.

But I did my job, wiping down their windows and filling the tank with gas, and when the driver came back, combing his slick black hair, I half expected him to pull a knife or gun out on me.

Just because he was black, I hate to admit.

He didn't.

"Say, uh, you know of any joints around here still serving food this time of night?"

"There's an all-night diner about ten miles west on that road," I said.

But I hadn't looked at him, and he noticed that.

"Young man, do I make you nervous or something?"

"No, not at all," I said.

"Then why aren't you looking at me when I'm addressing you?" His expression was severe.

"I don't know. Just doing my job."

"Uh-huh," he said, looking me over. Then he made some remark under his breath to his friends, about "crackers" being everywhere.

"Where you from anyway, boy?"

"New York City."

"New York City? No kidding? Why, we're just getting back from a convention there."

"Yeah?" I said, somehow relieved.

And suddenly it was as if we were friends.

"That's right. Ours was held at the super deluxe Marriott on Fifty-fourth Street in Manhattan. You heard of it?"

"Sure." I hadn't, but what else was I going to say?

"We had a hell of a time!"

And then he smiled.

"Don't know if we did the right thing going by car, but my brother here"—and he pointed to one of his friends—"just didn't want to fly. Thinks of jets as some kind of airborne hearses."

And they all laughed.

That's when I figured out they weren't going to rob or kill me.

"What kind of convention?" I asked.

"Oh, just the one and only annual meeting of the United Brotherhood of Morticians and Mortuary Workers."

"Really?"

"Yes, sir, you stab them and then we slab 'em," he said, laughing. "Yes sir, it was a fine event!"

Then, after he had paid me and had gotten behind the wheel again, he dangled his hand, clenched in a fist, out the window.

"Hey, what do you think I got here?"

"I don't know."

"Say 'Open sesame.'"

"What?"

"Just say it!"

"Open sesame," I said.

And he unclenched his hand.

Three crumpled one-dollar bills were in his palm.

"Take them, little fella. They won't bite."

I did.

"And next time, when some black folks come driving through here, be more respectful, will you?"

I nodded.

Then my would-be killers who turned out to be nice-guy morticians drove away.

Because of the light, early mornings were the best. That's when the local farmers would drive in with their tractors for diesel fuel. They were always telling me jokes, but also talked about the things they worried about, like how rising property taxes were making their lives difficult.

And how the big conglomerates were always trying to buy them out cheap—for chump change.

I guess everyone had their problems.

Usually, when my shift ended, there would be someone around to give me a lift back towards the farm. On a nice day, even if I had to walk a mile or so, I didn't mind it at all. I'd take my time, stop by this little stream, and kick off my work shoes, just soak my feet in the water, get drowsy from the churning sound. Or I'd go exploring the back roads of neighboring farms, checking out the cows and the white-bellied swallows circling the barns, all kinds of birdsong coming out of the trees. And then, feeling like I was no longer Rico but some other kid, like Tom Sawyer or Huck Finn, living another life, I'd keep walking along, still amazed to find myself in such a place.

Part 5 **BACK TO SCHOOL FOR EVERYBODY BUT ME**

nineteen

AUTUMN CAME ON its own kind of walk.

School buses were suddenly tooling along the back roads picking up farmers' kids, and most everyone in the house, starting their new classes at college, cleared out in the mornings. And thanks to Gilberto, Jimmy, wanting to put some bucks in his pocket, finally got a part-time job in a sign shop in town, painting logos for stores, hand-lettering price charts for a supermarket and FOR SALE notices for a real estate company.

Most days I was usually left alone in the house with Rex as my best pal. I didn't sleep much. Tossing and turning, I'd be thinking that I should be going to school myself. I was almost tempted to enroll in one of the schools in town, but I knew that would be as good as turning myself in 'cause they'd certainly find out that I was a runaway.

So I tried to teach myself instead, heading off to the library in town, picking up volumes on every subject under the sun. My room became a super mess, what with paperbacks and comics and clothes and loaned-out books thrown all over the place. I was a guitar-playing bookworm. But did I care? Hell no! And I had started to let my hair grow long. That was a real plus, like I was being free. My own *man*. So if I wanted to I could wear nothing more than a T-shirt, a pair of coveralls, and sneakers day after day, without my Moms screaming about me being a disgrace. I even bought a new pair of wire-rimmed eyeglasses, à la John Lennon, which I saw in the window of the Happy Eyes optical shop in town, on sale for twenty-seven of my hard-earned dollars.

I guess I was turning into a hippie, just like those guys I'd see in ponchos walking down the street in Janesville, wearing Indian beads around their necks and flashing me a peace sign with their hands. I liked all that, but somehow I still felt that I didn't really fit in.

Anyway, come autumn, we cleaned the outhouse again (no comment) and, among other things, in early October a carnival came to town.

I was at the station one night when that carnival's fleet of flatbed trucks came rumbling off the highway in a procession, hauling these big canvas-wrapped loads to the old state fairgrounds, at the other end of town. For a few weeks, what had been this empty and weedy field blossomed into this sparkly, lit-up amusement park with a carousel, little kids' teacup rides, a Ferris wheel, and even a dinky roller coaster. And all kinds of booths and stands went up, featuring games of chance, the sorts I'd see at a church bazaar back home or at the festivals in Little Italy.

In a place where not much ever happened, the carnival was a main attraction, and by the weekend those grounds were teeming with people from nearby towns, eating caramel apples and cotton candy.

Come Saturday, me and Gilberto drove over there to check that carnival out. Wendy had gone up to Madison to visit some friends, but that didn't seem to bother Gilberto at all, like he had something up his sleeve. Driving in, he kept saying that the day promised to be "Mighty tasty" and "Peachy keen!" stroking on his goatee, deep in some happy thoughts.

As we were bopping our way through the crowds, Gilberto seemed distracted, smiling a lot and tipping his lacquered hat at people in his friendly way, while definitely looking for a particular someone. I couldn't figure out what was going on with him until we reached the main ticket booth.

Standing in front of that booth and looking a little nervous but definitely fine was that elusive farm girl, Dierdra. In a pair of tight blue jeans and a heavy lumberjack's shirt, she was a picture of health and wholesomeness, buxom, rosy-cheeked, with braided pigtails and a pretty Nordic face.

She waved hello. I guess she had been waiting for him.

"Looky here," Gilberto said to me, happily. "I'll see you later, all right?"

"Sure," I said, a little surprised, thinking we would be hanging out.

"But keep it under your hat, won't you?"

"You know I will," I said, even if I was already feeling really bad for Wendy.

"And remember what I told you, man," Gilberto said, winking at me as he went off to meet her. "Don't be shy around the chicks, huh?"

So that afternoon, while strolling around the carnival grounds, I decided to assert my shy-assed self, nodding and smiling at a lot of girls who happened by, like Gilberto would have, without much luck at first.

Then it happened. While waiting in line to get on the Ferris wheel, I made myself say something to the pretty blonde in front of me. She was eating cotton candy and kept touching a little butterfly barrette that she had in her hair. The cotton candy matched the color of her sweater and sneakers.

"Howdy there," I said, tapping her on the shoulder. "You from around here?"

She turned, wiping some of that sticky cotton candy from her lips.

"Sort of," she said, in a soft voice. "I live over in Whitewater, about twenty miles from here. You ever been there?"

"Uh-uh. What's that like?" I said, trying to sound super interested.

"Oh, it's just a pretty little town," and she looked down at her sneakers.

As the line inched forward, I said, "Anyway, I'm Rico."

"I'm Sharon, but my friends call me Sheri," she said.

"That's a cool name."

"You think? Half the girls around here are called that."

"But it fits you."

"I suppose," she said, sighing.

Then, as she was about to take another bite of that cotton candy, she held it towards me, saying, "You want some?"

"Okay." I took a bite. God, that was sweet—even felt some little cavity acting up—but I just said, "Thanks!"

Then she looked away again, talking to me, but not talking to me. She told me she had been waiting for a friend, Gina, who hadn't shown up. Then silence. Try as I might, I couldn't come up with anything else to say to her. Man, was I lame.

"Rico, what's that from?" she asked shyly after a while.

"It's just short for Ricardo, or Richard," I said, still feeling that little cavity going *ouch* from the sugar juices.

"Ricardo?" she said with surprise. "Is that Spanish?"

"Yeah, it is. It was my grandpop's name."

"What kind of Spanish?" she asked.

"You ever hear of Cuba?" I asked, feeling kind of proud.

"Sure," she said, thinking about it. "Isn't that where that Ricky guy on the TV comes from?"

"That's right," I said, nodding.

"And that's where you're from?"

"Nah, New York City. Can't you tell?"

"Uh-uh," she said. "You look like you could be from around here."

"Well, I'm not," I said, feeling oddly offended. "No way—I mean, New York just ain't like here. Like, it's dirty and noisy and crowded with crazy people. You gotta always be watching your back, what with all the junkies around, you know?"

"Jeepers," she said. "It must have been really hard growing up in a big city."

"You best believe it!" I said, trying to sound street-smart and cool. (But "jeepers"?)

By then we had gotten to where the concession man was taking tickets, and calming down a bit, I said, "Hey, since you're going on this too, you wanna ride with me?"

"I guess so," she said, shrugging.

When we had climbed into the car, I sat across from her and she just stared at me, checking me out, and flashing a little smile from time to time. Her face was so freaking pretty! And for some reason, that kind of made me nervous.

Once the concession man pulled on some lever, we

started to rise, going so high up we could get a good look at the countryside for miles around.

"So where are you staying?" she asked me.

As we came to the top, I pointed north to where I thought Gilberto's place was.

"You can't really see it from here, but I live on a farm over that way with some friends," I said.

"A farm?" she asked.

I didn't tell her the whole story, just that I was visiting my old pal Gilberto.

"He's a really great guy," I said. "And so are the other folks staying there. But I'm like the youngest, you know?"

"How old are you?"

"Sixteen, but I'll be seventeen come next summer," I said. Like that was a big deal. "And yourself?"

"I'm fifteen," she said, finishing off her cotton candy.

Then I told her about my job at the gas station.

"Which one?" she asked me.

"The Clark's on Main Street."

"Yeah, I know it," she said.

And then she just looked off. Like I said, she had a nice face, and even if she was wearing a sweater, I could see that she was curvy underneath in all the right places. But I wasn't paying attention to just that. There was something about her eyes—clear blue with tinges of green—that had all kinds of stuff going on inside them.

Like all kinds of smarts.

And at the same time, they looked a little sad, like I knew my own did, when I wasn't having some smart-assed thought lurking inside my head.

Still, getting her to talk wasn't easy. I really had to pick her brains.

She didn't tell me much.

Only a few things.

Her mother was a high school teacher; her parents were divorced; her dad lived in Janesville, her mother in Whitewater. She'd been dropped off at the carnival by one of her older brothers, who was going to pick her up at half past five.

We ended up hanging out the rest of that afternoon. First we spent an hour roaming through the livestock displays, and she really loved that. Knowing her stuff, she could name all the different breeds of animals there, every kind of heifer, and sheep, rabbits, chicklings, and fowl. (You never saw that stuff displayed in your school

gym in New York City. Folks would be eating them up!)
Then we tried some of those carnival games. I decided I
had to win her something, tossing rings, shooting at tin
ducks, and putting down dime after dime on numbers,
and never hitting one, no matter how many times the
concession man turned the wheel. Whenever I lost, I
tried again, until finally I hit a number and won her a big
pink teddy bear.

That made me feel boss, even if it would have cost
me less to have just bought her one.

Altogether, it was turning into one of the nicest days
I'd ever had, until I decided to sample every food in
sight. While she was perfectly content with just a hamburger and a Coke, I ate two corn dogs, an ear of butter-
dipped white corn, a hamburger, and some peanut brittle,
followed by a dairy-whipped ice-cream cone with candy
sprinkles, stuff that I devoured just because I could,
without anyone—like my Moms—to get on my back. I
was holding up all right, until I got it into my head to go
on this ride called the Wild Hammer.

Which brings me to another rule:

When you've eaten too much and are trying to impress
a sweet girl with your derring-do, forget about it.

The Wild Hammer was made up of two cages at either

end of a beam that spun clockwise into the air, slowly at first and then more and more quickly, until the cages themselves went spinning around, so that things started to fly out of your pockets. This was not the smartest thing I've ever done.

Strapped in and facing each other, we were lifted upside down and sent tumbling like we were in a space capsule or a cyclotron. And once that ride really got going, five of the pukiest minutes of my life began. At first I just started laughing and yelling with joy the way most folks do while getting whipped around in a tumbling cage at a thousand miles a second, but after about a minute or so, with everything churning around inside me, I started throwing up like crazy, streams of mashed corn dogs and candy sprinkles and all the rest shooting every which way inside the cage; that stuff flung everywhere, as in *splat, splat, splat.*

That's when I learned what kind of good-hearted girl Sheri was. Even though the concession guy yelled at me and he had to hose down the cage and we were both covered in gunk, she couldn't have been nicer about it. We ran to find the restrooms, and we each spent about ten minutes inside cleaning up over the bathroom sinks. I finished first and was waiting outside for her, feeling embarrassed as hell when she walked out that door.

But was she pissed off?

No.

She just smiled, kind of shrugging, and when she came up to me, the first thing she said was, "Well, I'd been hoping there'd be new kinds of rides this year. . . . You sure found one!"

Still, I could barely say anything after that. When it came time for her to meet up with her brother in the parking lot and we said good-bye, I got the nerve up to give her Gilberto's telephone number at the farm and told her that she could also call me at the Clark's station if she ever wanted to do something. To my surprise, she said she would.

I couldn't wait to tell Gilberto about the girl I met. But I didn't see him until the next morning. He was by the kitchen table, reading a newspaper.

Coffee was brewing.

"So did you meet anyone yesterday?" he asked, grinning.

"Yep," I said. "This really nice, super straight, 4-H club kind of girl."

"She good-looking?" he asked, turning the page of his paper.

"I'd say so."

"Way to go!" and he reached over and slapped me five.

I almost told him about the throw-up incident, but decided not to.

"And what about you?" I asked him.

"Oh man, I'll tell you," Gilberto said, smiling, "but let's go out on the porch." I guess he didn't want to take the chance that Wendy might hear him.

"So when I left you," Gilberto began, "me and that girl Dierdra walked around the carnival for a while, but she was so uptight about someone seeing us together that I took her driving in my truck, talking about all kinds of things. Then we found this spot way off the beaten track, and well, to make a long story short, even with all my sweet talking, that girl was like some kind of Fort Knox."

"Say what?" I asked. Gilberto rarely admitted such a thing.

"Yeah." And he shook his head as if he still couldn't believe it. "But it was like a start, right?"

"I guess. But what about Wendy?"

He looked at me as if I were being the straightest Goody Two-shoes in the world.

"Rico, Rico, Rico," he finally said. "It's the hunt, the desire, the dream! Hey, didn't Martin Luther King Jr. say we should all aspire to our dreams?"

"He was talking about civil rights, Gilberto," I told him.

"I know, I know," he said. "But you can't blame me for trying, right?"

Then he looked out over the fields, which were aglow with sunlight, taking it all in.

"The thing is, Rico, me and that Dierdra—that'll probably never happen. But there's just something nice about being around someone like her—like she's old school, one hundred percent American in a way you and I will never be, you know?"

Even if I didn't exactly know what to make of his wanting to mess around on Wendy, I could sort of understand where he was coming from. Like, just getting next to someone so different from yourself was kind of thrilling.

Heading back into the house, I couldn't help admiring the guy, and I had to give him credit. Whatever happened between him and Dierdra, it was probably the first time that any farm girl around there had ever even dared go out with a bona fide one hundred percent

New York City Puerto Rican, let alone one with an ice-skating scar down the side of his face.

About a week later, just as the street outside the station filled with those flatbed carnival trucks on their way to some new destination, the phone rang. I thought it would be my boss, Mr. Jenkins, checking in on me, but it was Sheri, finally calling.

Her voice sounded friendly, but quiet, like she didn't want to be overheard. She was half whispering. I had to keep asking her to speak up, and because she called me at a busy time, the station customer bells sounding every few minutes, I had to keep putting down the phone. I kept expecting her to be gone each time I went back to the phone, but she hung in there. After a while we could finally "chat"—another word I never heard in New York.

I told her that I was messing around with some comic-book stories.

"Drawing them?"

"No, like writing them," I said. "But I got other things that I want to write too."

"Like what?"

"Like science-fiction stories. You ever read that stuff?"

"Not really," she said. "But my mom, she's an English

teacher, and I've read just about everything else—from Jane Austen to Mark Twain."

"Mark Twain? I love that dude! Do you?"

"I do," she said. "I think he's great."

And then I told her about how much I really liked that Huck Finn novel.

"I mean, that story, man,"—and yes, I actually called her "man"—God, I was lame!—"is like one I feel I've been living."

She giggled. "But why?" she asked.

"Well, it's like this. If you ever end up cutting out from a place, or even think about it, like I did from New York City, you suck up that Huck Finn story—with all the stuff about 'lightin' out'—like it's your own."

I didn't know if it made any sense to her, but Sheri said, "Wow, I can really see that."

Then I felt like telling her about all the other books I liked, and even about comic characters like Superman and Adam Strange, the sorts who turn around one day and find themselves in a completely different world, and it struck me that lots of the books I read were kinda about the same thing. But then I realized I was going on too long about myself. I decided to follow Gilberto's advice about how best to get next to a girl.

Like just by listening.

"Anyway, Sheri, forget about me," I said. "How are ya doing?"

"Okay, I guess," she said softly.

Then nothing. Okay, say anything, I told myself.

"Well, I want to apologize for puking all over the place when we were at the fair," I began, "but—"

"Aw, Rico," she said, cutting in. "I know you didn't mean to. I mean, if you had wanted to, that would be something else, but . . ."

She didn't finish the sentence. Suddenly there was all kinds of racket on her end, like someone pounding on a door and a voice shouting through that door, but all muffled. It was weird. Something crashed and I heard the telephone dropping to the floor, and then just a dial tone.

A half hour or so went by. In that time I heard two Eagles songs and some other country music claptrap over the radio. I took a leak and fueled up a twelve-wheel diesel truck, the burly driver, wired out of his mind on speed and feeling his hammy arm for his pulse, anxiously asking me if I had any "downers" to spare. I didn't.

(But I sold him two beers from the station's stash to help calm the guy.)

Wondering about Sheri, I would have called her back, if I had her number.

I pumped gas into two more cars, checked their oil, and squeegeed the crushed insects off their front and back windows. Then I just sat by the office desk, watching the telephone.

I just wanted to hear from the girl.

Then, at about eleven, the phone finally rang.

It was Sheri. She sounded like she was about to cry.

"Are you okay? What's going on?" I asked.

"Well," she said, "I called to invite you to a Halloween party my best friend, Gina, is throwing here in town."

"A party? Sounds cool," I said.

And she asked me to write down an address.

Check.

"But what's going on with you?" I asked.

Whispering, she said, "Ah, I can't tell you now. I'm with my dad."

Then I heard some more shouting in the background.

"Sorry, Rico, but I got to go."

"But why?" I asked.

"It's my dad. He's in one of his moods."

And she hung up.

* * *

The next night, when a blue Cadillac came tearing into the station, I was surprised to see Sheri, her eyes all red as if she'd been crying, sitting in the front seat beside a man who I supposed was her father. He was a tough-looking guy, square-jawed and cleft-chinned, with steely eyes and a crew cut that made him look like a Marine, sort of like Sergeant Rock of the comics. But while Sergeant Rock was a good guy, there didn't seem to be anything nice about Sheri's Pops. Asking for gas, he was slurring his words and smelled like whiskey big-time.

"Just give me a tank of regular," he said, getting out and immediately clutching the door to get his balance.

Man, was he loaded.

Normally, when I saw an "inebriate" behind the wheel, as Mr. Jenkins, a by-the-rules guy, called them (or a "*borrachrón*" in Spanish, to quote my Moms)—not someone just buzzed on a few beers but really really plastered—I'd call the state police to let them know that a drunk was on the road. (Just a month before, near Milwaukee, a vanload of Lutheran kids on their way to early-morning church services with their pastor was hit head-on by this drunk driving on the wrong side of the road.) But when I saw how miserable Sheri already was,

I let that shit go, just hoping that his house in Janesville wasn't very far away. But then I changed my mind when I saw him fumbling around the ground, looking for his wallet, which had tumbled from his hands with everything falling out. I got really worried. So while the tank was filling, and he went off to use the men's room, I shook my head at Sheri, slipped back into the office, dialed up the state police, and told them I had someone who shouldn't be driving at the station. They said they'd be right over.

I went back to the car, and seeing him behind the wheel again, I tried to stall for time.

"You want me to check your oil, sir?"

"No, I don't need that. Just tell me how much, would ya?"

I did, then I gave him his change. The few times I looked over at Sheri, she was practically shrinking down into the seat, like she wanted to disappear, a feeling I knew pretty well.

Then, as he was about to start the engine, I told him to wait. I began wiping down his front windows.

"Hey, come on, buddy," he said. "I don't have all night!"

I decided that I had to be up-front.

"Look, sir, I really can't let you go off driving in your condition."

"My condition?" he said, this nasty look on his face. "Mind your own business, will ya!" And he started his engine. "Now get out from in front of my car!"

He looked like he meant it.

"But sir," I said, trying anything. "Have some coffee, on the house, okay?"

"Just get out of my way," he said, the engine rumbling.

But, thank goodness, just then a white state police cruiser, sirens wailing, lights blinking, pulled into the station, two troopers getting out and approaching the car.

"Is this the guy?" one of them asked me.

"Yep."

I expected them to go the whole nine yards with him like I had seen them doing with some others— giving him a Breathalyzer test and making him walk the line—but as soon as one of the troopers, shining a flashlight into the Cadillac, saw who it was, he took his hand off his holstered belt and said, "Hey, Tom. I mean, of all people you should know better than to be driving around like this."

"Yeah, I know, I know," he said. "I suppose you're gonna run me in, huh?"

"Now, hold on," the trooper said, leaning his head through the open window. They talked for a few minutes. I couldn't hear what they were saying. Then the trooper walked over to me.

"Look, son, we really appreciate the call you put in to us, but we're not going to put this fellow through the wringer just because he's had a few. What we *will* do is get him off the road and home."

"Uh-huh," I said.

I couldn't understand why they were cutting him so much slack, but they were. Motioning to Sheri's father to slide over, one of the troopers started the engine up, and with the state police cruiser following behind, they drove out of the station, Sheri looking back at me through the window, her eyes really sad.

Later that same night, the station phone rang again. I snatched it up.

It was Sheri and she sounded terrible.

The first thing she said was, "Oh, Rico, I'm so embarrassed."

"Hey, you don't have to be with me," I said. "But what

was that all about? I've never seen the troopers letting anyone off so easy."

"My dad's a district attorney in town. He knows everybody."

"But that still doesn't seem right," I said. "He could've killed someone."

"I know," she said. "But he usually only drinks at home. It's just that when he went over to talk to my mom, they had a big argument about alimony and—"

She told me how that argument put him in a really bad mood, so bad that when they stopped somewhere for dinner on the way back to Janesville, he had a couple of double scotches, then drove to what they called a "package" store out here to buy a pint, which he drank down while they were pulled over on the side of the road.

"He's not a bad man," she said. "But once he starts up, there's no stopping him. It's just awful."

I still couldn't figure out why the state troopers would let him off. But then I thought about all the cops who used to hang around Mr. Farrentino's bar and looked the other way, when they knew that all kinds of illegal stuff was going on. I guess Sheri's Pops had the same kind of pull around here.

"Well, the main thing is that you're all right," I said. "But why did you come by the station?"

"I told Dad to. It was on the way, and I guess"—her voice was cracking—"I wanted you to see how he is sometimes."

For once I felt like I was on familiar ground, at least when it came to having a Pops who drank.

"Are you with him a lot?"

"Two weekends a month," she said. "But he wants me to be there more."

"And do you?" I had to ask.

"Rico, he's my dad!" she said. "I want to, but . . . but I just hate being around him when he's like that. He gets so mean."

"Does he hit you or something?"

"No, it's not that. It's just that he changes on me all the time. He's nice one second, and then he starts screaming at me the next."

Sounding like she could barely catch her breath, she went on. "He breaks things and gets so mean I just have to lock myself in my room. And sometimes he scares me half to death by pounding on the door."

"But can't you get your mom to do something about it?" I said, trying to be helpful.

"Rico, he knows every judge in the county."

"Damn," I said.

Hearing the desperation in her voice, I decided, even if it might be embarrassing, to tell her about my own Poppy.

"Sheri, I know where you're coming from," I said. "My Pops, he drinks a lot too. . . ."

"He does?"

"Yep, like all the time. And it always tore me up too." Just thinking about my Pops was doing a number on my guts. "It's just freakin' rough seeing your Pops that way. And you can't do a damn thing about it."

"It's just so hard!" she cried. I don't know what buttons I pressed, but a real storm of tears came pouring out of her, so many that she must have put the telephone under a pillow, because suddenly I couldn't hear much at all.

"You there? You there?" I kept asking.

She picked up the phone again, sniffling.

"But let me hip you to something. . . ."

"What's that?" she asked.

"Bitch that it is, you just got to know that it's not your fault if your Pops drinks too much. Some folks just get that way," I said while tapping a cigarette out of a new pack, off the shelf. I didn't smoke much, but I was so agitated that I lit one up. I put it out after a few puffs.

Man, that shit was jive.

"Let me ask you something else."

"All right," she said, sighing.

"Are you him?"

"No."

"Then don't be so down on yourself," I told her, thinking of all the times Gilberto said practically the same thing to me. "I mean, that shit won't get you anywhere."

"But it's scary," she said, her voice still raw.

"Damn right it is," I told her in my own coolest voice. "That's why folks like you and me got to be looking out for one another, you hear?"

Somehow just my saying that calmed her down.

"Rico, I do feel better now," she said after a moment. "Thank you!"

"Ah, it ain't no big thing," I said, like I was from the projects. "I've been there, that's all."

Just then a Pontiac came driving into the station.

"Look, Sheri, I got to go now. A customer just came in. But do me a favor, get some sleep, huh? And just remember—if you need me, you know where I am, okay?"

* * *

I spent the rest of my shift thinking about stuff.

Like how even a sweet girl like Sheri was going through all kinds of hassles. It kind of opened my eyes up to what I had been through back in the city. Hearing the hurt and panic in her voice, like she would do anything to get away from her Pops, even if she loved him, sounded the way I'd felt—as if she were a kind of mirror on myself. Like how sometimes you have to do some things that you don't really want to, just to get away from all the hassles, even if you're probably hurting your folks.

It made a lot more sense to me now.

In my case, it wasn't just about avoiding military school, but another thing.

Like, night after night of seeing your old man messing himself up will do that to you and make you wish for another life.

And it makes you feel that if you can't help him out, then maybe you can help someone else. Like Jimmy.

But the thing is, was I really helping myself?

Because not a day passed when I didn't wonder if my Pops was even worse off because I had split. And that nagged at me, along with just missing the good stuff back home, and wondering if folks like me and Sheri were just stuck with the kind of crap that nobody should have to ever put up with, but don't have any choice about, except maybe if they run away.

twenty

BY THE TIME Halloween rolled around, the trees—oaks, elms, and hickories—had started to shed their leaves, big piles of them covering the yard, and the nights became cooler, the whole world yawning like it was getting ready for the good sleeping months of winter. Pumpkins and piles of smaller, funky-looking squashes started popping up on people's porches, and in town all kinds of ghoul and witch displays were hanging in house and shop windows.

It was definitely festive, but not like what I had known back in the city.

Man, but I used to love those Halloweens!

I'd put on some cheap costume, cover my face with colors, and stand outside the subway exit, usually with Jimmy, hitting up people coming home from work for loose change, and then we'd go from building to building and from apartment to apartment on our block doing the trick-or-treat thing and making out like bandits, our bags filling with all kinds of candy, change, and even sometimes a loose cigarette or two.

But I'd always had a rough time deciding what to wear.

One year I tried to be Zorro, but that was ridiculous. I mean, I had to make myself, a Latino, look Latino. It was crazy.

Another year, I got me a clear plastic face mask and poured glue all over it, setting it on fire so it melted down. In that I looked like a radioactive zombie—way more convincing than my being a Zorro.

At least people, not being able to see my real face, couldn't come at me with all their jive attitudes.

I guess that's why I had a thing for superheroes who wore masks—like Batman, Daredevil, and the Flash. You could never tell what they really looked like, and I kind of envied them for that.

So for Gina's party—which thankfully happened to fall on a night when I didn't have to work—I just didn't know what to get dressed up as. But with Bonnie and Wendy helping me out, I came up with a pirate costume:

a red polka-dotted bandana around my head, a fake mustache, a vest, Curt's baggy red pantaloons (a souvenir from Marrakech), a pair of black knee-high fishing boots that we found in the barn—the best we could do—one of Gilberto's black big-buckled garrison belts, and as a final touch, some clip-on ring earrings. Oh, and yeah, a gold cardboard dagger that Bonnie made for me.

That night there was a full moon and all kinds of freaky lightning storms moving into the area from the west. The TV weatherman suggested that folks should stay at home. Yeah, right. It was Halloween!

Wendy offered me a lift in her red Toyota to Gina's place, reciting one of her new poems along the way. She did that a lot with me, like I was some kind of kindred poetic spirit. All sorts of poems about her black skin, her black soul, her black rage—it was like each of those poems was a little jewel box into which she put that part of herself. Otherwise her blackness wasn't anything she ever talked about; her poems were like her own secret identity.

I got to thinking that out here in Wisconsin, it was like I had my own secret identity too. I got to wondering if Wendy even knew I was a *cubano*. So as we bumped down the road, thunder sounding in the distance, I just came out and asked her.

"Yep, I know," she said, as hail started to come down hard, bouncing against the asphalt and hood, like beads of overheated cooking oil in a frying pan. She pulled over to the side of the road and yanked on the emergency brake. "But, to be honest, Rico, I would have never figured that out without Gilberto telling me. No offense, but you seem just like some nice white kid, even if you do cuss it up sometimes."

"Well, that's a drag," I said, feeling about a million different ways at once. "But you're right, I definitely don't look it."

"You're cute, anyway," she said, pinching my pirate's cheek.

Then she asked me a question I had answered a million times before.

"Are both your parents Cuban?"

"Yeah," I said.

"But are they both white like you?"

"Nope, it's just one of those things that landed on me, because I had an Irish great-grandfather, you know?"

"Yep, I actually do," she said. She looked at me

intently. "I don't know if Gilberto ever told you, but my mom is white and so are my two brothers. I'm the only one who took after my dad's side!"

I couldn't believe it!

"Really? Did that ever bother you?" I asked, while all that hail kept pelting down like bullets, the car's hood sounding with a thousand pings.

"Hell, yes!" she said. "Especially at school. When I was growing up in Denver, most kids were nice to me, but now and then I'd get a certain kind of nasty look from some of them, no matter what else was coming out of their mouths."

She was going through her purse, looking for a joint.

"It was sort of the same for me, except like an opposite thing," I told her. "I mean, I've always been taken for a white dude!"

"Uh, Rico, hate to tell you," she said, lighting the joint. "You kind of are." She blew some smoke out, coughed, squeezing her nose to keep the rest in, and then passed the joint to me.

"But that's just on the outside," I told her, barely taking in more than a token puff.

"Well, that might be true, but you don't sound Latino

any more than I sound black when I'm talking!" she admitted as I passed the joint back.

While she took another drag, I was swearing to myself that I could talk that street shit as good as anybody if I had to—but I guess that really had nothing to do with sounding like a Latino, with an accent and all that.

And knowing the Spanish language inside out.

And how to dance the mambo and all those other steps and carry yourself with the right body language, all the shit I didn't have going for me.

But even so, I still felt like I was. Latino, I mean. It was too confusing to explain.

"Tell me something," I asked her. "You ever get any static from black folks about the way you are?"

"To be honest, aside from my relatives, growing up I hardly knew any. But since then, I have, and that's crazy too."

She laughed.

"Straight, buttoned-down Negroes, like my father— he's a doctor—they like me fine and dandy, like I'm the way all black girls should be: boarding-school bred, nice-mannered, good vocabulary, all that stuff. But the 'brothers,' now that's a different story!"

She was shaking her head.

"I mean, no matter how black I make myself look—I could be wearing a silver Tina Turner miniskirt, high go-go boots, and sporting the biggest Afro—once I open my mouth, I become an *Oreo* to them."

"An 'Oreo'?"

"Yep," she said. "Black on the outside, white on the inside. And let me tell you"—and she really started sucking that joint up—"it's like nobody wants to let you into their club."

I couldn't believe it. That's exactly how *I* felt. "But why's everybody so messed up?" I had to ask. I rolled the window down a crack because the smoke in the car was thick, like being inside a cloud.

"I don't know," she said. "That's just the way it is." Then, smiling, she added, "But you know who's got that all figured out?"

"Who?"

"Gilberto. The more I'm around that guy," she said, "the more I think I should be like him."

"Gilberto?" I asked, as half the sky continued to fall on us.

"Yep, Gilberto," she said, shivering a little and turning these knobs on the dashboard to turn on the heat. "He's practically as dark as me but doesn't give a damn about what people think. Just rolls with whatever comes his way. Never looks back and never thinks he's black," she said, giggling, while tapping some ashes into the dashboard tray. "I mean, he's not the deepest person in the world, but maybe that's why he's happy most of the time."

Then she took another toke, shrugging.

"Wish I could be like that, but I'm not," she said. "I just think too much."

"I'm with you on that," I said.

Then she asked me if I wanted a shotgun. I didn't want to seem uncool, and so I said I did. With that she put that joint into her mouth backwards. The lit end was balanced inside on her tongue, the dry part sticking out of her lips, her mouth not three inches from mine, so that she could shoot a concentrated stream of smoke up my nose.

But, just then, outside it started crashing and booming big-time, again and again like cannons. The sky all dark in one moment, and then a sheet of white in the next, like in a horror movie.

Then as she was about to blow that smoke up my nose, we heard this really loud boom of thunder from just above us, and then another *boom*, and everything around us started glowing in a blinding way, the whole world flashing white, static charges shimmering on the hood, a little horizon of yellow light floating outside the windshield for a few seconds, before going away.

Tingles shot through the rubber mats beneath our feet.

With a scream, Wendy spit out the joint and grabbed me, really tightly. I could feel her heart beating hard.

We sat there petrified, like the car might explode. When it didn't, Wendy moved back to her seat.

"Oh, but my goodness gracious," she said, putting her hand to her throat. "Is that what I think it was?"

"Yup," I said, my hands still shaking. "I do believe we were just hit by lightning."

"But, how come we're not all fried up like fritters?" she asked, patting at her chest like she was trying to put out a small fire.

"Maybe because all the electricity shot through the frame and we're grounded by the rubber tires," I told her, having heard from truckers about their getting hit by lightning while on the road.

"But shit," she said. "That was freaky."

"You said it."

"I nearly peed in my pants."

"Me too."

Afterwards, when the thunder sounded more distant again, and you could see the moon through these rushing thready clouds, Wendy almost seemed embarrassed by her reaction. But I was thrilled, not over the way she had put her arms around me, but because a car with people in it could be hit by lightning and survive, like in a science-fiction movie, that whole thing giving me all kinds of ideas for a new kind of comic-book character.

And maybe because it had happened on Halloween.

"Rico," Wendy asked me when she had finally gathered herself. "Do you still want to go to that party?"

"If it's cool with you," I said.

"Well, okay," and she sighed. "As long as this damn car still works."

Turning the key and pumping the gas pedal, she tried to start the ignition.

Once, twice, and then a third time, nothing happening. Oh please, Lordy Lord, I was praying to myself, let the car engine start.

I didn't want to let Sheri down.

But when Wendy tried the fourth time, while new

flashes of lightning were rolling across the horizon like fireworks, the sky glaring in sections, the engine started revving up, and here we were, soon on our way to town, electricity having jostled our minds and souls.

Gina's house was on one of those streets that looked like just about every other, lit jack-o'-lanterns glowing in the window, cars parked up and down along the sidewalks.

Heading towards her front door, I could see through the windows all kinds of costumed partiers dancing. A shapely female devil, in tight red leotards, a cape, and holding a trident, waved me in.

twenty-one

OKAY, TRICK-OR-TREATERS, listen here—a quiz:

First question:

When I walked into Gina's house, dressed as a Mr. Jolly Roger—or whatever the heck I was supposed to be—thunder still booming in the sky, and I followed Miss Devil (Gina in disguise) into her living room and through a crowd of Midwest, hush puppy–wearing, beer-chugging, Halloween revelers, over to Sheri, who was sitting on a couch in a dimly lit corner, can you guess which kind of costume she had put on?

a. A harem-like and very revealing *I Dream of Jeannie* outfit.

b. A ballerina's ruffled tutu and soft velvet shoes.

c. A hobo's crumpled hat, bulbous nose, over-
large pants and shoes.

d. A fairy-tale princess's royal gown.

e. None of the above, like she hadn't bothered
to wear any costume at all.

Second question:

If, like myself, you went into the kitchen, and found
that both the refrigerator and the iced-up sink were
filled with bottles of beer and wine, and then went down
the hall, ducking your Jolly Rogers's head under all these
hanging paper jack-o'-lanterns into the bathroom to find
a bathtub filled with ice cubes and even more beer; and
if you could smell wafts of pot in the air and saw all kinds
of tipsy ghouls, vampires, and other creatures of the
night dancing like crazy and making out in the corners,
would you say:

a. Parents were home.

b. Parents weren't home.

c. Who the hell cares!

Third question:

Say you're from New York and you've been struck by

lightning, but remain uncertain of yourself—even if you think you have electrical charges emanating from your body—and you want to impress the Midwest girl you once threw up on, would you:

a. Sit with her, while all this loud rock-'n'-roll music is playing, and just make all kinds of small talk about how nice it is to see her? And then go off to bob for apples, or to play pin the tail on the donkey like a nice, girl-respecting guy?

b. Or, even if she's leaning her head on your shoulder and sipping beer through one of those squiggly-centered plastic straws, and sometimes stops to give you a kiss, do you act like an idiot or jump all over her, since you're in a dark corner?

c. Do you practice self-restraint, saving all your electrified pent-up energy for "later" when you're in your own lumpy bed?

d. Do you get restless and, even if you're shy and she's shy about dancing, take her out onto the floor?

e. And once you do, and the word has gone

around that you're from New York City—I
mean you're like manna from heaven 'cause
nothing too exciting happens around
here—to impress your girl, no matter how
jive your moves, do you start to invent
dances with names like the "Manhattan
Monkey" and the "Harlem Slide," with all
kinds of outrageous jerky steps, and somehow carry them off—so much that folks
start applauding?

Fourth question:
Say you're this guy, dressed up as a pirate—a sort of
pirate—and the sweet Midwest girl you really like, after
drinking all night, kind of tells you that she'll be staying
here at her friend's place and that you can also stay if you
want to. Do you, at two in the morning of All Souls Day,
tell her:

a. Oh but, Sheri, I really, really would love to,
   but, damn I just don't know. I mean we've
   hardly been hanging out.
b. I would but I think you're a little too tipsy.
c. All right—if it won't bug you out, okay?

Final question:

a. Do you spend hours making out with her on the couch before getting a lift home from a totally whacked-out zombie on his way to Beloit?

b. Or do you actually head upstairs with her, to mess around big-time, for a while at least, until she falls asleep in your arms—and *then* you sneak out to catch a last-minute ride home?

Well, whatever your answers, no way am I telling you what really happened that night (it's the *cubano* outhouse-digger's rule), but I *will* fill you in on what happened when I eventually got back to the farm and looked out my bedroom window. By then, in the middle of the night, the worst part of the storm had passed, but I could still see these occasional flashes lighting up the distance. And that made me think about what had happened earlier to me and Wendy.

What if this white dude is in a car with a black dude when it gets hit by lightning? And what if the lightning magically fuses their bodies and souls together, so that suddenly they are one person, capable of becoming white or black at will, and with all kinds of superpowers?

Then I refined the idea a little.

Maybe the black guy is a dark Latino and the white dude is a sandy-haired guy like myself. And instead of just having these two friends in a car when they get hit by the lightning, what if I make them twin brothers, who look exactly the same except for the color of their skin?

I couldn't even begin to sleep.

"See, the whole thing is that this guy can change his appearance at will," I told Jimmy the next day. "Latino in one moment, white in the next. Like Clark Kent and Superman. But in his case, he just scopes the crummy world out for instances of prejudice and all that."

Jimmy listened, adjusting his glasses. "Sounds sort of cool. And what would this superhero be called?"

"How about 'Dark Dude'?"

"Hey—like what those guys in the projects used to call you?"

"Yeah, only he's got superpowers."

"All right," he said. "You write a script, and I'll see what I can do."

"For real?"

"Yeah. I can't promise you anything, but I'll give it a shot."

Man, that made me happy as hell!

That's what I worked on for the next few weeks, when I wasn't thinking about Sheri.

Part 6 **HAPPY HOLIDAYS**

twenty-two

AFTER HALLOWEEN SHERI and me started to hang out whenever she could, like maybe every other weekend, when she was staying with her old man. And sometimes, she'd take a bus in after school for a few hours and we'd walk down Main Street, getting ice-cream sodas at the pharmacy or going around town looking for old comics. I had put an ad into the local newspaper, offering to pay up to a quarter apiece, and every now and then someone would call me at the house about having some to sell, and we would head over to check their comics out. I was hoping to find some old classic superhero comics, but even the kind of comics people chose to read out in Wisconsin was different. I mean I had never seen so many *Donald Duck* and *Little Lulu* and *Bugs Bunny* comic books—really wholesome stuff—in my life!

Now and then, I'd hang with her at Gina's place, watching TV—she was a big *Dark Shadows* fan—or we would sit reading books. And while we messed around a bit sometimes, we mostly hung tight: Like she would just want me to hold her, especially when she would be getting all upset at the thought of having to go home to her dad. I'd have to tell her to stop chewing on her fingernails. I mean, they were a mess and a half! The one time she came by with Gina to meet the crew, she got the official nod of approval from Gilberto, who thought Sheri was the prettiest thing. And coming up to my crummy room, Sheri just beamed: "Oh, Rico, this is so nice!" Then she plopped down on my lousy mattress and cuddled up under a blanket like she never wanted to leave.

But, of course, she had to.

(Okay, so you're probably thinking, how lame can this guy be? And, at the same time, you're probably wondering if I went for it, right? Well, like I said before, if I did, I wouldn't tell you, and if I didn't, let me put it this way: If you looked into those blue eyes and saw all that pain in them, you'd best believe your heart would be breaking too. I mean, you just wouldn't be looking to get behind that in the same way you might with other girls, okay?)

* * *

As the weather got colder, I didn't see her as much as I would have liked. Without a car, that long-distance stuff wasn't so easy. The trees looking starker and starker, the sky turning a silvery gray, flocks of birds—going *caw caw, caw caw*—flying south. Like, everything out here, already way slow when compared with zipping city standards, slowed down even more, people disappearing into their homes, little clouds of chimney smoke sprouting all over the countryside, and most of the livestock kept inside the barns.

And it could suddenly get cold as a bitch.

On Thanksgiving Day, when we had a nice feast in the house, the porch thermometer read fifteen degrees. And with the ground already covered in a few feet of snow and the wind blowing across the fields like a MF, you had to have some really good reason to go anywhere.

It was bad enough that I had to be at the gas station on such cold nights. With the sun going down around five in the afternoon and that darkness lasting until about nine the next morning, I spent my shifts thinking I was in a terrible dream. I was always shoveling snow off the driveway. And just pumping gas and scraping ice off the windshields became as awful as anything one could do. Worse than cleaning the outhouse, even. But at least the office and the station bathroom were warm, and I didn't have to deal with how freaking cold it could be back at the farmhouse.

Freaking cold is actually an understatement. In early December a glass of water I left on my sill froze solid, and the *insides* of my windowpanes were coated with ice.

I mean, I had one steam pipe in the corner of my room, but it just couldn't do the job; I'd put my half-frozen hand on it, and it didn't feel any warmer than a piece of toast.

I'll say it again: It was cold—or let me put it another way.

You know that expression "numb-nuts"? Well, that must have originated out there.

The heating in that old house was so bad, we'd have to keep the potbellied stove burning with wood all day. Everybody had to wear long thermal underwear— Gilberto told me they used to be called "union suits"— or walked around with blankets draped over their shoulders. As for the outhouse room? Once you went down that drafty hall and opened its door—and saw one of the funny notices that Curt had put up under a picture of President Nixon saying, "When you go, think of sending him your truest feelings by way of natural telegrams"—you may as well have walked into an ice box. Made me feel really sorry for the girls: Guys could at least run out and take a leak just out the door, but the girls didn't have that luxury, if it can be called that.

The worst for me was that I couldn't even play the guitar: The strings were too cold to handle.

Probably just what the old-time farmers had to go through, I'd think, wondering what on Earth I was doing there.

Still, it was nice to go out with Gilberto for some cross-country skiing, to see a horse pulling a sleigh, its reins jingling, coming up the road. And there was that frozen pond, where we'd all go ice-skating, even Jimmy—trying his best and often falling on his ass—giving it a shot, stuff he'd never do in New York.

The wildest thing was once that snow came down, it stayed. And feet of it! Bundled in a heavy coat and sweater, I'd go stomping through the drifts, and each time I did and I found my boots sinking down, I'd feel like my old New York self was getting slowly swallowed up, like I was becoming someone else.

twenty-three

SUDDENLY, IN NO time flat, Christmas Eve rolled
around, and damn, was I happy that I didn't have to work
that night. In fact, Mr. Jenkins closed the station up for
the next three days, the one time of the year he did so.

And he gave me a ten-dollar bonus and a case of
Yoo-hoo.

I couldn't wait to get back to the farm, our living room homey as any nice Christmas in a magazine,
the tree me and Gilberto had cut down looking all
magical.

A few days before, we had gone off into the woods
at the far edge of the farm, snow falling off the tree
boughs around us. We were wearing these lumberjack-
looking beaver-skin hats, the sort you could buy at a
tag sale for nothing. Gilberto carried the axe. When we

came to this patch of nice pines, most standing about seven feet high, Gilberto put his hand on my shoulder and asked me, "Which one do you like?"

And that tore me up, because that hand on my shoulder thing is just what my Pops used to do with me when we'd head out to buy a tree, and then he'd say those same words. Just thinking about that and how my Pops, being all kindhearted, used to buy these ratty Charlie Brown trees from this poor Puerto Rican guy on 109th, even if they were half dried-up, just to help him out, made me pretend that I had gotten something in my eye for a second.

I ended up choosing a plump Scott's pine, with pretty blue-green needles, even if it was kind of scraggly in some places, like it needed some tender, loving care. Within the hour, we had dragged that tree home and put it up in the living room. We started decorating it—with ribbons and old what-have-you kind of trinkets, and lots of cheap dime-store ornaments. The only fancy thing we put on the tree was an aluminum star that Wendy found somewhere. Bonnie had gone through the trouble of threading cranberries to string along its branches. Then we put up a couple of strands of old bubble lights that Gilberto had found at a junk shop in Janesville, and dripping with two boxes worth of tinsel, that tree blinked, laughed, breathed, and posed for our delight like a movie star might.

But the more festive the house got, the more I started remembering things I didn't want to be remembering: how I counted each day leading up to Christmas when I was little and held my breath like I couldn't wait for Santa Claus (which my Moms pronounced *Santa Clow*, as in "Ow!") to come along, and how my folks were always telling me that he'd climb down the fire escape from the roof, where his reindeer were hanging out, to reach us; and like it was Santa Claus who gave me my one toy a year. I really believed in him and didn't let go of that shit until I was eleven, being a little slow in growing up.

And the smell of the pine brought back other smells—of the rum drinks my Pops concocted for the zillions of visitors we'd have coming through the apartment during the holidays, dozens of little kids running up and down the hall, their Pops and Moms dancing away and totally wrecked out of their minds in our living room. And the food! Our tables would be covered with all kinds of food—'cause nobody turned up empty-handed. There would be boxes of honey-drenched or cream-covered pastries, boxes and boxes of *pasteles*, cold cuts, roast pork, beer fizzing, folks drinking, and yours truly here sitting in a corner and taking everything in.

At the farm, come Christmas Eve day, we made a punch, a wild concoction of orange and cranberry juice, with cloves and cinnamon, and a few quarts of vodka and gin and sherry, to which we added some orange slices in the end (as if they mattered). Bonnie and Curt had come up with some beaucoup reefer, so our living room smelled like burning wood, gooey pine sap, and sweet weed.

We held an open house that day, and a bunch of Gilberto's pals came by: students from his college, a lot of hippies, a few guys with their wives from his job at the brewery—some of them staying for a few hours; most of them, aghast after taking a look around at the messiness of that household, quickly leaving.

None of us could complain. The hippies left behind hash brownies or a pint or two of Jack Daniel's. One buzzed dude offered Bonnie, with whom he was rightly and instantly in love, a few tablets of what he called "Christmas wonder," which, I think, she gobbled down without a second thought. But even the straighter folks, like the guys from Gilberto's job, brought us bottles of booze, not to mention home-baked cookies.

By four o'clock we had so much stuff by way of refreshments that even the draftiness of that house didn't bother any of us. Wendy and Bonnie were dancing with abandon in front of the stereo. And a turkey, roasting in the oven, with all its fixings in a big pot, smelled really good. In a way, with even Jimmy sitting contently beside Polly, things could not have been better.

Come evening, it had started to snow again, a nice feathery snow that just made the outside world seem as quiet as a church.

I sat around, enjoying the tree and smelling the pine cones burning in the potbellied stove, but then I started thinking about home again, and our own better days at Christmas: the fun of going to midnight Mass with a lot of the neighborhood kids, most of them a little woozy on booze, and coming back to the apartment to find that the party was still going on; of hearing my Poppy laughing; of seeing him dancing in our living room with my Moms, and finding that there were still platters of *yuca*, *tostones*, and yellow rice, and honey ham and chicken and *lechón* out on the kitchen table; of having a tasty late-night snack with Isabel—of all the nice things that I took for granted.

"You okay, Rico?" Gilberto asked me, squatting down beside my chair.

"Yeah, yeah, man. Why you asking?"

"Well, everyone's having a good time while you're suddenly looking super serious."

I shrugged. "I don't know. I was just thinking about my folks, it being Christmas Eve and all."

"So why don't you just call them? Hey, I'm sure they'd be really happy to hear from you. After all, it's *La Noche Buena*, right?"

Yeah, the night to be hanging out with the family.

"Come on, you know I can't."

He was confounded by that.

"Okay, do what you like. But I'm going to call my Moms right now."

There was only one telephone in the house, this old boxy thing hanging on the kitchen wall.

"Oye, Mommy, Feliz Navidad," Gilberto began.

A few words rasped though the phone.

And then, shocking me, Gilberto spoke only in Spanish for the next ten minutes.

Afterwards I felt stunned.

"You speak Spanish?"

"Of course, Sherlock. You think I'm a dummy?"

"But you never did around me."

"Man, you're not remembering right. I always have, with your Moms. But otherwise, why the hell would I?"

"I don't know. But damn."

"Rico, I spent the first seven years of my life in P. R. What else would I have spoken?" he said, tugging on his goatee. "Anyway, why don't you just call your Pops and Moms. I mean, it's Christmas!"

Yeah Christmas, it gets you all sappy, like goo from a tree. Calling my folks? I didn't know, but maybe because it was Christmas I thought that my Moms—I wasn't worried about my Pops—wouldn't be too hard on me.

Like I said, Christmas gets you sappy.

Still, I sat for a long time, thinking about making that call, and then, going back and forth in my head and having a few more glasses of punch, I decided to give it a try.

But I could hardly remember the number, our telephone having been a new thing that was only installed after my Poppy had gotten sick.

I tried a few different numbers before getting through.

It was about nine o'clock in New York, I figured.

I got more nervous each time it rang, wondering just who might pick up.

After the fourth ring, my Moms answered.

"*¿Diga?*" she said in this voice that was both hard and sad at the same time. "*¿Quién habla?*"

"Mommy," I said. "It's me, Rico."

"*¿Quién?*" she asked as if she couldn't believe it. "Rico?"

"Yeah, *mamá*," I said.

She gasped.

"*Ay! Ay! Ay!* Rolando, wake up, it's our boy!" she called to my Pops in Spanish. But wherever he was—I pictured him in the kitchen, dozing before the table—he did not come to the phone.

"*Pero mi hijo,*" she continued. "We thought you were dead!"

"No, *mamá*, I'm not," I said, puzzled that she could even think such a thing.

"*Gracias a Dios!* Thank God!" she kept repeating. "We've all been so worried—and your *papá*, *el pobre*, if you could see how he has been suffering!"

"I'm sorry, *mamá*," I said, wincing, her words bringing months of worry down on my head. "But I did what I had to do. I told you that in the note I left."

Then, wondering if she had understood my English, I tried to repeat myself in my half-assed Spanish. But that was a huge mistake: I had somehow slipped the word *aguantar*, or "put up with," into the sentence, so that what I managed to say was, "If I left home, it was because I couldn't put up with things anymore."

And then all the joy and relief in her voice left her.

"Ah sí," she said flatly. Then: "You should tell that to your *papá*, but he can't even get up to the telephone—he's been drinking so much because of what you've done! . . . But, *dime*—tell me—where are you?"

"I can't tell you, *mamá*, but I'm okay, *entiendes?*"

"Yes, I understand. You are somewhere far away and don't care at all about your family!"

I was thinking that it just wasn't so. In fact, if anything, I was caring too much about them. But I just didn't know what to say.

She sighed. *"Ay, por Dios*, to think that you have turned out to be such a bad son . . ." And then she started really laying into me, her voice so loud and angry that I had to hold the phone away from my ear.

"But, Mommy," I tried again, "I only called to say 'Merry Christmas' and to let you know that I was all right." But she kept on and on.

"*Ah sí*, Merry Christmas while we're here *sufriendo* with worry. Are you having a good time, wherever you are?"

"But, *mamá*, I only meant—"

"Oh the shame! *La vergüenza!*" she said, going into all kinds of things, like wishing she had never been so "easygoing" on me, her spoiled-rotten son.

"No Cuban son would do what you have done, abandoning his family the way you did. No, only *un americano loco*"—a crazy American—"would be so heartless. But I will pray to God that he fills your head with some common sense and that you will understand the wrongs you have committed—the sins against your father, and the pain you have brought us. Oh your Poppy, he almost suffered another *ataque de corazón*. . . ."

I couldn't take it anymore. "Okay, okay, *mamá*, I hear you, but I have to go. Please, tell Poppy and Isabel *'Feliz Navidad'* for me."

And then I just hung up, wishing I hadn't called at all.

* * *

I sat down on the floor by the Christmas tree feeling like I had just been sideswiped by a bus.

If I were alone somewhere, I probably would have started crying.

I tried to put on a good front, but I guess I didn't do a good job.

Gilberto, pretty much figuring that my call had not been a pleasant one, started patting my back and giving my tight shoulders a squeeze, like in a massage. Leaning down, he picked out a package from under the tree, tossing it onto my lap.

"I know we should wait until tomorrow, but open it, my bro," he said. And he patted my back.

Inside that box, in a nest of crinkled paper, was this red corduroy shirt, loud as any I had ever seen.

"That's so you can show off for your girl Sheri."

"How very cool, Gilberto," I said. "Thanks a lot."

So I gave Gilberto his present: the fattest Swiss Army knife I could find in the hardware store in town.

"You must have been reading my mind," he told me, flicking out its different blades. "It's just what I needed!" With that he gave me a big bro punch in the shoulder. Then, going with that flow, Wendy handed me two brightly wrapped presents.

"Here, Rico, since we're at it," she said. "These are for you."

"For me, really?" I asked.

"Yep," she said. "Go ahead, open them."

They were collections of poetry, one being by Langston Hughes, of Harlem fame, and the other called "*Versos sencillos*" by this famous Cuban writer, José Martí, whose name I grew up hearing, but whose stuff I had never read.

"I got that 'cause you told me that you come from a Cuban family and I figured you'd like it," she said.

"You best believe that," I answered, truly touched. I looked through the Cuban book.

It was all in Spanish!

As I quickly glanced over the poems, their words hit me like scrambled messages from another planet. I nodded anyway, as if I could understand what I was looking at. "Yep, José Martí," I said to Wendy, as I turned some pages. The thing is, my folks never bothered to teach me how to read anything in Spanish and that hurt just then, in the same way that I was bugged by the fact that I had trouble rolling my *rrrrr*s. Bet you anything that Huck Finn would have felt the same way if he opened his mouth and was mistaken for a Northerner.

Even so, half-assed as I was at being a *cubano*—and even if my Moms had just done a number on me—as I sat there, with that book in my hands, I felt like I was holding a tiny stove or a beautiful dove cooing away. Somehow—I can't explain it—just knowing that it was written by a Cuban made me feel good, like it was warming the room.

"Look inside," she said, breaking my spell. "I wrote something special for you."

"Yeah?" I said, turning to it.

On the inside of the cover, in a very pretty blue ballpoint pen script, was this:

For Rico,
Young as you are
What you can't now see
You will surely be
A wonderful person
Warm as light
Of special individuality.
Merry Christmas,
Wendy

I gave Wendy her present, a pretty hand mirror I'd found in a crafts shop in town. It had all fancy twirls along its handle, and its head was shaped like an oval, just like her face. In my fantasies, she'd look into it and see just how beautiful she was, instead of frowning the way she did sometimes when I'd catch her staring at herself in a mirror.

Frowning like I was on that Christmas Eve.

"My goodness," she said, glancing quickly into it. "Rico, this is the nicest mirror anyone's ever given me!"

Then she kissed my cheek, and that sort of made me feel a little better.

It wasn't long before everybody was opening presents.

From Bonnie and Curt, I received a wooden recorder and two sets of guitar strings. In turn I gave Curt a copy of the Beatles' White Album and Bonnie a pretty silk scarf.

Polly gave me a nice writing pen, and we both had to laugh, because I had gotten her one too!

But the present I worked the hardest on was Jimmy's. He must have been a little embarrassed when I handed him a big box, because he hadn't gotten anything for me. (I just didn't expect anything from him, though, Jimmy being Jimmy.) Inside were all kinds of pens and bottles of inks and heavy-grade bristol board, a T square, tracing paper and pencils and kneading erasers, all the things the cartooning books from the library said he would need to illustrate a professional comic script.

Okay, so I was trying to nudge him about the Dark Dude thing—I mean, he hadn't even started to work on it.

"Aw, man," he said, going through the box. "Why'd you have to do that?"

"You know why. So that we can do our thing again," I told him. "And other stuff will be coming. I got a light box on order from this shop in Madison, and I've had my eye on a drawing table in town. It's used, but really nice."

And I swear, a few tears seemed to come into his eyes.

We hung out, playing games like Parcheesi, Chinese checkers, and backgammon, Christmas carols and rock-'n'-roll songs coming out the phonograph, that punch in plentiful supply. And even if I couldn't get my mind off my family and the way my Moms had made me feel worse than I was already feeling, at least one more nice thing happened that Christmas Eve.

Sometime past ten thirty, Sheri called me from her mom's house in Whitewater, and just hearing about how she had spent that night with her relatives, away from her dad, all cozy and shit, and the nice dinner they had, with a fireplace blazing, her voice sounding happy, did me good.

"I just wish you could have been here," she told me.

"Me too," I said.

And I almost told her about what happened when I called New York, but she was in such a good mood, I didn't want to lay anything on her, except that we'd had one hell of an all-day bash at the farm and that I would have loved to have her around. But like she told me, Christmas was a family time.

"I know what you're saying," I said. "You don't have to explain a thing."

"Well, Merry Christmas, Rico. Hope you have a wonderful one," she said before hanging up.

One more last thing about that Wisconsin Christmas Eve. Past midnight, with the snow still coming down, Bonnie got it into her head that it would be wonderful to go outside and commune with nature. But she didn't have too many takers. Gilberto and Wendy had gone to bed, while Polly and Jimmy were perfectly content to just sit warming themselves by the stove. I didn't particularly want to get off my butt either, but a little buzzed and still smarting big-time from that telephone call, I couldn't put up much resistance when Bonnie floated down from outer space and, grinning like crazy, pulled me off the couch.

"Come out with us, Rico," she said. "Let yourself go for a change."

And she hauled me over to the entranceway where my winter coat was hanging off a hook.

So I followed Bonnie and Curt into the snow. Poor Curt, tall and thin and shivering, stood off to the side, his hands in his pockets and stomping his feet, while Bonnie, high on nature, began turning in circles, her face tilted up towards the sky, feeling the snowflakes against her skin. I was fascinated by how happy she seemed to be, but felt sort of foolish about turning in circles myself. I mean, I didn't really feel like a kid anymore, and I guess I wasn't much of a free spirit. But she came after me, grabbing my hand, and then, taking hold of my shoulders, started to turn me around and around.

And so I went along with her.

"Oh, Rico, make a wish," she said. "A Christmas wish and maybe it'll come true."

Well, I did, hoping for something beautiful to happen—and in a way it did: When I stopped turning I saw a herd of deer, somehow looking bluish in that light, bounding across the field, a wonderful thing to see, even if it had nothing to do with the wish I had really made that Christmas Eve.

Part 7 **THE SPRING**

twenty-four

I'M GONNA SKIP through most of that winter. I'll just say it was like we'd been hibernating and holding our breath and waiting for the snow to melt and for spring to come. (I mean it: We had a fifty-inch snowfall that year.) And slowly it did, little buds starting to sprout in the trees by early April and wildflowers blooming in the fields by mid-May.

Suddenly birds were chirping away, and butterflies, with their three-month lives (according to the *Farmer's Almanac*) went fluttering through the yard. With spiderwebs dropping down from the porch roof where icicles had hung, Rex, his tail wagging, went crazy sniffing around everywhere again. By then all the grayness of the landscape just started fading. It was like you had been looking at a pencil drawing of a farm, only to see it suddenly bursting with watercolors. Like some artist had gotten his ass up to bring new life to that world.

The worst thing about that winter, though, was that I hadn't seen much of Sheri. We sometimes met up in town to catch a movie, but mainly we talked on the phone. And mostly about how she should keep her head together about her Pops. The good news was that the guy tried to reform himself and didn't have a drink for two months that winter; the bad news was that when he fell off the wagon, he went crazy again. I don't want to keep talking about how low she got when that crap was going on, but I'll say just one thing: If I could have shipped that guy off to Siberia or put him in a rocket to the moon, I would have.

So our thing went like this: When she was upset, I tried to cheer her up and make her feel good about her-self, while Sheri, listening to my stories about my life in New York, wanted to do something nice for me. Shocked when I finally told her that I was a dropout, she wanted me to meet her schoolteacher mother.

"Rico, maybe she could pull strings and get you into a school around here. Wouldn't that be great?"

I didn't know. As bored as I was with working at the station, I kind of liked being independent. But I was also just scared about meeting her Moms. I'd never met a girlfriend's Moms before, due to the fact that I had never had a girlfriend.

It was in late March—a few days into that spring— when Sheri invited me out to her mom's house in Whitewater. Snow was still on the ground, and it was a real pain getting out there. Hitchhiking along those still icy roads, it took me forever to find their house at 12 Bluebird Lane.

But when I did, I was amazed.

Sheri's house looked like a fairy-tale cottage, the roof covered with snow and icicles hanging everywhere. Even though I was freezing, it took me a while to get around to knocking on that door.

Sheri let me in.

And talk about a nice and homey-looking living room!

All the furniture looked first-class, not a piece dragged in from the street: a nice big color TV, an upright piano, a fireplace ablaze, all kinds of family pictures everywhere.

And one of the walls was filled with just books!

"Mother," Sheri called into another room while I was warming myself by that fire and thinking what a nice house Sheri had. "Rico's here."

Well, I was nervous, but not the kind of nervous when you think you might get beat up: I just wondered if Sheri's Moms would like me. I'd even trimmed back my hair a little for the occasion, and put on my best shirt and sweater and cleanest jeans, so that I wouldn't seem too scruffy.

Sheri's Moms, Mrs. Pearson, soon popped into the room from the kitchen. Pretty and blond like her daughter, she had her hair done up, with pagoda-like curls, as if she had just come from a beauty salon. And like a Betty Crocker kind of lady, the sort to bake cookies and apple pies seven days a week, she was wearing an apron and bringing in a tray of sandwiches and other stuff for me.

"So you're Rico, the boy my Sharon's talked about."

"I guess that's me," I said, feeling shy as hell.

"Well, make yourself at home," she told me.

Then she sat me down on the couch, and while I went at that lunch—man, I was hungry after being out in the cold—she got right to the point of my visit.

Not about me seeing Sheri, but the fact that I had dropped out of school.

"Rico, everything Sharon's said about you makes me think that you're a bright and considerate young man.

Surely you understand how important a diploma is. So I can't help but wonder why you left school before getting yours."

Wow, what a question to answer not two minutes after meeting her.

Then I thought, What the hell. I told her my story about feeling hassled to death back at Jo Mama's, and how I just couldn't take it anymore. Then I talked about my situation at home, and about my Pops getting sick and my Moms always being hard on me. Sheri's mother nodded as if my every word was meaningful, sometimes smiling when I would use a New York City word, like "jive" or "lame." Once I told her all that stuff, she did not BS around, cutting quick to the chase scene of my visit.

"You're a runaway, aren't you?" she said, looking me straight in the eyes.

I nodded.

"Well, that's none of my business, but, may I ask you a question?" she said, pouring herself some coffee. Then she sat down across from me.

"Sure," I said, now feeling like I wanted to run out of the room.

"If you could enroll in a school without anyone asking questions, would you?" she asked.

"You mean here?"

"Yes, here," she said. "Besides teaching English classes, I'm the assistant principal of Whitewater High," she said, smiling. "And I know all the big guns in these districts, and—"

As she went on, I started thinking ahead. Like, to just what would happen if, by some miracle, I ended up in a Janesville or Whitewater high school. I had another few years to go. Let's say I did great . . . I would get an academic diploma, and then, if I had some financial help, I'd get into one of the colleges out there, and then—the thought shocked me—maybe I'd get a good job and marry someone like Sheri, and then, wall to wall, I would get swallowed up by that world. I just felt my heart beating faster and faster at the thought.

Then, after that microsecond, I tuned in again.

". . . if you wanted me to, Rico," she went on, "I could pull some strings and arrange an enrollment for you—no questions asked."

"Thank you, Mrs. Pearson, but I got to think about that," I told her in my most respectful voice. "I mean, I've always figured that if I ever went back to school, it would be in New York."

When I said that, Sheri, sitting by the fireplace,

looked over at me, a hurt expression on her face.

"So," Sheri's Moms said, "if a Wisconsin school is out, are there any in New York that you would like to attend?"

I went through all kinds of schools in my head.

The Bronx High School of Science was too brainy for my taste.

And short of going back to a Catholic high school like Cardinal Hayes, the only public school that, if the truth be told, really ever interested me was the High School of Music and Art, up on Convent Avenue in Harlem.

I told her so.

"Music and art?" she asked me.

"Yup," I said.

"Well, Rico," she went on, smiling. "While you may think we're all hicks out here—I happen to have a few colleagues from my teachers' college who are highly placed in the New York City education system. It wouldn't be any trouble for me to speak to them, should you want to go back to school in New York. If you are serious about pursuing this avenue, just let me know."

"Avenue"? "Pursuing"? What was it with some people? Me? I didn't want anything more than just to feel right about myself.

twenty-five

IT WAS LATE May. About one in the afternoon. I was hanging around the living room, trying to read the book of Cuban poems Wendy had given me for Christmas, when the door swung open. I looked up. It was Gilberto, home early from his job as some kind of inventory clerk in Milwaukee, a gig he had taken towards a "hands on" credits course for a business program at his college.

"What are you doing back home so soon?" I asked, glad to put the book down, so many of those Spanish words going over my head.

"I just quit my job."

"But what happened?"

He walked into the kitchen for a beer. I heard the cap popping off the bottle with a *shhhh*, and then he came back in.

"Let me tell you . . . ," he began, as he stretched out in a chair.

And then he explained the whole thing. One big boss told another boss to fire this guy whose arm had been crushed when this beer keg rolled off the back of a truck, and that boss ordered Gilberto to break the news. The thing is, he just wouldn't do it.

"Rico, you know that my Pops was a union organizer in New York? Before he got murdered, he did all kinds of things to improve conditions for the Latinos working in the sweatshops of Fashion Avenue. He got them a minimum wage and some other benefits."

I nodded, remembering how his Pops was always lecturing the older kids of the neighborhood about the importance of having principles.

"So I walked into the big boss's office and told him that it wasn't right for him to be firing someone because of an accident that wasn't his fault. In fact, I told him it was pretty f—king cold that the guy didn't even have medical benefits. Well, that MF"—and he finished off his bottle of beer with one mighty swig—"he just smiled and thanked me for voicing my concerns."

"Is that when you quit?" I asked him, as he got up for another beer.

"Uh-uh," he said. "After that, I thought about what my Pops would have done, and so I put together a petition asking for better sick pay and health coverage for the workers, but they were so scared of being fired, Rico, that not a one of them dared sign the thing. Let me tell you, it was like pissing in the wind."

That cracked me up: pissing in the wind? I'd never tried it.

"Anyway," he continued, halfway to emptying another bottle, "once that shit got back to the big boss, he called me into the office and accused me of being a commie agitator, but I just smiled at his ass, got up, and told him he could go screw himself, at which point, Rico, he called security and had them walk me out of the plant."

But he was smiling away. His tie was loosened, and he looked relaxed as hell.

"So that didn't bug you out?"

"Hell no! I had a boring job anyway. Keeping tabs on how many cases and kegs of beer go out on trucks ain't exactly big-time fun," he said, taking another swig. "Besides, I've already found myself a way cooler gig."

I could only imagine. I grinned and waited.

"You know those horse stables over by Roaring Brook Road? It's like a riding academy? Well, a guy in my basic lit class works there part-time, and this very morning he hooked me up with a job as a horse groom. The pay ain't great, but I'll be able to learn all about horses, even ride them, and if I get good enough, maybe end up becoming a riding instructor myself. And *that* pays!"

"So, you'll be making like a cowboy?" I asked, doing this Hopalong Cassidy thing in my chair.

"Yep. So the hell with that old job! I like being in the open air more anyway. It'll be way better than being cooped up in a plant."

I was happy for the guy. And glad that he was landing on his feet. Just seeing his easygoing ways, I wished I could be more like him, letting shit roll off me, and never looking back.

Oh, yeah. There was something else that happened that day. Like Gilberto letting me in on a little secret.

"Come out with me for a second," he said suddenly when he came back into the living room after changing his clothes. "But you got to keep what I'm gonna show you under your hat."

"Okeydokey," I said, using another Midwest term I'd picked up. What's he up to now? I wondered.

We went out into the yard, Rex following us. Beyond all the junk and into a field of corn, where new but sickly stalks were rising up out of the soil despite their neglect, we went down a narrow path for about a quarter mile. We came upon this cultivated plot of land where stood a crop of healthy-looking plants, most about a half-foot high or so and resembling, in my mind, the kind of poison oak bushes that grew in Riverside Park.

"What do you see there?" Gilberto asked me.

"Uh, plants?"

"Well, okay, Einstein, but what kind?" he asked, grinning.

I walked around. There must have been a zillion of these plants growing. They were thin-stemmed but flourishing, their leaves delicate with slightly brownish tips. I bent down to touch one, but I still didn't have any idea of what I was looking at.

"Okay, I give up. What's the story?" I asked him.

"The story, *mein dummkopf*, is that you are standing in the midst of a quarter acre of homegrown, all-American weed."

"Say what?"

"This, Rico my man, is marijuana in its natural state," Gilberto said with his hands proudly set against his ribs like he was the Jolly Green Giant.

"When did this all happen?" I stammered, marveling at the giant *huevos* on the guy.

"When Curt asked me one day if he could throw a few seeds down to see if anything would come up. I told him, why the F not," Gilberto said, beaming as we moved through those rows. "And, wouldn't you know it, within a few weeks some plants started coming up. I mean, this stuff is way easier than growing corn! Even the insects, for some reason, don't give a damn about it." He laughed. "They don't call it weed for nothing!"

"So, when did you plant all this?"

"In late April. Curt did most of the work."

"But how come you didn't ask me to help?"

Gilberto shrugged, smiling. "Hey, I've been saving you for outhouse duty!"

I made a face.

"Besides, we just wanted to keep it quiet."

We kept walking through the rows.

"The coolest thing is that unless you know it's out here, you wouldn't be able to tell," he said, stroking his goatee like a good-hearted devil. "If you look from the house or the driveway, all you see are the old cornfields."

"Well, that's for sure," I said, still stunned that I hadn't had a clue. "So what are you going to do with the stuff?"

"We don't even know if it'll be any good, but if it turns out to be beaucoup, we'll keep some for us, the rest we'll sell. Curt knows a lot of people."

For the first time in a long while, my radar flicked on.

"But aren't you worried about getting busted?"

"Like, who's going to know? You gonna tell anybody?"

"No!"

"So, what's there to worry about?" he asked me, putting his arm around my shoulder and walking me back to the house.

twenty-six

THOSE PLANTS GREW quietly, without a peep. So quietly I'd even started to forget about them. But then one Sunday morning in early June, Gilberto asked me what I would be doing that day.

I was sitting on the porch steps eating a piece of buttered toast with jelly.

"I'm going out to Whitewater for a picnic with Sheri's family. You know, to meet them for the first time."

"That's too bad, Rico," Gilberto said, "'cause today's the day."

"For what, cleaning the outhouse again?"

"To gather up the Lord's bounty," he said, grinning like crazy.

"The Lord's what?" Then it hit me. "Oh, you mean—Oh!"

"Yep, today's the day," he said, rubbing his hands.

"Damn, wish I could help," I said. "But I can't be canceling on Sheri. I think it would really blow her head."

"Aw, don't even sweat it," Gilberto said. "Between me and Curt and Jimmy, it'll be like a snap. You just go do your thing, all right, little bro?"

And, even if I didn't still have a fuzzy-ball crew cut like I used to, he rubbed my head for good luck.

By late morning, just about everybody in the household had dragged their asses out of bed. Bonnie in a blue nightshirt, yawning and stretching her fine body out in the kitchen. Wendy, still sleepy-eyed, coming into the living room in fluffy slippers and holding a bowl of granola. Polly and Jimmy sat sipping herbal tea (!) by the kitchen table, while Gilberto and Curt, completely psyched and in coveralls, were already out by the barn gathering their tools—shears, shovels, and trowels, some wheelbarrows, too. As I was leaving, I saw Gilberto, whistling happily and heading out the door with several boxes of black, heavy-duty garbage bags.

Like he had told me, it was the day.

＊　＊　＊

I walked about half a mile along the road from Gilberto's place. Coming to Route 26 going east, I stuck my thumb out. Maybe because I was wearing coveralls and had my guitar with me, all kinds of vehicles drove by, but then, the county sheriff, this guy named Nat, the coolest cop I'd ever met, pulled up in his brown Oldsmobile, rolling down his window and saying, "Hey, Rico, hop in."

It wasn't my first lift with him. Sometimes when I got off from my shift at the station and he was just starting his own, with not much to do—it wasn't like that town was a hotbed of crime at eight in the morning—he'd pick me up and drive me over to the farm. We always talked about music. And even if he wore a brown uniform and a big-ass sheriff's badge on his lapel, and had a .38 in his holster, he was about as opposite from an NYC cop as one could be. His black hair was long, falling over his ears, and he had these thick Elvis sideburns. The Grateful Dead or Jimi Hendrix was usually blaring from his tape deck. A peace symbol dangled off his rearview mirror. And I swear that just about every time I rode with him, the insides of that Oldsmobile smelled like pot.

"So, Rico, where you heading?" he asked me that day.

"Out to Whitewater," I said.

"Oh yes sirree, Whitewater, a great little town. What's going on there?"

"A picnic," I said. "With my girl's family."

"Ah, sweet love," he said, kind of daydreaming. "How's that working out?"

"Pretty good, I guess."

"You guess?" he asked, shaking his head. "Well, whatever you have going on in the romance department, be careful. Me, I had it all, traveling all over the state playing with different groups when I was a kid like you. I mean, that was beautiful, son, but once you settle down, watch out!"

"What do you mean?"

He laughed.

"Well, if you aren't careful, you'll turn around and find yourself married with three kids on a farm somewhere."

"That doesn't sound so bad," I said, trying to stay with him.

"And it isn't. When I get home at the end of the day to my Nancy, it's just about the happiest feeling in the world. But sometimes, when all this stuff is going on, with one kid being sick, and the other not doing so well in school, and the other throwing tantrums, I sometimes feel like getting the heck out of there."

"Wow," I said.

"Yes sir, wow," he said, coming to an inter-section—ahead just miles and miles of farms, one after the other. "When I'm driving sometimes, I just get a hankering"—another midwestern word I never heard in New York—"for the wide-open spaces. Just wanting to hit the road and experience whatever might come my way without having to think about anything else, you know?"

"I guess I do."

He was always philosophizing around me. And always happy to share his life's story. That day he told me about how he once hitched a ride to Boulder, Colorado, to participate in a music festival, and how he liked that town and being near the Rockies so much, he almost stayed there for good.

"And I would have, except for one little thing—my then girlfriend was expecting our first." He shook his head. "And that changed everything, Rico."

He glanced over at me and almost had a look of

longing in his eyes. Like his eyes were telling me, *Be careful what you do, son*. But then he smiled and, pulling over to the side of the road, dropped me off by the route to Whitewater.

"Now, you take care, Rico, and have yourself a nice day," Sheriff Nat said as he drove off.

I caught another ride with a bakery truck—all that fresh bread smelling really nice—and I got out to Whitewater just before noon.

Sheri was waiting for me by her door, her mother beside her.

The first thing I did was to give Sheri's Moms a peck on her cheek, but despite her friendly Betty Crocker demeanor, she just barely squeezed out a smile. I think she was annoyed that I hadn't acted on any of her offers.

Anyway, we got into her station wagon and drove off to a state park, about half an hour away, a really pretty place that looked like something out of a storybook, with a big lake and a waterfall cascading down these rocks. Sheri's family was waiting for us under the shade of this massive oak tree, where some tables had been set up. She had two older brothers,

Chuck and Randy—tall, lanky, blond guys, who wore the crispest clothing I'd ever seen in my life. Their little kids were running around blowing soap bubbles and chasing puppies, while their wives prepared the food.

It was a completely wholesome kind of event, as all-American as apple pie, with a barbecue grill and blankets neatly spread out on the lawn by the pretty lake. Unlike the kinds of outings I used to go on with my family to Coney Island, it was quiet, no portable radios blasting, no folks passing around bottles of beer, no impromptu dancing, but also, no fights or drunk people pissing in the water. I mean it was civilized.

I had to put up with a few mild "somebody around here needs some money for a haircut" kind of jibes, but I was kind of having a good time, anyway. I took a rowboat out with Sheri, feeding pieces of bread to the ducks and swans that floated along. I tried archery. I played horseshoes. Her brothers seemed to like the fact that I was quiet.

"For a hippie, he isn't too bad," I heard one of them say, joking to his wife as he saw me fiddling with my guitar.

His remark hit me like a slap to the back of my head. A hippie? Me?

When I was little, it was *"el pobrecito"*—or "the poor little guy"—'cause I was sick.

And then, because I was so much lighter than my cousins, they nicknamed me *"el alemán"*—or "the German," besides the old standby of "Pinky."

Then there was "a fairy nice fellow" and "mama's boy" and "douche bag" because my Moms kept me on a tight leash.

Then "whitey," then "jive MF," and, oh yeah, that other name, "dark dude," down in the projects.

I stared off at the lake. It looked all tranquil, with the tree boughs and sky reflecting so prettily off its surface. But what was underneath?

I washed down a big, thick, juicy hamburger and some potato salad with lemonade, and walked out to some rocks by the lakeside. Just below the surface ripples, fish slithered like phantoms in and out of their secret hiding places. And in that quivering water, I saw my own face looking back up at me, but all distorted, and in an instant, it hit me that I looked a lot like my Pops.

And then I thought about my Poppy getting up to

go to work, even if he didn't feel like it, and I wished that he could be sitting right there in my place, taking it easy.

And I wished that little Isabel could have been there too, eating up a storm: that potato salad, hamburgers and sausage sandwiches, corn on the cob all slathered and dripping with butter (and there was no more delicious corn anywhere than in Wisconsin—I mean for those folks, corn was like our plantains!), Isabel would have liked that! I could just see her eating five ears, with a big grin on her face.

Then my Pops again. I wished he was lying out on a blanket in the shade, half asleep with his stomach full and a nice breeze to make him all relaxed.

Even my Moms was part of the picture. I could see her sitting by the lakeside, with a sun hat on her head, her feet dipping into the water and laughing when the ducks came by—my Moms calling out to Sheri's folks in Spanish, even if they didn't understand it, *"¡Ay, ay, ay, los patos! Mira los patos!"* and just happy because she was out of the goddamn city.

But that was just inside my head.

With the fresh air, the aroma of grilling meat, the little birds that came swooping over the water, and all the trees around seeming to breathe—with everything nice, nice, nice, I should have been really enjoying myself.

Somehow, I couldn't.

Then Sheri called out to me. She wanted me to play the guitar for them. So, we had a little singalong.

"Oh, Susannah," "Row, Row, Row Your Boat," and "If I Had a Hammer" were the kinds of songs they asked for; you know, the stuff that in real life would make me want to throw up. But that was what they were into, even the littlest of their children, who didn't really know the words, joining in.

It was sweet.

It was wholesome.

It was one hundred percent American.

And, man, I couldn't wait to get back to the farm.

Her family seemed to like me, though, and by the time it started to get dark, Sheri's brothers had gotten used to the idea that I was going out with their little sister.

Later, her oldest brother Randy offered to drive me back.

Sheri sat beside me in the front seat. The farm was about an hour away and, as I said, it was getting dark.

* * *

And thank God for that.

Thank God because while making small talk with Randy I asked him, "What do you do, anyway?"

"Well," he said, shifting gears. "I got me a little Cessna that I fly around sometimes on the weekends. And I like a little softball game every now and then. But what I mainly do is work for the state police. I run the desk here in Whitewater."

"Really?" I said, thinking, Holy shit!

"Yes, sir. Sergeant Randy Pearson at your service. Got a revolver and holster under the back seat." He must have seen my expression because he laughed. "Does that make you nervous?"

"Not at all," I said, feeling nervous as hell.

"Anyway, you have to direct me to where you're staying. I don't really know that stretch over there."

When we came to the dirt road leading up the hill to the farm, you couldn't see much of anything. The only lights were those coming from the car's headlights and the house itself. It was a moonless night.

And thank God for that, I say again.

Because just as we had come to the top of the dirt road and had pulled in towards the house, we hit something, loud thumps sounding under the chassis. We all got out of the station wagon. Shining his flashlight on the ground, Randy said, "Some bozo's left a pile of garbage bags right plumb in the middle of your drive-way."

Goddamn! And kiss my ass good-bye, I was thinking. Like maybe those garbage bags were filled with all those marijuana plants. My poor stomach suddenly twisting, and my mind cut ahead to everybody in Gilberto's house being marched off to jail, including me.

"Hold up, I'll move them," I offered, like I was trying to be super helpful.

"Nah, it'll be easier if I back the station wagon up," he said, since a few were partially stuck under the wheels.

So he backed up. Then he got out again.

"Not a great place for your friends to leave their garbage, Rico," he said. "Here, let's move it over to the side of the road so no one else drives into it."

He picked up two of the bags and tossed them over to his left. I grabbed four more and did the same.

Then I hurriedly thanked the sergeant for the lift, and Sheri for the nice afternoon. As I got my guitar out the back, I told her I hoped to see her again soon. Then I heard the porch door slap open.

Gilberto had stepped outside. He walked over to say hello.

"Hey, Sheri," he said to my girl. "You all have a good time today?"

"Oh, I think we did," she said in her quiet way.

And then he shook hands with her brother, introduced himself.

Everybody was all smiles.

Then her brother backed the station wagon around. Just before taking off down the dirt road, he stuck his head out the window.

"Rico, it was good meeting you," he said. "I expect you to be nice to my sister, don't forget that."

"Easiest thing in the world," I said.

The moment they were gone, I grasped Gilberto's arm.

"Uh, Gilberto, do these bags have what I think they have in them?"

"Yes sirree, they certainly do. So far we've filled up about fifteen of the suckers, and we're not even done. We're gonna have a buttload of Wisconsin home-grown."

"So, ah, why were they sitting in front of the house?"

"I don't know—we just piled them up there, that's all."

"Uh-huh," I said. "Well, when we came in, we kind of ran into them."

"Oh man! Did they break?"

"No, but we had to move them off the road."

"Yeah, so what's the big deal? At least the bags aren't broken."

"Well, the thing is, Sheri's brother is a state trooper."

"He's a what? And you let him drive you home? Are you stupid?"

"I didn't even know that until we were halfway here. What could I do, jump out of the car?"

Then Gilberto gave me a bad-assed look, his face glaring yellow under the porch light. For a moment I almost thought he wouldn't even let me into the house. I guess even guys like Gilberto have their moods.

"So, after seeing Sheri all this time, she never told you?"

"Nope." I shrugged. "Hey, Gilberto, I'm sorry. I didn't know!"

"For crying out loud, Rico. Next time you come back here with strangers, do your homework first, okay?" Then, pushing the porch door open with his boot, he went inside, shaking his head, like I was the biggest doofus in the world.

That's all he said about it, but that night I kind of felt bad, not just because I had almost messed up, but because it was the first time I thought that Gilberto might be getting tired of having me around.

Part 8 **JIMMY'S PROMISE**

twenty-seven

THIS MIGHT SOUND funny, but, a few weeks later, when we had to clean the outhouse, to get back on Gilberto's good side I acted like I was actually excited about it, as if I was an old hand already, and just so thrilled about shoveling out that goop again. "I hear and obey!" I told him. (Okay, it was a "white lie.") This time, though, we had a smaller crew—just Gilberto, me, and Curt dealing with that sludge. (A little advice on behalf of the United Outhouse Cleaners of America: Get yourself nose plugs, my brothers.) On that day Jimmy was nowhere to be found, and believe you me, Gilberto was none too happy about it when Jimmy told him he just didn't have the time. He said that between his work at the sign shop and other jobs, he could hardly even hang out with Polly, except at night, when, uh, he stayed in her room.

Like I said, Gilberto wasn't too happy to hear that.

"So, what's up with your boy Jimmy?" Gilberto asked me. "What, he's suddenly too good for us?"

I just shrugged, shoveling more of the sludge out.

"Jimmy's just into this whole new thing. I mean, he's come a long way, Gilberto—thanks to you and—"

But he cut me off.

"Does he think *I* like having to do this?"

"It's just that Jimmy's been busy lately," I said, trying to defend him.

"Well, you should tell him to lose the attitude he's had lately."

I was thinking that if only Gilberto had seen how down and out Jimmy used to be when he was shooting H, he'd feel really good about how much Jimmy had changed. And he really had. For one thing, he'd stopped smoking—Polly being a health nut. And he had become a much more careful dresser—Polly always dragging him up to Madison to good clothing stores. He'd bought himself two new pairs of eyeglasses, leaving the Scotch-taped pair behind forever. And he even wanted to look like an artist: bought himself a beret and instead of that red bandana, took to wearing a silk scarf, like some Frenchy in a movie.

I had to admit, I was sort of missing the guy. I guess there can never be too much of a good thing, but the fact was that, to my freaking surprise, Jimmy was turning into one heck of a success story. He never even wanted to talk about the old neighborhood. He was doing so well that just about everybody in Janesville was seeing, in one place or the other, his artwork. He was all over town. If you went down Main Street and saw the new Brown Cow ice-cream shop sign, that was Jimmy's. And so was the Chuckling Chicken, Mr. Friendly's Hardware with its talking hammer and saw, and the Bouncing Baby maternity shop. He was becoming known as a local Picasso of "store signage." His boss even offered to hire him full-time, with a raise, but Jimmy already had other things going. Like painting flower-power designs and "Rocky Mountain High" sunsets and rock band logos on vans, skulls and bones on motorcycles, and racing flairs on hopped-up stock cars, like the one that my boss, Mr. Jenkins, kept in the back.

He was so busy that I was starting to get worried.

Not about Jimmy—I was happy that he was coming up in the world—but about his illustrating *Dark Dude*.

Like, I'd see him in the yard working on some biker's Harley, painting a devil's face along the gas tank; I'd see him getting picked up at the farm by someone he was doing a job for, carrying a box filled with brushes, cans of enamel paint and spray paints, and vanishing for most of that day. He had even come down to the station with me a few nights, working on Mr. Jenkins's T-bird, painting lightning streaks along its side, and an atomic explosion on the hood.

Okay, I admit it. I was getting a little jealous. And maybe a little pissed. I mean, months after he had promised to illustrate *Dark Dude*, back at Christmas, it still wasn't done. It was barely started! The first page, just half-finished, with a super "splash" in pencil of a masked, two-toned hero bursting through a glass door, a lá Jack Kirby, still sat pinned to the drawing board, my handwritten script, lying in the same spot, untouched and unmoved, week after week.

After a while it began to drag my head.

I didn't want to make a big deal out of it, so one morning I got home and just took that script up to my room, stashing it away in a drawer.

In my head I wrote "R.I.P." on those pages.

And it got me thinking. After nearly a year out there, what did *I* have to show for myself? Okay, I was trying out something new, living out there, and I did have Sheri

as my pal, but I just wasn't getting anywhere, not like
Jimmy.

But was I going to hassle him about it?

No way. I mean, he'd come so far from his dope-
shooting days, I just kept my trap shut and did my usual
thing.

Every time I saw Jimmy, we still slapped five.

And I still sat with him on the porch—our countrified
"stoop"—drinking beers in the late afternoons. I never
mentioned that story, not even once, and I was amazed
that he hadn't noticed the script was missing.

But, one day, he finally did. Coming up to me, he
looked all upset.

"Why'd you take them pages, Rico?" Jimmy asked me.
"I was gonna get around to them, I swear on my mother!"

Yeah, right, I thought.

"What can I tell you," I said, trying to be cool but
feeling my face grow hot. "I just got tired of looking at it
sitting there, that's all!" Then I let it all out. "It's like you
don't take me seriously, like you still think doing a comic
is some stupid little kid idea."

He was kind of stunned; I was on the verge of
losing it. Like a stupid little kid. But I couldn't stop.
"So just forget it, all right, Jimmy?" I yelled, getting up

from the porch like I had something better to do. "It's no big deal."

But I somehow pressed some kind of button.

"Hey, hold up, Rico. I'm really sorry," he said, coming after me. "It's just that I've been so damn busy lately between the shop and all these other jobs I've been doing." He glanced at me, a look of pure wonder in his eyes. "The folks around here actually like my stuff."

And that memory, the one of his Pops throwing him a dime for one of his drawings, came back to me. I needed to let him speak his piece.

"Don't sweat it. It's cool, all right?"

"No, it's not. Look, I had some jobs lined up this coming weekend, but I'm gonna blow them off, just to work on your story, all right?" He paused for a moment, then said, "I wouldn't have any of this if you hadn't hauled my ass out of the city. I owe you big-time."

"Are you being for real?"

"Yeah, man, I swear on it," he said, crossing his heart.

And we slapped five.

But there was an itty-bitty catch.

"Like, I know I can do it in one weekend, but I could use a little help," he said, playing with the scarf around his neck.

"Uh-huh," I said, giving him a look, imagining all these little schemes churning away inside his head. "Like what kind of help?"

"Remember them little white pills you once got at the gas station? You know, that truckers' shit?"

"White crosses?" I asked.

"Yeah!" he said enthusiastically. "Get me some, and I'll be primed for three days!"

White crosses were a kind of speed. Harmless-looking because they were smaller than aspirins, those white pills, marked by crosses, taken two or three at a time, were strong enough to keep truckers wired and awake during entire three-day cross-country hauls. So wired that half the times you saw a tractor-trailer rig turned over, or crushed against a wall, it was because the driver had lost his mind. It was teeth-grinding stuff. The few times I tried just one at the station, I felt weird for hours and couldn't sleep afterwards.

"I don't know, Jimmy," I hedged. "I mean, you been doing so good lately."

I mean, I didn't need him to illustrate the story that bad.

He got testy.

"Oh yeah? What are you, my mother now?"

"No man, but—"

"Here's the thing," he said. "Polly's gonna be away this weekend, and if I can just be left alone for a few days, I'm pretty sure I can finish the whole thing. I swear, it would be just a one-time thing."

Yeah, I thought. It always starts like a one-time thing.

"I don't know, Jimmy," I said, shaking my head.

Then he got an idea.

"How about we flip a coin?"

"Say what?"

"Yeah, like let the man upstairs decide for us, all right?" he said, pointing towards the sky.

"I guess so." I shrugged.

He took out a quarter.

Heads was yes for the white cross; tails no.

Jimmy flipped that quarter way high, let it bounce down on the grass.

It came up tails: no white cross.

Still, Jimmy spent most of that weekend hunched over that drawing board, with a pencil and kneading eraser in hand, drinking beers and cranking out the panels. I was amazed: A cartooning book said that a single page was a really good daily rate for a professional comic-book artist, but he drew up ten pages in two days, and without any of them little pills.

And he penciled in all the dialogue and thought balloons and captions. Giant WHAMS! KABOOMS! and ZZZZZZZZS! exploded across the pages.

But it had a price: Come that Monday, he couldn't get up for work, just slept through most of the day. Come Tuesday, though, he was back on his feet and feeling proud as hell.

So was I. Those pages looked great!

I would have mailed them on Monday, but I just had to hang on to them for a while, looking at them about every chance I got. I couldn't believe how professional they looked.

Come Wednesday, I bought a big padded mailing envelope and went over to the post office in Janesville to send the pages out to that comic-book company in New York City, special delivery.

Passing the envelope over to the postal clerk, my hands were shaking.

So, after that weekend, I was really appreciating the hell out of my man Jimmy, getting my two cents in about how great we would be as a comic-book team.

"Just think about it, James. You and me going back to New York first class! Showing folks we turned out to be something! Now, wouldn't that be great, huh?" I said happily. I couldn't wait to hear back from DC Comics.

But one late afternoon, when I brought that up again, Jimmy's head was somewhere else. He just didn't want to hear about it.

"Rico, before you start going on and on, there's something I got to tell you."

"Yeah?" I said.

"Come October, I'm gonna be nineteen, and, well, I got to be thinking about my future and all."

"Yeah, so," I said, feeling wary.

"Thing is, me and Polly, we been talking about other things."

The way he said it made me feel like I was about to have a carpet pulled out from under me.

"I mean, Rico, I like it out here," he said. "It ain't perfect. But man, nobody hassles me, and I'm making some bucks doing that diddly sign work. And you know what else?"

"What?"

"I'm only a semester short of my high school diploma,

and Polly—well, you never even really ever sat down to talk to the girl, have you?"

"I guess not," I said, a little embarrassed.

"Well, she believes that I can be doing all kinds of things. Like going to a college and stuff, even if I didn't graduate from high school—"

"Thanks to your Pops," I couldn't resist adding.

"Yeah, well, she . . . she thinks I can get into a college anyway, 'cause of my artwork." Then I swear I saw him actually smiling. "What I'm telling you is that for the first time, I got me some possibilities." He had substituted gum chewing for his cigarette habit, so he took a Wrigley's out of his pocket and popped it into his mouth. "Like, did you know that Polly's from Seattle?"

I didn't.

"We talk about going back there one day, if we end up together. But I'm just as fine with staying out here." He had one hand in the other, cracking his knuckles. "I just don't have anything to go back to in New York, that's all."

And I looked at him. He'd gone through so much crap. What *did* he have to go back to?

His lousy Pops.

That dark basement.

Water bugs.

Rats.

His Pops punching him in the head.

No money.

Skag.

Junkies.

Scratching all over.

That dealer Clyde, from the projects.

Static, static, static.

And I knew he was right. He really didn't have anything to go back to.

"But let me hip you to something about yourself," Jimmy was saying. "The day *you* go home, no matter how mad your folks might be, in the end they'll be jumping up, all happy to see your ass. Crazy as your Moms might be, she loves you. And they all do, Rico, and that's saying a whole lot!"

He was chomping on that stick of gum.

"So I know I got to find that shit somewhere else. It surely ain't waiting for me in New York."

All right, so I was getting the feeling he was cutting me loose, and didn't say anything, which is another way of saying a lot.

"Look, I had to tell you, sooner or later," he went on.

"It's just something I've been thinking, that's all." And maybe because I was looking crestfallen, he added, "You and me are still a team. But even if that comic-book stuff should turn into some kind of thing, I got to be scoping out the bigger picture. Like, am I gonna be for real about life one day or just another bullshit hangout artist?"

The only thing missing was the kind of inspirational music you hear in some of those sappy movies.

"And that's something you should be thinking about too, Rico. I mean, are you gonna be hanging out here forever?"

I shrugged, Sheri's Moms's offer coming back to me.

"I don't know, man."

"Well, you best be getting real about it," he said, just as Polly came out of the house in her sunbonnet, a sketch pad in hand.

"Come on, Jimmy," she said to him, smiling sweetly. "The light's great right now!"

Jimmy got up to join Polly. "Catch you later, Rico."

"Yeah, later," I said.

One thing about being on a farm is that when you start feeling lonely, you can always find stuff to do. Like spraying insecticide, mowing the lawn, pulling up clumps of weed growing by the fences, and going over to the barn to check out the laundry lines on which we had hung the pot plants to dry—they called it "curing"—and to make sure that weed crop wasn't getting moldy. Even if I didn't know what I was doing, I would pinch those leaves to feel if they were getting any drier. And if I found a plant that seemed to be getting there, I'd drop it into a wooden box in a corner of the barn so that Curt, being our resident expert, could look it over later and decide whether it was worth grinding up and giving it a tryout in a pipe.

So that day, after talking with Jimmy and looking around in the barn, I just felt like taking a walk, not on the main roads, but along the foot trails and dirt roads of neighboring farms and woods. Since I didn't have to go to work that night, I wasn't in any kind of hurry. I passed by this abandoned farmhouse, with an old wagon in its yard and its storm cellar doors turned up—it could have been the farm Dorothy lived on in *The Wizard of Oz*.

And I then laughed out loud: I was living on nearly the same type of a farm!

And something about being in the countryside made me feel a little bit like that kid Huckleberry Finn, except—and I laughed out loud when I made this

connection, damn!—my Jim had left his slavery behind.
At least I had done one thing right, even if my man
Jimmy would be moving on without me one day.

Yes indeedy, that blew my head, 'cause it made me
think about my own future, and I wasn't too hot on that.

I was glad I had brought along a bag of peanuts, which
I'd stashed in the pockets of my coveralls. Each time I
saw squirrels or chipmunks hustling around the trees, I
stopped to feed those little dudes. I especially loved it
when the squirrels would come down the tree trunks and
approach me, their tails pointing up and wriggling, their
cute toy-sized mugs quivering and shit.

"Eat up, you guys," I said, tossing them the peanuts,
and thinking about how my Pops used to do the same
thing in Riverside Park when I was little, my Pops getting
all happy about seeing the squirrels there.

It hit me so square I thought I would turn around
and see him standing behind me, leaning over a fence
and feeding them squirrels too. He'd once told me about
growing up on a farm back in Cuba, with all kinds of
animals around.

"What kind?" I'd asked.

"Oh, cows and pigs and chickens and horses. And we
had mango and avocado trees everywhere." Then he got

all wistful. "When I wasn't much older than you," he said, "I was already riding horses and visiting our neighbors' farms. People were nice, not like they are here."

My Pops then smiled, a beautiful but sad smile.

And then I thought about my Pops on a horse, as a young man, all happy, instead of looking so lost when he'd come home from the subway after work, with big perspiration stains on his shirt and his tired face looking like he'd just been in hell.

I guess you can't turn off your brain.

And that's hooked up with your heart.

And the heart with the soul.

Man, somehow, even in the midst of farm country, I was feeling low.

I kept walking, maybe for an hour, checking out the cows who would come right up to the fence when they saw me, their collar bells clanging. And the butterflies that would sort of loop along with you, like keeping you company.

I decided to cut through a cornfield, about a half a mile wide, on the other side of which was a meadow. Beyond was another road that led back to Gilberto's place. Soon, I was walking between all these rows of six-foot-high cornstalks, too tall for me to see over them. It was kind of cool to see nothing but corn and sky. But after a while, as I got deeper into that field, I just couldn't tell where I was. It was like the sky and hill that I had seen just a few minutes before had vanished, rows and rows of cornstalks surrounding me.

That field was hard to move through, even if I stayed on the narrow tracks of clumpy earth alongside the corn rows. Thinking that I was heading in one direction, I'd see a break in the stalks and go that way. And then seeing another, I would do the same, over and over again, until it hit me that I was lost.

And let me tell you, boy did that feel like I was inside some weird dream.

I told myself to be cool and not to panic, but just thinking about getting stranded in that field, in the pitch-dark after sunset, really scared me. I mean, when it got dark out there, it got really dark. Like, you couldn't see a thing. And so, instead of just walking, I started running, figuring that if I stuck to one direction, I'd have to come out somewhere.

Sweat poured off my face.

It was steamy inside of there, almost like a jungle.

My heart was pounding.

My hands got nicked from hitting the stalks.

I imagined crazy things.

Like the cornstalks suddenly moving around on their own, like in a science-fiction movie about plants from outer space.

A headline in the local gazette: "Teenage Boy Eaten by Corn!"

My Moms somehow knowing about this, even if she was far away.

"You see, Rico!" I could hear her saying. "You really don't know what you're doing!"

My Pops calling to me from the distance: "This way, boy. This way!"

And then, just as I was swearing that I was the biggest dope in the state of Wisconsin, I saw sunlight breaking through some rows ahead, and so I ran even faster and, gasping for breath, finally burst out into that meadow.

Then this crazy thing happened.

In the far distance, way over the other side of the farm, I could swear I saw my Poppy riding a horse along the dirt road. He was in a cowboy hat, sitting high and proud in the saddle, his posture erect. I blinked my eyes, thinking I was maybe having heatstroke or something. But when I opened them again, the rider on his horse, like an elongating shadow, kept coming closer.

And then I realized that it wasn't my Poppy, but Gilberto himself, with a wide grin on his face and a cowboy hat upon his head, mounted on a chestnut mare. I mean that guy was like a chameleon.

Little by little he drew near.

And you know what? Seeing him made me feel so happy I started running towards him.

"Holy Jesus, Gilberto!" I said, feeling a little out of breath. "Where the hell'd you get a horse?"

Gilberto smiled, patting the side of that horse's head.

"Rico," he said. "Meet Sally. Of all the horses I've been grooming over at the Roaring Brook Stables, this one horse and me have been getting along so well that I'm thinking about buying her for the farm."

And Gilberto stroked that pretty horse's neck, and if I wasn't imagining things, she snorted back in appreciation, tossing her shaggy-maned head.

"So you're really into this horse thing," I remarked.

"You best believe it."

Proudly he added, "Sally here is three years old."

Then the horse, immense as she was, saw a white-winged butterfly fluttering by and took a few steps back in apprehension. Gilberto pulled gently on her reins, saying, "Whoa, girl, whoa." When she'd calmed down, he offered me a ride.

"On the horse?"

"No, on a freaking flying saucer. What do you think?"

"You're kidding, right?"

"Come on and try it!"

Climbing down off Sally and holding her steady, Gilberto told me to put one foot in the stirrup and then to lift myself up onto the saddle.

"Now what you do, Rico, is press your legs against her torso a few times," he told me.

"What's that do?"

"You weigh like twelve pounds to her," he said. "But when you do that, she knows you're there."

I did, and it hit me then that this warm-muscled creature under me was probably the sort of horse that my Pops used to ride in Cuba. And I thought about how I'd love to tell him I'd ridden one too.

Nervous and as uncertain as I was, I asked, "And so, now what?"

"Just pull up a bit on the bridle, and say 'Chuck, chuck.'"

"'Chuck, chuck'?"

"Yeah. You can say anything, really. It's the tone of voice that does it."

So I went "Chuck, chuck," and tightened my legs. Then, thinking about what my Pops might have said, I added, *"¡Andale!"* and just like that Sally started moving forward.

At first we went around in a little circle with Gilberto leading us. Then we started going along one of the dirt roads that cut through the back fields, and for just a few seconds I had the strangest feeling about what my life might have been like were I raised in Cuba instead of New York City.

I would have worn a *guajiro*'s straw hat and white pantaloons, and I would have never spoken even a word of English. And instead of fields of Wisconsin corn surrounding me, there would have been sugar cane plantations and palm trees everywhere I looked. And I would have never listened to the Beatles and Bob Dylan or read so many comics and science-fiction books: I would have been me, but nothing like a hippie, and certainly not the kind of kid who gets lost in a cornfield.

"So what do you think?" Gilberto asked me as we approached the farm. "Isn't riding the most tasty thing?"

"Sure is," I said, my butt aching like hell.

Then I climbed down.

"I got to get her back to the stables," Gilberto said. "But any time you want to, come on over and I'll let you practice, okay?"

Then he swung up onto the saddle, and with his cowboy hat cocked over his brow, Gilberto rode off like a vaquero of old—while I was feeling like things were definitely cool between us again.

But you never know when something new will be coming down on you. A few days later, we were driving by the Dietrichs' farm on the way to the station—Gilberto giving Dierdra a friendly wave with his hat and a few honks. She was sitting beside her father on their porch, looking all forlorn.

"It's the ones who get away that kill you the most!" Gilberto said, shaking his head.

Then as we passed their silo, which looked like a giant ding-dong, he said he wanted to talk to me about something important. I was bracing myself for a new lecture about who knows what.

"So what's up?" I finally asked him.

And Gilberto got all serious.

"I don't know how to put this to you, Rico," he began.

"But I was talking to my Moms on the horn last night."

"How's she doing?" I asked.

"Really great," he said. "Just bought herself a little getaway near Mayagüez, in west P.R., you know, with the money I gave her. But that's not all we talked about."

We had come to a railroad crossing just as red lights started to blink and a divider came down to halt all traffic—namely us. A train was barreling along the track, the engineer blowing a horn, the *chugga, chugga, chugga* as its cars flashed by us, too loud to talk over.

Then it passed.

"See," Gilberto went on when it quieted down and the divider lifted. "We were talking about the neighborhood, and when I asked her what was going on lately, she told me this thing about your Pops."

We crossed the tracks.

"Aw, man, what?" I asked, worried that he might have had another heart attack.

"Just that every time she runs into your Pops on the street, it's like he's so broken up that he can barely speak."

Man, I didn't need to hear that.

"And that got me to thinking," he said.

Uh-oh.

"I mean, Rico, it's been a year since you came out

here, and well, even if I love you, my little bro, the way it's been going down with your folks—it just doesn't seem right to me." And he shook his head.

To be truthful, I was a little miffed to hear him say that. I was already feeling bad enough, thinking about my Moms and Pops every single day, but—damn my luck—once again, even one of my best buddies wasn't seeing me for who I was: just somebody trying to get along, without hassling anyone else.

"But it hasn't been easy for me, either," I told him. "You think I like hearing that my Pops is so messed up?"

Gilberto pulled over just then and turned to me.

"Rico, don't you know that you're goddamn lucky to still have your Pops? If I still had mine, I would be kissing the ground."

I had no answer to that. And I didn't even look over his way: I just wanted to get the F out of his truck. I mean, as much as Gilberto had always said he would be always watching my back, I got the feeling that right now he was just blowing smoke up my butt, by not being straight and telling me he wanted me to go. I couldn't understand why he would—I'd been paying him rent for the longest time, at first for both me and Jimmy, and I was getting along with everybody in the house. And when it came to cleaning the outhouse, did I once ever complain? Hell no. I just got down into that shit and did the responsible thing. Like, I was pulling my weight and stuff, big-time.

But there he was, laying a trip on me.

"Rico, the thing is," he went on, "you can't string your folks out forever. Doesn't your freaking conscience ever bother you?"

"Well, sure it does," I said. "But, goddamn, if you think I want to stay out here and turn into some countrified white-bread MF, you got that dead wrong too. I mean, I'd have to be out of my freakin' mind!"

Gilberto rubbed his nose, thinking.

"Calm down, I ain't attacking you. I'm just trying to help you."

"Making me feel worse isn't helping. And it ain't right! Why can't you lighten up on me and let me decide for myself what I'm gonna do?"

When I looked at him, in his lacquered cowboy hat, it hit me that he was blissfully unaware of just how much he had changed. He was still Gilberto, with a whole lot of girl hound in his heart, and a good guy, but at the same time, I didn't think he had any idea of how far he was already drifting from what he had been about. Like, he was becoming less Puerto Rican and more a Midwest guy every day. And maybe that's what I was afraid was going to happen to me.

"Fine. If you gotta know," I told him finally, "I've been thinking about all that stuff, and Gilberto, I know what I'm gonna do, but I just don't know how I'm gonna do it, okay?" Then I couldn't help myself. "And . . . well . . ."—I glanced over at him—"I'm kinda scared."

"Of what?"

"Hey, of ending up in reform school. And my Moms, all right? I mean I can't imagine them forgiving me." There was something else. "And besides, I don't know how I'd break it to Sheri, you know?"

"It's up to you," he said, starting the engine up again. "You can either be a man about it, or a wussy, but I'll tell you one thing, I got my own conscience too. And for me, this whole thing is starting to make me feel bad—real bad—for your folks."

"So are you kicking me out?" I asked. "Because if you are, that ain't right either. Just let me decide, okay?"

"Yeah, yeah," he said, holding up his right hand, like he was trying to ward off some evil spirits.

Then we drove to the station in silence for the rest of the way.

✳ ✳ ✳

I'd settled into a chair in the gas station office, trying not to get too bummed by my conversation with Gilberto. If he only knew how I messed around every night, during the quiet hours, trying to write a letter to my parents, and the questions I was always asking myself. Would I address it to "Mom and Pop" or "Mommy and Poppy" or "*Mamá y Papá*"? And should it be in English or in Spanish, even if my Spanish was half-assed? Or how I was studying a Spanish grammar book, and had gotten me a Spanish dictionary that I kept in the station and fiddled around with, not only trying to read those poems by José Martí, but trying to write that letter in Spanish, by translating my English with that dictionary. But the problem was, I just didn't know what to say.

I'd write, *Dear Mom and Pop, I know you are probably mad at me, but I want you to know I'm sorry, and miss you very much.* But then I'd cross that out and begin again: *I wanted you to know that I'm okay and have been worried and sad that I upset you....* I'd cross that out, and no matter whatever approach I took, in Spanish or English, it just never seemed right. I was always asking their forgiveness, but then when I would think about it, I would wonder what I was asking them to forgive. To forgive me for just trying to get out of a home life that was breaking my heart to watch? Or for wanting to cut loose all the kick-ass nastiness of the city, or for wanting to avoid Pepe's military school—but that was the least of it. No, that wasn't what I wanted to say. It was more about how, in getting some distance from them, I could see there was both the good and bad in my life, like there was nothing I could do about the way I looked, and nothing I could do about the creeps of the world. And that yeah, I missed them big-time, and knew they really cared for me, even if they couldn't understand where I was coming from and that I never intended to take them for granted . . . and . . . on and on.

I'd circle around that shit, over and over again. And even though I couldn't bring myself to actually finish a single letter and mail it, just thinking about them so much, and that I had done a really coldhearted thing, without realizing it, well, that was slowly clearing my head of the bad feelings. Like, I had to do right by them, and by my own self, no matter what would be awaiting me. But like I told Gilberto, I just didn't know when.

twenty-eight

I HAVEN'T TALKED much about how religious my Moms was: Going to church on Sunday to hang out in the house of "*El Señor*" was always one of the high points of her week, the one place where she seemed to really find some peace of mind, and the day when she was most mellow, until something would throw her into a worrying mood again. She always had sayings, though, and one of them was that God sometimes helps you out in your decisions about life, and well, even if I didn't know what that big superhero in the sky was all about, that night, He sent down some of His darkest angels to further hip me to myself.

They came into the station at about three in the morning, in two cars with Pennsylvania license plates.

Four white guys in one, and in the second, three more, all of them dead drunk.

"Fill 'er up," one of them said to me.

They were in their twenties, most of them with slick black hair. Some were pudgy, some were muscular, all of them were staggering around.

A little alarm went off in my head.

Even with the state troopers coming by at least once during the graveyard shift, you sometimes got a really creepy feeling from some folks, just from the way their eyes looked, or from their body language. Or the way they regarded you. If your hair was too long or your manner wasn't manly enough for their taste, you just knew that trouble was coming. That night, while I was filling up their tanks, I could just tell that one of them, this husky dude boring holes into the back of my head with his eyes, had it out for me.

But, you know, I was trying to be a pro.

"You want me to check your oil?" I asked him when he had gotten out the car.

"No," he said, malice in his eyes. "But tell me something." He stood right in front of me, thrusting his chest out.

"Yeah?"

"What's it like to be a stone faggot?"

"You're kidding me, right?" I said, taken aback.

"Why would I be kidding with a chick like you?" and he laughed.

I put my hands up.

"Okay. Forget that I asked you anything," I said, starting to walk around him.

I headed back towards the station office, planning to call the troopers. But then this fat guy, standing behind the mean one, blocked my way.

"Where you going, sweetheart?" the fat guy asked me.

"Just to get some rags, that's all."

"Uh-uh," the guy said. "I don't think so."

"All right, all right," I said, stepping back.

"So what's that in your pocket, a purse?" the mean one asked.

"Say what?" I asked.

"You look like you should have a purse."

"Listen, I don't want any hassles, okay?" I said, trying to keep calm.

"Hey, Miss Fairy here doesn't want any trouble," he said to the fat guy. "Maybe we should haul him over to the side, and dick him up the ass! What do you guys think?"

And they were laughing and laughing.

Then he grabbed me by my hair, pulling it really tight in his fist, like he wanted to rip it out.

He smiled again, and I could see his rotten teeth.

"So, if you're not a girl, why's your hair so long?" he said, pulling my hair tighter.

"I don't know."

"You don't know!" he said angrily. "Isn't it because you're a little pussy?"

And he took out a lighter, which he clacked open, a high blue flame shooting up. Jesus, if he was going to torch me, he'd blow the whole place up. The running gas pumps were only a few feet away!

"Put that out!" I shouted. "It'll catch on the fumes!"

He looked over at the pumps.

"I'm not bullshitting you," I said to make the point again.

"All right, so I'll wait," he said, clicking the lighter lid shut. Then he just leaned against his car, staring and making kissy-kissy sounds at me.

I glanced quickly up and down the road—not a car was in sight.

As I stuck the nozzle into the second tank, I didn't want them see how my hands were shaking really bad and that I had to use one hand to hold the other steady. By then, my stomach was hurting, it was so much in knots.

In a few minutes the pumps clicked off. As I put the spout back in place, that mean guy started with the lighter business again.

"Anyone ever burn off your pretty hair, faggot?" he said, shoving me and waving that lighter in front of my face.

I didn't say anything, just kept looking off, hoping that someone would be coming along. No one did. It was a dead stretch of the night, in the way you would never find in New York.

"Hey, I asked you a question, queenie!" he said, jamming his finger into my chest.

"No," I said, stepping back again.

"No, what?"

"No one has ever burned my hair off," I mumbled under my breath.

I was really scared by then. And when you get scared, all kinds of crazy thoughts come into your head.

Like why was this prick walking around, when all kinds of good folks weren't?

And where the hell was God?

And where was a lightning bolt when you needed it?

And why did cops always turn up when you didn't need them?

And would these guys be acting so tough if they found themselves in the projects along 125th Street and had to deal with some really hard-ass dudes, instead of peace-symbol-wearing Rico?

Stepping towards me, the prick started flicking the lighter around my ears: I could smell the tips of my hair singe.

"Come on, man, be cool!" I said, jumping back.

And then he told the fat guy to hold me and even as I started to yank my arms away and felt like punching him, I knew that if I did, I'd just make things worse.

By then the other guys had joined them.

"So what do you fellows think? Should we give Blondie here a nice trim to remember us by?"

While the fat guy held me, the mean one grabbing hold of my hair and flaming on his lighter again, I truly believed they were going to really mess me up.

But instead of lighting my hair on fire, he just started punching me, his fists hitting my jaw, then my stomach, the guy smacking me so hard that I thought my head had fallen apart. He kept saying, "How about that?" and "Does it feel good, princess?" hitting me over and over again, even when I'd slumped to the ground.

Then the MF tried to kick me in my temple, but I raised my arms just in time to block him.

Looking up at his hateful face, and believing I was going to die, all the stuff I would miss hit me.

Like comics. And them novels.

John Carter of Mars.

Guitars. Spaceships. *Mad* magazines.

The *Playboy* centerfolds.

Huckleberry Finn.

And food:

Juicy hamburgers, french fries.

Thick roast beef sandwiches.

Ice cream (pistachio) and chocolate bars.

Those coconut-covered Good Humor bars.

My Moms's flan.

Her *lechón* and *arroz con pollo*.

Chorizo and egg sandwiches, fried *plátanos*.

And more:

Like the sky.

The birds. The sun. The stars at night.

The murky ocean off Coney.

And people, too:

Yeah, Gilberto, Jimmy, maybe even Sheri.

But my family the most.

Whap!

Like he kept on punching me, again and again.

Spitting at me.

"You f—king filthy hippie!"

"Poppy!"

Boom.

"You little princess!"

"Mamá!"

Whap!

"Faggot!"

Crack!

And on and on until I felt like throwing up.

Like die, die, die was in his eyes.

And I couldn't help but wonder what the guy would have done if he had known I was a spic on top of being a hippie scumbag.

But then, one of the guys, this tall fellow who had this pained expression on his face—the only one who did not seem amused by what was going on—walked over and said, "Come on, Joey, it's not worth it. Leave the kid alone."

Then the mean one looked at him, as if that other guy was suddenly the new fairy. And they just stared at each other for a few moments, like those gunslingers in the movies do before a showdown.

"I mean it, man," the tall one said. "We don't need the trouble."

"Aw, I gotta use the can anyway," the mean one said, rubbing his gut and shooting the tall guy a look that was not friendly.

So he went off to the restroom. Five minutes went by, with the other guy watching me. By then, the tall guy had gotten into the back of one of the cars, an expression that he deserved a better life and a better set of friends written all over his face. And then the others followed, except for the fat guy, who continued to stand over me, making sure I didn't slip off to call the cops.

Finally, the mean one came out from the men's room. But instead of heading back to his car, he stepped inside the station office, where, looking around, he yanked the telephone line out the wall.

Then he finally came over to me.

I had gotten up to my knees, spitting blood onto the pavement.

"So what do we owe you, *dearie?*" he asked, with his lips pursed at me.

Surprised that he had even asked, I somehow added up the totals.

"Sixteen twenty-five."

He laughed.

"In your dreams, princess."

And he sucker-punched me, leaving me doubled over. He might have punched me another time if one of the guys hadn't started honking a car horn at him.

"So long, you little faggot," he said, heading to his car.

Then, behind the wheel, he started his engine, and giving me the finger, drove off, the other car following.

While I dragged my ass over to the office, waiting for the state police to make their nightly stop, I remembered something that my guitar teacher, Mr. Lopez, who lived downstairs from us, once told me while we were hanging around on the stoop.

"You're a kid, Rico, but if there are two things you have to learn about life, it's this. Number one, whatever problems you think you have, believe me, there are people with problems much worse than your own. And the second thing is that no matter how many idiots you think there are in your life, as you grow up, you will discover that they not only never go away, but multiply, for the world is filled with them."

"So what do you do?" I'd asked him.

"What you do is try to be the most decent person you can be, even if it's hard. You got to do the right thing, always, even when you don't particularly want to. At least then you'll know that you aren't one of those people who go around messing up things for everyone else."

But recalling such wise words didn't mean much to me then: With the exception of the tall guy, who had tried to keep that mean one from doing much worse things to me, I just wished all of them dead, hoping their cars were going up in flames in a drunken highway wreck somewhere on the interstate.

On top of everything else, once the state troopers had come and gone, I still had to take care of business in the station, attending to my regular duties, like cleaning the johns.

The ladies' room only took a few minutes to mop down, but the men's room was something else. That creep had not only shattered the bathroom mirror but had relieved himself on the tile floor, mucked-up wads of toilet paper stuck on the walls. He was so sick he'd even scrawled "You Suck Faggot!" with his own filth across the inside metal door.

When I was done hosing that stuff down, I sat in the office again, the word "faggot" and all that ugliness—even out there in wonderful Wisconsin—settling in my mind like a message. Were they sent to me by *El Señor*? I wondered. And why did it happen at all? And then, when it came down to it, what was I doing, wasting my time dealing with creeps like them?

Just a little after eight, this guy Tim came into the station to take over from my shift. Tim was very midwestern, hayseedy but handsome, and very clean in his language. I never heard him use any curse words, but that morning, when I told him how I'd gotten beat up, he said, "Well, dang, Rico, I guess there are scuzzballs everywhere."

"Yep," I said, nodding even if I didn't know exactly what scuzzballs were.

"How are you getting home, anyway?" he asked me.

"I guess I'll thumb it," I said, holding my side, which was aching.

"Are you sure you're okay?" he said, looking really concerned.

"Yeah," I said. "But I'll tell you, Tim, after last night, I gotta wonder how long I'll be hanging around here, let alone coming back to the station tonight."

"Tell you what," he said. "I'll work that shift for you."

"You sure, man?"

"Yeah, I'll square it later with Mr. Jenkins."

"Well, thanks," I said, feeling like I wanted to cry.

So, leaving the station, I crossed over to the other side of the road and stuck out my thumb. Most days, while hitching a ride home, I'd walk about a third of a mile along the road to a McDonald's to buy myself some breakfast, but I felt too cramped up and kind of sick. And as pretty as that morning was looking, with the sky a magazine-picture blue and everything smelling so green, it just didn't seem that way to me at all.

I had been standing on the side of the road for a few minutes, feeling about as blue as blue could be, when I saw Sheriff Nat's Oldsmobile heading my way.

Pulling over, he stuck his head out the window.

"Where you headed?"

"Home, I guess," I said, wondering where that really might be. Man, just then all I wanted was a little peace and calm. My Moms . . . my Moms used to do this thing when I was little—wash my hair over the sink, her hands feeling soft on my neck, her fingers rubbing my scalp. She'd smile and look at me with big-time affection—all that good stuff happening before I got sick. I must have looked like I was under some kind of spell, because Sheriff Nat asked me, "You all right, Rico?"

"Yeah," I said coming back.

"Well, hop in," he told me, patting the front seat beside him, where his hat was sitting.

But I hesitated. I mean, messed up as I was feeling, did I really want the county sheriff coming by the farm, particularly with all those pot plants hanging in the barn?

"Aw," I said, "I don't want to be taking up your time. But thanks anyway."

"Hey, I talked to one of the state troopers about what happened at the station last night. I know what you've been through." Leaning over to the passenger side, he opened the door. "So, just get in"—and he patted the seat beside him again—"and that's an order!"

I got in, not having much choice and wishing that I had made up some story, like that I was waiting for Gilberto to pick me up. But that wouldn't have held water, as they say out here. After all, I had been trying to thumb a ride.

"Your place is off Route Twenty-six, that right?" he asked me, taking off.

"Yep," I said, racking my brain and trying to remember if anyone had shut those barn doors last night.

"Would you like a little music?" he said, fiddling with his radio.

"Yeah," I said, pressing my hands between my legs to stop them from shaking.

Nat glanced over. "They really messed with you, didn't they?" he said, finding a country station. "But you try and relax, all right? You're okay."

"It's just that I didn't think that those kinds of things happened around here," I said, trying to stop the shakes.

"Oh, it happens, anywhere there's people," he said. "If you knew the number of felons, thieves, rapists, drug dealers, and murderers who pass through these parts, your mind would go spinning."

Then, as he drove along at a leisurely speed, his left

hand dangling out the window and occasionally giving a wave to the farmers we passed, I tried to lighten up, but I just couldn't get my mind off that barn. But then I remembered how the inside of that Oldsmobile sometimes smelled like pot, and that made me feel a little better, like maybe, even if he saw those plants, he might look the other way.

But that was some mother of an iffy thing.

By the time we were only about half a mile away, I was really holding on to my seat, my hands gripping the leather under me.

"Look, kid," he said, patting me on the knee. "About last night. Just write it off to a bad piece of luck, that's all."

Or a message, I thought.

Soon enough, the Oldsmobile was going up the driveway. I was doing a countdown from ten to one in my head, like I was about to blast off in a spaceship, and I closed my eyes, waiting for the moment when I would find out whether Gilberto, and probably the others, would be going to jail.

Just as Sheriff Nat was pulling up to front of the house, I opened my eyes and looked over at the barn. Rex had his hind leg lifted, peeing against the barn door.

Which was shut. Rex came bounding towards us, his tail wagging.

Thank you, Lord, for that shut door, and dogs that pee against shut barn doors. Thank you, thank you, I kept saying to myself, over and over again.

Hearing us, Gilberto stepped out onto the porch, a cup of coffee in hand.

"Jesus, Rico," Gilberto said, seeing my bruised-up face, galloping down the steps. "What happened to you?"

The sheriff told him the story.

"Aw, man," Gilberto said, all upset. "Who did it?"

"A bunch of white guys," I said. "I guess they were greasers."

The sheriff looked highly amused, and I realized he was smiling over the fact that a white guy had just put it that way. "Take care of your young friend here."

"I will, Sheriff," Gilberto assured him.

"That's Sheriff Nat, to you," he said as he got back into his car. Starting the engine, he had a piece of advice for me.

"Rico, you take care now, and just remember, as bad as you might be feeling, it could have been much worse." He pulled down on the brim of his hat. "There was that station attendant near Chicago, a sixteen-year-old kid, who got shot in the head a few days ago, during a robbery."

Well, that really cheered me up.

Then he tipped his hat at us and drove away.

With that, Gilberto's expression changed. I wouldn't say he was angry, but he was looking at me like I was crazy.

"I'm sorry you got beat up last night, but what's with you and the fuzz, anyway?" he said, pushing open the kitchen screen door.

That morning, everybody was super nice to me. Jimmy just took one look at the bruises on my face and did this very un-Jimmy-like thing, which was just to put his arms around me and say, "My bro, my bro!" Then Wendy came up behind me and started rubbing my back, saying, "Oh, you poor guy" and "Boy, do I hate those people." Bonnie made a kind of ice pack for me, putting some chopped-up cubes inside an old hot water bottle to help bring down the swelling on my head, and Polly offered me some painkillers she used for that time of month stuff.

Curt offered me a toke off a joint, rolled from the homegrown.

But all I wanted to do was drink a beer or two, or three, or four.

To untangle the knots in my gut.

After everyone left, I stood by my window with its wonderful view of the countryside: the farms, the cows, the cornfields, the silos, the barns, the pretty blue sky, and the wisps of cloud drifting through it like they were your own little friends.

Then a solitary puff of cloud came, floating slowly by, as if it were looking for a place to belong. And, man, I must have been weirded out, 'cause I was thinking that if I were a cloud, that one would be me.

For a week or so, I tried to hide my bruises with flesh-colored pimple cream. I just got tired of being down at the station with all them people looking at my mug and asking me about how it got messed up. I almost quit, especially when Mr. Jenkins wanted me to pay for the lost gas and the cost of replacing the bathroom mirror from that night—I mean, talk about being jive! But when he saw my face turning purple and the way I looked at him like he was a cheap and unfeeling bastard, he finally let that shit go.

It became harder for me to drag my ass down there.

And once I did, I'd spend those nights wishing I could be somewhere else. I'd ask the long-distance truckers just where they were headed on their cross-country hauls, the names Albuquerque, Phoenix, Denver, and Los Angeles pulling me in one direction, Philadelphia, Boston, and New York in another. Then I started to think how Sheri's Moms had offered to help me get into a good school like Music and Art back home, and that I should get off my ass and finally write that letter to my folks. But my mind kept racing: What if I showed up at my door and my Moms and Pops wouldn't want to have anything to do with me? Or instead of giving me hugs and kisses, the way I dreamed they would, they put a beating on my ass—as if that hadn't happened enough. And what if Sheri's Moms wouldn't keep her word, and I ended back at Jo Mama's or worse, down in Florida, learning military-style discipline and stuff I don't think I'd be too good at.

Talk about feeling hassled.

All I knew was that I needed to calm myself down. So I started dipping into that *Huckleberry Finn* book again, loving the hell out of those descriptions of him and his man Jim floating on a raft on the Mississippi River, and I wondered what that bad-ass kid would do if he were in my place. Yeah, he was about a thousand times cooler than me, and his drunk Pappy was way meaner than mine, but would he stick around?

Or light out, hitting the road?

Or would he be heading on home?

Part 9 **IT JUST BE THAT WAY SOMETIMES**

twenty-nine

IT WAS EARLY July when a letter came in the morning mail. When I saw it sitting on the kitchen table, I instantly knew that it was from the comic-book company in New York—a picture of Superman, his arms akimbo, was printed on the back of the envelope. But I didn't have the heart to open it just yet. I had to work up the nerve—and anyway, if it was bad news I'd be miserable all day, so I figured I'd wait for Jimmy to come home first.

I got a cup of coffee and wandered into the living room, where Curt was filling up small plastic bags with the homegrown.

Just a few days before, he had hauled in the last batch of decent pot from the barn. As far as I could tell, his get-rich scheme hadn't quite worked out, not the way he wanted. Like 75 percent of that stuff had either wilted, like old lettuce you find in the bottom of a refrigerator, or gotten moldy, like hard old lemons growing that fuzzy cotton stuff on their skin. The rest, about ten pounds' worth, had to be sold off at hippie-friendly prices and fast, on Gilberto's orders.

(That was about twenty dollars an ounce. Always doing math in my head, I figured he and Gilberto would be splitting about three grand or so, maybe more, depending how it was sold.)

Gilberto didn't want to deal with having it around anymore—particularly since he had seen this helicopter flying over the area a couple of times. Rumor had it that it was a DEA chopper looking for pot farms.

Besides, as he was planning to buy that horse Sally for the farm, he needed the barn, his plan being to convert it into a stable where he could put all that hay and alfalfa and oats, or whatever the heck else horses ate. Ready or not, he told Curt to clear the last of that weed out of there.

But it was still a righteous amount of weed, even if everybody had been helping themselves to it. Jimmy smoked that reefer like cigarettes when he was hanging around the house, and Bonnie and Curt did too.

Gilberto liked a toke or two on occasion, but he was mainly a beer man. And Wendy, she would smoke now and then, but not in the same way she used to before we got hit by lightning—as if she didn't want to tempt fate again—sort of taking quick little drags and blowing out that smoke just as fast. Polly wouldn't even go near that pot—she just didn't like anything that messed with her mind while she would be drawing.

Ditto for me: Soon as I had more than a few tokes—which I would take so as not to seem too straight—all these weird thoughts started coming at me.

Mostly about my folks.

I could be listening to the Grateful Dead, with this really pretty light coming in through the window, the kind that seems rich and plump, in which you can see little dust motes floating like angels through it, and just like that I'd feel that my Moms and Pops were somehow nearby. Even when I knew they were just in my head, if I had smoked too much, I could swear they'd be talking to me:

Rico, where are you?

Rico, why did you leave us?

Rico, when are you coming home?

It all spooked my ass, big-time.

So, when it came down to that weed, I'd mainly pretend to be dragging on that shit. Nope, it just wasn't for me.

Kept in a suitcase in a closet—along with a bunch of plastic bags and a small scale—that pot took over Curt's life. With the word out at the local colleges and communes, and among his and Bonnie's musician friends from Janesville to Madison, hardly a day went by without at least two or three cars coming to the farm.

And sometimes folks would be calling up out of the blue.

"Hello, my name is Johnny so-and-so, a friend of Derek's, who knows Polly's friend Cherise from art school. Is Curt there?"

Even some of the bikers Jimmy knew from his painting jobs came by. What can you say when you see a half-dozen big-ass Harleys zipping up, with their engines burping and blasting, along an otherwise quiet country road towards your house? And these huge dudes, dressed in black and wearing leather hats, come knocking on your door?

Like, "Yes sir! By all means, do come in!"

I mean, it was crazy, all kinds of folks coming over, just about every day, hanging around in the living room, listening to music and trying that weed, compliments of Curt, who was selling off those ounces like they were corn dogs in an amusement park.

But that day, come about four in the afternoon, while I was sitting around with Curt and Bonnie, wondering if I should just bite the bullet and open the letter, and about ten minutes after Gilberto had come home from his job at the Roaring Brook Stables to take a shower, a car pulled up, a blue Chevy convertible, its sideboards all dusted over from traveling the dirt roads.

I heard the car's doors slam, then a knock on our door.

"Hey, Rico," Curt said, "would you get that, man?"

"All right-a-roony," I said, going to the door.

Two scarecrow-thin white dudes with the longest hair I had ever seen in my life stood on the porch. Their hair reached down to their waists. One, the dark-haired dude, had this wicked Mandarin-looking, Fu Manchu mustache, and the other resembled a Viking prince, with curly blond hair just rippling down in waves over his chest. They were both wearing Mexican ponchos and all kinds of silver-and-turquoise jewelry. I mean, they looked very cool.

"Peace, brother, and good afternoon," the blond one said in an English accent, holding up two fingers in the shape of a V. "Does a Curt Svenson live here?"

"Yeah," I said.

"We're just up from Mexico way, and friends of our acquaintance have told us that Curt might be able to help us replenish certain supplies."

"Replenish?" I wasn't even sure what that meant, but I got the drift.

"Wait a second," I said, calling into the room. "Hey, Curt, you want to come over here and talk to these guys?"

Being tall himself, Curt came out to the entranceway and sort of stretched his lanky frame all which ways, with one hand practically touching the ceiling, the other pressed against the opposite wall.

"What can I do for you?" he said.

And the English guy answered, "Well, firstly, peace to you, brother. My name is Rodney and my companion here, he's William," his friend squinting and smiling slightly at the mention of his name. "We have come here bearing you gifts."

And the English dude dug down into one of his pockets and pulled out a big piece of hashish. It looked like a sheep pellet.

"Accept it, my brother," he said, "with all our good wishes."

Curt sniffed it, to see if it was for real. I guess it was, because he smiled, asking them, "So what can I do for you?"

"Well," the Englishman said. "A little bird told us that you were selling some beaucoup cannabis, and so," he said, bowing a bit and making a regal gesture with a sweep of his arm—like, I thought the guy must have been totally stoned—"we thought we might be able to avail ourselves of your resources, and to pay you well for them."

Curt and I exchanged looks—these guys were seriously weird, but he was already so used to all kinds of folks coming to the farm, most of them harmless, that he hardly hesitated. "Okay, come on in," he told them.

And so these guys came into the living room, the dark-haired one, I noticed, looking around everywhere. Music was on the phonograph, and Bonnie, sitting on the couch watching some soap opera on TV with the sound all turned down, was knitting. Gilberto, in the shower and singing "You've Lost That Lovin' Feelin'," could be heard loud and clear, along with some operatic, if slightly off-key, *La, la, la, la*s.

Everything seemed to be cool, copacetic even. The two dudes were sitting opposite Curt when he handed them a lit joint. He was proud of our crop, that weed being pretty strong. So the Englishman, taking a puff and leaning his head back against his chair, just started laughing, like he was having all kinds of wild dreams.

"So—so—how much," he said, coughing, "do you have?" and he started doubling over, his face turning red. Seeing him, I couldn't help but to think about Jimmy in the old days. Then he gathered himself, his friend heartily rapping him on the back.

"Like, how much do you have?" he asked Curt again.

"I don't know," said Curt. "Maybe about seven or so pounds left."

The Englishman reached into his pocket, pulled out a wad of one-hundred-dollar bills, and pushed it across the trunk towards Curt.

"Count it, brother," he said. "But I guarantee that when you do, you will be looking at five thousand of your American dollars, understand?"

Curt was amazed.

"But I must see the merchandise first," the Englishman said, grabbing the wad back.

And with that, Curt, shooting me excited glances,

went off to the closet where he had stashed the suit-case.

Gilberto, done with his shower, passed by the living room, a white towel around him. "Howdy, dudes," he said to the strangers. Then he disappeared.

By then Curt had brought out the suitcase: It was one of those lacquered cases, with all kinds of unknown memories attached to it that Gilberto had found along the side of a road. Proudly, confidently, Curt laid it on the trunk and clicked it open. Laying side by side in a row, each pound was neatly wrapped in a plastic bag.

The English dude's blue eyes widened.

"Excellent," he said to Curt. And he nudged his friend with his elbow. "How wonderful; isn't it, William?"

And then he started fishing around inside his pon-cho for something, and just like that, his manner changed. He wasn't smiling anymore, and his soft, some-what crazed, Jesus-like eyes grew hard, and it hit me that the guy was probably a narc and that I would be spending the next few years in some jail cell or reform school. But no, he did not pull out a badge. What he did pull out was a gun, a freaking .45, just like the .45 I once saw this guy Poppo carrying around the neighborhood in a brown paper bag!

Pointing that gun at Curt and me, he just grinned, saying, "Well, gentlemen, thank you for the delightful visit." And while his friend grabbed that suitcase, the suave Englishman backed away towards the door, his gun cocked, and saying things like "If you come after us, I'll surely shoot you."

A few moments later, their car tore ass out of our driveway.

It seemed like it was out of a movie.

But that was only part one.

Part two had to do with one of those sayings. Something like "You can take the boy out of the city, but you can't take the city out of the boy." And that must be true, because as soon as Gilberto walked into the living room and heard about what had happened, he just looked at me and said, "Come on, Rico, let's go."

I don't know what he had in mind, but even when I told him that those guys had a real gun, Gilberto just went off into his room and came out holding a baseball bat and an air rifle that shot BBs.

"You're kidding, right?" I asked him. He shook his head.

"What else are we supposed to do? Call the cops?

No. We're gonna chase those suckers down. No way am I going to let them get away with that!"

I never realized that Gilberto could get so worked up, but folks who grow up poor just don't like to get ripped off. Even if what was stolen is a certain something that would land you in a jail.

So we got into his truck and followed their skid marks—easterly—until we saw that they had cut over onto a dirt road and were circling around the far side of a field, a few miles away, a cloud of dust rising behind their Chevy. And with that, Gilberto really floored the pickup, and we were racing after them like maniacs. It was kind of thrilling and scary at the same time: I kept wondering what Gilberto would do in the event that we actually caught up with them, like pull out his air rifle and shoot it out, or smash up their car with the baseball bat, all their bullets somehow missing us?

In any case, as we were speeding along, maybe doing seventy miles an hour on a local road, we heard a siren. I looked behind us and thought, Holy crap!

It was Sheriff Nat, in his brown Oldsmobile, trailing us.

So we slowed up, pulling over to the side of the road. Gilberto slid the air rifle under the seat.

Walking towards us, Sheriff Nat kept his hand on his

holster until he recognized who we were. He just started shaking his head. Tipping the brim of his hat, he said, "Uh, hate to bug you guys, but can you tell me why you're in such a big hurry?"

I looked at Gilberto; he looked at me.

Finally, Gilberto came up with a story: "I just needed to burn off some steam. Had me a fight with my girl."

"Uh-huh," he said, like he didn't really believe a word of it. "And the baseball bat, what's that about?" he said, looking into the cab.

"We were just gonna hit some balls later," Gilberto said. "Right, Rico?"

"Yeah."

"Look, guys," Sheriff Nat said, after a moment. "I should be giving you a speeding ticket, but we'll let this one be a warning. Don't let it happen again, okay?"

"Yes, sir!" Gilberto said.

And then Sheriff Nat got back into his car.

By then, the dust cloud, and with it all that weed, had vanished into the distance.

It was just one of those win-some, lose-some days.

Poor Curt was crushed about the stolen weed, but once he had calmed down, Gilberto didn't really seem to care. "If it wasn't meant to be, it wasn't meant to be," he said, shrugging and heading out of the house with Rex.

With all that excitement, I had forgotten about that letter from New York, until Jimmy walked in, just after six, his face a little crestfallen, having heard about the lost pot.

"Yo Jimmy," I said. "Got a letter today."

"What kind of letter?"

"From that comic-book company," I said, picking it up off the table.

"So what's it say?" he asked. I could hear a tinge of excitement in his voice, for all his cool demeanor.

"I haven't read it yet. I was waiting for you."

"Well, shoot, man," he said, popping open a beer.

It might be strange to say, but just then, as I was about to tear the envelope open, I was feeling more tense than I had when that guy had pulled out the gun. Like the future of one of my little dreams was on the line.

I mean, my hand was actually shaking and my heart started beating faster.

Was it good news?

Nope.

Like, if I was a tree, I would have been falling; a stone in a pond, sinking.

This is what it said:

Dear Ricardo,

Thanks so much for sending us your and Jimmy Ortiz's terrific story! Compliments on both the artwork and script! All of us here at DC were very impressed with its dynamic energy!

However, as much as I personally liked the basic premise of your character, which I thought was great, my boss, the company manager who makes all the final decisions, felt it was "too ethnic" and thus not appropriate to our usual all-American superhero roster.

I wanted to give it a shot, but unfortunately comic-book sales have been falling off lately: Even Superman hasn't been selling the way he used to. And my boss is just too cautious to stray away from the tried and true. But I am fairly certain that the Dark Dude will get his due one day.

With sincerest regrets,
Julius Schwartz

P.S. Keep on trying!

It wasn't a horrible note, but it wasn't great.

Like I said, it was one of those days.

Of course, I had to tell Sheri about that comic-book dream being down the drain, but that was the least of what was bothering me. As we bopped through town the next Saturday, looking in shop windows and eating pistachio ice-cream cones, I didn't have to say a word: deep inside she already knew. Now and then, she'd smile, but sadly, and give my hand a tight squeeze like she never wanted to let it go. Oh, but let me tell you, my fellow dark dudes (and dudettes), her sweetness gave me enough pause that I began waiting for another sign that would tell me what I should do.

So early the next morning, with outhouse duty awaiting me later that day, I went roaming around the farm and through the little meadow of wild flowers where my man Jimmy and Polly liked to sit and draw. With birds chirping everywhere, and the trees breathing and stretching out their limbs big time, everything seemed so beautiful, like in one of those nice dreams that remind you of the summertime when you were a tiny kid. It was so beautiful that even the butterflies, looping merrily over the grass, seemed as happy as happy can be. But you know what? Even in the midst of such a pretty spot, the saddest things will get in your face, like the red-breasted robin I found laying by a tree, its wings twitching slightly and its startled BB eyes looking numbly at the sky. I couldn't help but scoop it up into my hands—its little heart pulsing wildly against my palm. Okay, it sounds stupid, but I started trying different stuff to bring it around—like blowing breath at its beak, rubbing its tummy, even talking to it—"Come on, please, please, wake up, little fella."

Just as I was starting to feel that I was wasting my time, and had put it down, the little guy popped back to life. At first, it sort of staggered around in circles like a drunk on twiggy legs, and then, shaking its ruffled feathered head, it began flapping its wings, as if to see if they were still working. Then the robin looked up into the blueness of the sky, and, just like that, it flew away, to where little birds go.

I have to tell you—that felt good. And it also made me think something else—no one back home was going to believe it when I told them about that bird, and, by the way, back home didn't mean the farm, back home meant back *home*.

A few days later, Sheri and me were sitting in the bus station. And God but that was tough. Sheri was crying and I was trying to act like it was no big thing and that it wasn't hard on me. But it was killing me to feel her swallowing down sobs as I held her tight, because no matter how many times I told Sheri that I would be coming back one day, I don't think she really believed it would happen. How could she—I didn't know if I believed it myself. It was just one of those corny things people say as their good-byes.

It gave me something nice to think about, though—getting back there someday. I mean, last night, I went outside at like 3 a.m., and looking at all of those crazy stars, so many that you'd swear that if you had superhero vision you'd see them stretching way over New York City, over Harlem even, I knew I wasn't ever going to see such a thing back home, even if they were gonna still be hanging out somewhere. And I knew I'd be missing that view. And Jimmy, man, I couldn't imagine being on the block without my man James, but at the same time, seeing him with Polly, painting in that field, all mellow; no way was I messing with that. And Gilberto was just starting to teach me how to keep my ass down on that horse of his, to really ride. I mean, getting out to Wisconsin was definitely one of the coolest things I'd ever done, and, at the same time, there was a lot of shit too, and not just the outhouse kind. As Gilberto once put it, what might look easy doesn't always turn out that way. But, heck, as they say out here, didn't I get hipped to certain things? Like, no matter where you might be—on the Mississippi, the planet Mars, a farm in Wisconsin, or in a messed-up big city like New York—there'll always be people who are gonna get in your face. Life was going to kick your ass sometimes, because, you know what, where you are doesn't change who you are. I thought of that while I was sitting with Sheri waiting for the bus, feeling more like myself than I had in a long time—maybe ever.

But I had some other stuff to talk about with Sheri, what with her Pops drinking again: to remember that when things got bad, she should think of me and that we weren't who our parents were. After a while, though, we couldn't even speak and just kept holding hands and hugging. Finally, breaking that silence, I promised that we would write each other as often as we could, but that didn't make her feel much better. Sheri just kept sighing, nearly crying, but after a while, she calmed down, her sweet eyes, I swear, just welling up with good wishes for me. Then that bus pulled in, and before I got on, my guitar in hand, I just had to give her my own copy of that Huck Finn book, as a keepsake. What I had written inside that cover, I won't say, but it made that girl smile and blush and cry out, "Oh, Rico!" After one last good-bye, I climbed aboard, and the bus rumbled out of the station, my face pressed against the window. I watched Sheri waving and waving at me until I disappeared from view.

Well, I'll tell you my friends, leaving that place wasn't easy at all, but sometimes you've got to do what you've got to do. Doesn't take a genius to figure that one out, particularly if you've been getting a little tired of out-house duty. Yep, I was filling wheelbarrows with that wonderful outhouse ripeness for the last time, when I finally made up my mind to go. And once I did, no matter how hard things might turn out to be, I put aside my last shovel of you-know-what and went into the farmhouse, and after taking a freezing cold shower, I got on the telephone and dialed my folks' number in New York.

Hearing my Moms's voice, I took a deep-assed breath and—in my best Spanish—told her, and then my Pops, that I was coming home.

*　*　*　*　*

a note to readers

The publication of *Dark Dude* by Cuban-American Oscar Hijuelos marks an exciting moment at Atheneum Books for Young Readers. We intend to offer the finest literature of Latino inspiration to the world's readers, whether they be young adults or young-at-heart adults.

Atheneum/Simon & Schuster greets the largest and fastest growing ethnic community in the United States with enthusiasm by saying: Your voices, your dreams, your experiences, and your hopes will find expression in our books. We believe that the Latino community—so diverse in tradition, cultural sensibility, historical pacing, race and religion—is renewing the American spirit. We invite you to share with us in celebrating our new venture. Read this literature that defines a whole new world in a promising new millennium. *Saludos!*

—The Editors

Reading Group Guide

DISCUSSION QUESTIONS

1. What are some of the main challenges Rico and his family face living in Harlem? Describe Gilberto's and Jimmy's experiences as well.

2. List some of the characteristics, beyond the physical, that make Rico different. What charactcristics does he show while living in Harlem?

3. How does Rico fit into his environment in Harlem? How does the community relate to him? Consider the Jo Mama School shooting, and the drug dealing and heroin use with Jimmy.

4. How does Rico view his light skin color? How does his view change from when he is in Harlem to when he is in Wisconsin? Does he feel comfortable in his own skin?

5. Rico hit a low, where he wants to escape his family, school, and street life in Harlem. He asks Jimmy to show

him how to use heroin. How does this become a turning point in their lives?

6. The feelings of hopelessness for both Rico and Jimmy culminate in Jimmy catching fire. How does Rico rescue Jimmy? What do we learn about Rico?

7. Discuss the hitchhiking trip that Rico and Jimmy take as they run away from New York. Would this make you more or less likely to hitchhike yourself? Of all the characters they meet, who stands out most for you?

8. Exploring the bonds that bind a family is a major theme in this story. What torments Rico as he leaves New York? How does he relate to his family while he is in Wisconsin? How does the "family" in the farmhouse affect Rico and Jimmy?

9. Rico's favorite book is *The Adventures of Huckleberry Finn* by Mark Twain. How does his story parallel to that of Huck Finn's?

10. Arriving in Wisconsin feels like a dream to Rico and Jimmy. Describe some of their adjustments and

differences. How does Rico's feelings of being an "outsider" continue?

11. Gilberto is a major influence on Rico. How difficult is it for Rico when Gilberto moves from Harlem to go to college in Wisconsin? When Rico arrives at the farm, Gilberto is Rico's guide. Discuss the bond between Gilberto and Rico.

12. Blond, blue-eyed, educated Midwesterner Sheri becomes Rico's first real girlfriend. How does their relationship help both of them grow?

13. How do Jimmy and Rico feel when they complete the *Dark Dude* comic book and submit it to DC Comics? What does this show us about Rico? Discuss the outcome of the submittal and the letter from DC Comics. Were you surprised?

14. What do you imagine is the next chapter in Rico's journey?

15. What makes people who they are? Is it how they look? Their language? Their ethnic heritage? Where they grow

up? Discuss the elements of the book that support your answers.

ACTIVITIES

1. Rico and Jimmy create a comic book series with their superhero, the Dark Dude. Try creating a comic book. Create a superhero that reflects characteristics you would like to embody. Write or illustrate it yourself, or get a partner. There are good guides in *Dark Dude* on how to get your comic published. Do you think you could get yours published?

2. Regional language is a distillation that reflects ethnicity, culture, and class. The language of Harlem included "jive," "lame," and "dark dude." In the book, the language of Wisconsin includes "outhouse," "hankering," and "neat." Find more examples from *Dark Dude*, making lists of New York City words and Wisconsin words. What do these words reflect about the cultures and ethnicities they come from? Can you create a list of words that reflect your region's language? Compare it to other regions.

3. Find Internet images, books, and magazines that have pictures of Harlem and also of farmland Wisconsin in the late 1960s. Try creating a photo collage that reflects the two very different environments. Then make a list of similarities and differences. How strange would it be to move from one to the other for you? How might it change you?